Please Release Me

Please Release Me

Rhoda Baxter

Where heroes are like chocolate – irresistible!

Published 2016 by Choc Lit Limited
Penrose House, Crawley Drive, Camberley, Surrey GU15 2AB, UK
www.choc-lit.com

A CIP catalogue record for this book is available
from the British Library

ISBN 978-1-78189-300-5

Printed and bound by CPI Group (UK) Ltd, Croydon, CR0 4YY

To the staff and families at Martin House

Acknowledgements

I will donate 50% of the royalties I get from this book to Martin House Children's Hospice, here's why:

I was lucky enough to be able to talk to some of the families and staff at Martin House, a specialist children's hospice for families with children who have life limiting conditions. Most health conditions are life limiting in one way or another, but in this context, it means children whose life expectancy is lower than most. You'd expect heart-breaking sadness and death there, instead I saw hope, laughter, friendship and children playing. Together.

To the families who are supported by Martin House, it's an absolute life line. It provides much needed respite for parents who haven't had a good night's sleep for ages, it provides time for siblings of sick children to hang out with their parents without their sibling's needs getting in the way, it provides a place where parents can talk to other parents in a similar situation and, when the worst happens, it provides bereavement support. Friendships made during respite stays reach well beyond the confines of the hospice. If you want to find out more about this amazing place, check out their website: www.martinhouse.org.uk

I wanted to write a book that shows this positive side of hospices. Most people think of hospices as places where sick people go to die, but they are also communities and have ups and downs, frustrations and friendships just like any other community.

Government funding to these sort of places is scarce (and shrinking) so they rely a lot on fundraising efforts.

Please support your local hospice. They need you.

I would like to thank everyone at Martin House, families and carers alike, for all their help. I would also like to thank my critique partner, Jen Hicks, for nagging me to write more; Zoe Goodacre from South Wales Critical Care Network (@ZGoodacre) for advice on Sally's coma; Laura E James (@laura_E_james) for conversations about being a carer and how hard it is to move on; Mark English from Rock City in Hull (@RockCityClimb) for advice about the abseiling scene, to the Romantic Novelists Association (@RNAtweets) posse for being the best support network ever and everyone at Choc Lit who helped get this book from me to you. And of course, a big thank you to my family for supporting me and not minding that the house is a tip and it's fish fingers and baked beans for tea. Again.

Thank you also to the Tasting Panel readers who passed *Please Release Me*: Olivia F., Jo C., Fiona D., Izzy T., Sandy F., Jill S., Lucy D., Helena N. and Betty S.

Chapter One

They were lucky with the weather. Sally stepped out into the sunlight. A breeze blew her veil across her face and she laughed as Peter moved it out of the way. He took a long tendril of hair that hung in a carefully styled curl and tucked it behind her ear. The camera shutter whirred. That would make a nice photo. She turned to the camera, trying not to squint into the sun. She didn't want to look like she had wrinkles around her eyes.

'Can we have just the happy couple please?' said the photographer.

People skipped off the steps, leaving Sally and Peter alone to be photographed. Peter slipped his arm around her waist. His gaze locked on hers. He looked at her as though she were something precious and treasured and true. She felt a surge of hope. As long as he looked at her like that, she would be the happiest woman in the world.

Peter grinned at her and kissed her lightly on the lips.

'Perfect,' said the photographer. 'Now, can we have the groom's family, please.'

As Peter's parents and his sister and the bratty nephews were being arranged around her, Sally let her eyes wander over the people who were milling around at the bottom of the steps. They looked bright and cheerful. There were a few people from work. She noticed that a few of them were wearing the same shiny suits that they wore to work during the week. Cheapskates. A couple of Peter's female friends stood apart, resplendent in Miu Miu and perfect make-up. She wondered how many of them had been after Peter themselves. Hah.

The photographer touched her arm and gestured for her to move. She stepped back. Her gaze drifted to the back of the crowd. She froze. It couldn't be. She wouldn't dare.

The woman was wearing a shabby blue coat and a hat with a feather in it. Standing in the shadows, she looked like someone passing by who'd paused to look at the happy couple. When Sally's eyes met hers, she raised a hand a fraction and gave a little wave. Sally's throat tightened with anger.

'Sally?' said Peter. 'You okay?'

She looked at him and back to the spot. But the woman had gone. Like a ghost, she'd disappeared into the shadows. Sally looked back at Peter and forced a smile back onto her face. 'Yes. I'm fine. Just … you know. It's all so amazing.'

He tightened the arm that was around her waist. 'Isn't it.' His face shone with happiness. That was one of the many things she loved about him. He was so … trusting.

'I love you,' she said, and laid her head against his shoulder.

'Say cheese everyone!' said the photographer. He took a few shots. 'Thank you. Now, can we have the bride's fam … friends please?'

Next to her, Peter tensed. She smiled at him and watched the tension drain. 'Friends,' she said. 'I have lots of those.'

The reception was on a different side of the building. Sally excused herself and went to the loos. Being in a public building meant the toilets were down a draughty corridor. If they'd had the wedding in a church, things would have been worse. She picked up her skirts and hurried, her heels clicking on the stone floor. A quick glance over the shoulder reassured her that no one had followed her.

She was washing her hands when a cubicle door opened

a fraction. She straightened up and watched in the mirror. 'It's okay. I know you're in here.'

The woman stepped out, her expression a little sheepish. She smiled. 'You look beautiful Sal.'

'Thank you.'

'I always said your face would be the saving of you.'

'What are you doing here, Glenda? I told you never to come looking for me.'

The older woman's face crumpled, as if it wasn't crumpled enough already. 'I wanted to see my daughter get married. What mother could resist that? You wouldn't deny me that, would ya?'

Sally studied her. Her mother wasn't as old as she looked. The years of alcohol and bad eating had taken its toll on her skin. This was one of the reasons Sally rarely got drunk. She would end up all wrinkled and pruney. And she couldn't see Peter loving someone like that. Glenda smiled. Her eyes were teary. Sally relented, just a fraction. 'Okay.'

'He seems like a nice man,' her mother said, as though she were making a peace offering. 'You've done well for yourself there.' She came up to her and raised a hand. Sally drew away. 'In spite of everything, Sal. I just want you to be happy. That's all I ever wanted.'

For a moment there was flash of memory. Tenderness, smiles. Before. Sally looked at the thread-veined face and softened. 'I know,' she said. 'And I will be. Peter is rich and kind and he loves me.'

'Do you love him?'

She shrugged. 'I think so.' She would learn to. How hard could it be?

Her mother nodded. 'That's good to know.' She started patting her pockets. 'I got you something. For your wedding.' She pulled a folded piece of paper out of a pocket. 'Here.'

She took Sally's reluctant hand and pressed the paper into it. 'It's all I could get you. You might be lucky.'

Sally opened the paper and saw a lottery ticket. She felt the quickening excitement. If this was the winning ticket, she could pay off the little debt and buy Peter something nice. Like that watch he'd wanted. She looked up into her mother's red-rimmed, washed out eyes. 'Thanks. Glenda.'

Glenda licked her lips before she spoke. 'There was a time when you called me mum.'

'Yeah, well, not anymore.' She looked for somewhere to put the lottery ticket where Peter wouldn't see it. Wedding dresses had no pockets. You'd think that with all the flounces and ruffles, there'd be somewhere. In the end, she tucked it into the sleeve, just beyond the tight ruffle that clinched her wrist. She turned on a tap and quickly rinsed her hands. 'I have to go. Remember our deal. You can never, ever, come and see me again. Understand?'

Glenda put her hands back into her pockets. 'But what if you—'

'Never. Understand me? NEVER.'

A nod.

'Excellent.' Sally picked up her skirts and started towards the door. 'Bye.'

'Sal …'

She turned.

'You couldn't score me a drink, could ya?'

Sally took in the stooped shoulders and the plaintive longing of an alcoholic needing a fix. 'No.' She swept out and marched down the corridor, to her new life.

'Ready?' Peter held out his arm to her. The evening sun shone on his blond hair, turning it orange. He was still in his wedding suit. His eyes were full of smiles. He looked happy.

Sally laughed. Something bubbled in her chest. Happiness. This was what it felt like. To have limitless possibilities laid out in front of her. To know that she was married to Peter Wesley. She had security and comfort ahead of her. No more evaluating houses she could never afford. No more schlepping round extolling the virtues of the three bedroom semi, perfect for a growing family. Ready? Was she ever.

She shifted her bouquet into one hand and took Peter's arm with the other. She looked over her shoulder at the women who were self-consciously standing in a semi circle behind her. 'Okay ladies, here it comes.' She threw the bouquet one handed over her shoulder. She and Peter both looked round to see who caught it.

A girl in a tight red dress waved it triumphantly in the air. 'Nice one Maz,' said Sally. 'You next.'

Maz grinned.

People surged round and confetti rained down on them. Peter's father stood next to the car, which was decorated with ribbons and crepe streamers. He handed Peter the keys. 'Here you go son,' he said. He leaned in and gave Sally a peck on the cheek. 'Welcome to the family Sally.'

'Aw thanks Roger.' Sally's gaze slid towards Peter's mother. 'And Diane.'

Diane's smile didn't quite make it to her eyes. She gave Sally a quick kiss and gave Peter a hug. 'Be happy,' she said. Her hand lingered on his cheek.

'We will be,' said Peter. He opened the door for Sally and, when she'd dropped into her seat, helped her gather up the rest of the skirts. He then hurried round to the driver's side, waved to the guests and got in.

'Woo hoo!' Sally threw her arms up and laughed. 'Thailand, here we come!'

Peter laughed too. 'Glad to see you so happy, Mrs

Wesley.' He gave her a fond smile and returned his attention to the road. They were driving straight from the reception to the hotel. They had an early flight tomorrow. The party would have to go on without them. Sally was still in her flouncy dress, but she didn't bother being careful with it any more. She didn't need to now.

Peter pulled to a stop at some traffic lights. 'You look amazing,' he said, above the rasp of the handbrake.

'Thank you, darling.' She put a hand on his thigh, high up. 'So do you.' She slid her hand round, so that it was between his legs.

Peter gave her a sideways glance, his mouth twitching at the sides. 'Behave ...'

She pouted at him and moved her hand a fraction further up. The lights went to amber. Peter smiled again and removed her hand from his groin. 'Just a teeny bit longer,' he said, his voice full of warmth and promise, 'and we can relax, properly.' He released her hand.

'Ah, come on baby, live a little. A hand job. On your wedding day ...'

'Not while I'm driving, Sal. You'll get us both killed.'

'Spoilsport.'

The car sped off, round the roundabout and onto a slip road. Sally waited until they'd joined the carriageway. Peter was gorgeous, but he could be so square. Teasing him was just too easy. She reached across and pinched his thigh. He batted her hand away, his eyes firmly on the road. Something fell out of her sleeve and landed in his lap. The lottery ticket. Crap. Peter mustn't see that. She dived after it.

'Sally!' The car wobbled slightly before Peter got it back on track. 'What is the matter with you?'

'It's just that ... um ... you've got one of my tissues in

your lap.' She tried not to speak too fast. He hadn't noticed what it was yet.

'Ah leave it,' he said.

'Oh, but it's all a bit ew ...'

Peter shrugged a shoulder as though to say he didn't mind. 'I thought the whole ceremony went rather well.'

'Me too.' She kept an eye on the red and white square of paper.

Peter said something else. Then, 'Sally?'

'Pardon? Sorry, I was miles away then.'

'Sally is something wrong?'

'No. No. It's just been ... a big day.'

'Of course, you must be exhausted. Poor darling. Why don't you have a nap? We've got another twenty minutes before we get there. You could recharge a bit.'

'I'm okay ...' The paper slipped out of sight.

Peter shifted. He removed a hand from the steering wheel. 'What is that sticking into my leg?' His eyes still on the road, he picked up the folded paper.

'Let me take that,' Sally lunged across.

Peter frowned and moved the paper out of her reach, unfolding it as he did so. There was a pause. 'Sally. This is a lottery ticket.' The mellowness in his voice had been replaced with a sharp edge. 'Why do you have a lottery ticket tucked into the sleeve of your wedding dress? And please don't insult my intelligence by telling me you blew your nose on it.'

Sally kept her eyes on the paper. 'It was a wedding present. From ... one of my friends. She thought it would be cool if we won, with it being our wedding day and everything.'

'A ... friend.' He didn't believe her, she could tell.

'It's true,' she said.

He glanced at her, his anger wavering.

'I didn't buy it Peter. You know I wouldn't do that. GA rules. I know.' When he didn't say anything, she pouted. 'You're acting as though you don't believe me. I've never lied to you, have I? Don't you trust me?'

He looked at her again, a quick glance, but long enough for her to see that he felt bad. He was so easy to manipulate. Being married to him was going to be a dream.

'I didn't buy it. It was a gift,' she repeated, allowing a sob-like catch into her voice.

Peter frowned out of the windscreen for a moment and seemed to come to a decision. 'I believe you,' he said. 'And I'm glad you didn't buy it. But you understand you can't keep it.'

Sally tensed. She had no intention of letting that lottery ticket go. It could have the winning numbers. Peter was an idiot if he let go of a chance like that. 'Peter…' She put her thumb on the catch of her seat belt. She wouldn't be able to reach him while the belt tethered her.

'I can't risk you relapsing.' He pressed the button to lower the window.

He was going to throw it out of the window. 'No!' Sally lunged across him to grab the ticket. There was a screech of tyres and the scenery swung round. Sally had an impression of Peter's face, his eyes wide, his mouth open. All of it too close. Horns blared. Everything juddered and suddenly she was weightless. Flying backwards. Away from Peter. Everything in front of her went white. Something hit the back of her head.

Chapter Two

10 months after the crash

The hospice was called Holy Spirit Hospice, which always sounded faintly spooky to Grace. The building had once been a Catholic school, which explained the name and the spread of the large house. At some point there had been a circular drive that led to the front door, but hospices needed car parks and ambulance ports, so it was all concreted over now. Only the fountain near the entrance still remained. They had saved the beauty for the gardens at the back. The facade of the building spread out in two wings. It looked more like a hotel than a place where very sick people went to recover or die.

Grace strode in, barely noticing the ornamental plants that flanked the entrance.

The guard at the reception desk said, 'Evening Grace. Bit early today.'

'Evening Tony. How're you?'

'Are you going to this meeting later?'

'I certainly am.' Grace signed in, as she always did.

'They've changed the room where they're holding it,' said Tony. 'It's in the common room on third floor East.' He consulted a note on his desk. 'Same time.'

'Thanks.' She gave him a parting wave and headed to the lifts. The lift had just arrived when someone ran up and dashed a signature into the signing in book. Grace stuck her hand out and stayed the doors.

A blond man, holding a bunch of roses, gave her a grateful smile and got in next to her. Having pressed the fourth floor button for herself, she pressed the third floor button for him without him asking. They had seen each other before. She knew whoever he visited every day was on the long term palliative care floor.

The man thanked her and pushed his glasses, which had slipped down his nose, back up. They both avoided eye contact. Grace pretended to read a poster about a sponsored abseil down the hospital tower.

After a few seconds, Grace took a sideways glance at him. He was handsome, if a little drawn. His hair was getting a bit long, which made him look quite attractive in a young George Clooney sort of a way. Behind his small designer glasses, there were shadows under his eyes and a sadness that he wore around him like a cloak. Grace wondered who it was that he was visiting. A parent? A lover? She leaned forward a little to look to see if he had a wedding ring on his hand. Damn. He was wearing leather gloves.

He saw her peering and gave her a quizzical look. Caught out, Grace struggled for something to say. 'I ... was just admiring your flowers. Very beautiful.'

He looked down at the bunch of red roses. She had seen him with those a lot. Not every day, but often. 'Yes,' he said, carefully, as though considering the possibility that they were beautiful. 'I guess they are.' He shook his head. 'They were her favourite flowers. So I bring them in ... in case she can smell them.'

The lift reached floor three and pinged. The man seemed relieved. 'Bye.' He stepped out of the lift.

Grace watched him as he walked away, the bunch of flowers swinging as his arms moved. A lone figure in the long corridor. She wondered again whom he was visiting and how he must love her. The doors closed and Grace reflected that it would be nice to be loved that much. Especially by a man so good-looking. She sighed. What had got into her today? It was all very well admiring a handsome man, but to think about him in any other way ... that was just silly. He was, after all, just a stranger.

The lift stopped on her floor and she got out.

This floor was brighter and more cheery than the one below. It was meant to be a more sociable space and not look like a hospital, but it was hard to disguise the smell of disinfectant and old age, despite the air-fresheners that regularly hissed out the scent of fresh laundry.

A few elderly residents were being wheeled around in their wheelchairs. Grace greeted most of them by name. She had been coming here often enough to know them all. Most of them would leave within a few months, one way or another. Her mother had stayed here for just over a year, her life slowly leaching away.

She reached Margaret's room and knocked before going in. The room was bright and tastefully decorated. The staff had tried to make it as comfortable as possible, putting Margaret's photographs on the wall and using her bedding from home.

Margaret was sitting up in her bed, wearing the dusky rose slip dress, her grey hair neatly combed. A nurse stood next to her, changing the bag on her drip. Margaret's bad right arm lay, palm up, on the bed next to her. The IV line trailed out of it and was held in place with a bandage, so there were no sticky plasters to damage the paper-thin skin. Margaret was talking, the words slightly slurred by the droop on one side of her mouth. 'Absolute drivel,' she said. 'Why even put it on? It's not as though it even has a proper storyline.'

'Did someone leave Big Brother on again?' Grace went across to the other side of the bed and laid a kiss on the soft cheek. Margaret was small, with her skin stretched over delicate bones. She had once been firm and plump and formidable, but the stroke and age had shrunk her. She was, however, still formidable.

'No. It was some other reality thing. The language those young people used. I'm surprised they even let it on the airwaves.'

'Perhaps I should read you 1984 next.'

'George Orwell would be turning in his grave,' Margaret muttered.

The nurse caught Grace's eye and raised her eyebrows. 'Now, are you comfortable Margaret? Do you need me to adjust the bed at all?'

'I'm fine now, thank you Judy. Especially now that Grace is here. It will be good to hear a proper story.' She paused. 'You couldn't get me a glass of sherry?'

Both the nurse and Grace laughed.

'Nice try, Margaret,' said the nurse. 'You are a one.' She smiled fondly at the old lady. 'I'll leave you to your reading then. Got the call button within reach? Good. Just buzz if you need anything.' She looked up. 'I'll see you later, Grace.'

'Bye Judy.'

They watched her leave. Once the door had clicked behind her, Margaret said, 'She's worried about that son of hers. He's going to Afghanistan next week.'

'I guess he'd be in the front line too. Poor Judy. It must be horrible sending your son out to work knowing he may never come back.' Grace pulled the comfy chair nearer to the bed.

'What a waste of youth,' said Margaret. 'Still, it's better than sitting here waiting to die.'

Grace ignored the comment. She didn't want to get drawn into a conversation about the attractions of death

12

when compared to boredom. Margaret complained about being bored all the time. Yet she was constantly busy with watching TV, or catching up on gossip. She even insisted on being wheeled into the chair aerobics classes so that she could wave her good arm around according to the instructions and then stay for a cup of a tea afterwards.

'It's a short visit today Margaret. I've got to go to a fundraising meeting,' said Grace. She opened the cupboard next to Margaret's bed and pulled out a copy of *The Life of Pi*. There was a postcard stuck in it to mark the place. 'Ready?'

'No. No. Tell me about your day first,' said Margaret, leaning back and turning her head to look at Grace. 'What's happening out there in the real world?'

'You tell me,' said Grace. Margaret watched the news every day. She was better informed about world politics than Grace was. She also knew what films were out. What new books she wanted to read.

'How's work?'

Grace shrugged. 'Same as always.'

'And how is your assistant?' Margaret seemed to remember every small detail that Grace had shared with her.

'Okay, I think. She was going on about getting back into the dating scene.'

'Good for her,' said Margaret. 'It's a shame to waste your life looking back and wishing things had been different.' Margaret gave Grace a meaningful look. Her eyes, nestled in amongst the smile lines, were sharp. 'You should go out with her. Hitch your colours to her mast … as it were. Get out there and meet a nice young man.'

Grace opened the book. Margaret gave her this lecture every so often. She didn't need to hear it again. It was patronising and irritating. And true.

'You need to do something outside your comfort zone,' Margaret carried on. 'Get yourself out of this rut you've got yourself into.'

'Do you want me to read today or not?'

Margaret sighed. 'Only trying to help. It's such a waste that you're hiding away behind your work.'

Grace closed her eyes and composed herself. Margaret meant well. She had been friends with Grace's mother when she was staying in the hospice. When her mother died, Margaret and Grace had sort of adopted each other. Margaret was trying to carry on her mother's campaign to get Grace to settle down. 'I'm sorry. I shouldn't have snapped. It's just ... been a long day.'

'Sorry,' said Margaret, not sounding sorry at all. 'Perhaps you had better read. It's a wonderful book, this. Who would have thought a story about a boy and a tiger afloat in the ocean would be so enthralling? And the writing is so lucid.'

Grace removed the bookmark, settled back in her chair and began to read. Soon she and Margaret were in a lifeboat in the middle of the sea. The hospice, with its cheerful wallpaper and bunches of flowers and impossible-to-disguise medical equipment were all forgotten, for a while.

Consciousness returned slowly. 'I must be in the ambulance,' Sally thought. 'After the crash.' There had been a car crash. She remembered that much.

Everything around her was black. So black it was as though there was nothing above her, nothing below, nothing all around. The blackness was not threatening. It was a comforting sort of absence. Genuine nothing.

She should have been frightened, but she wasn't. She knew there were things that she wanted, needed even, but she couldn't recall what they were. So she relaxed. This was probably a dream and she'd wake up all too soon. In the meantime, she would enjoy this … she sought for a word; a name for this unfamiliar feeling of everything being as it should be. This … tranquillity.

Every so often there would be something. A distant noise. Or sense of her body. Arms and legs she knew she had, but couldn't move or touch or see. Like phantom limbs, they told her they were there and then melted away again.

It was a voice that caught her attention. A man's voice. Deep and soft and kind. Very kind. She knew that voice. He was important. Sally listened. Eventually a name came to her. Peter. That voice was Peter. He meant something.

She only heard his speaking in snatches. A word here and there, the cadences of his voice that resonated. There were long gaps when she went back to her lovely world of nothing and then, again, the voice. Eventually the sound of Peter's voice came in longer and longer snatches. Until she could hear whole sentences at a time. Then there were other voices. Women who said things like 'let's change those sheets for you Sally' and then said things like 'I went to that new club last night' or 'Our Gary wants to join the army. I don't know what to do. I don't want him to get shot'.

With the increasing clarity came the other stuff. The feelings. The frustration. She tried to move. To say 'I'm here. It's dark. Get me out', but nothing happened. She would have cried, if she could. Eventually, she learned to listen. She learned the different nurses' names. She waited for the gossip when they talked by her bedside. She knew by now she was in a hospital or something. She also knew that no one came to visit her other than Peter.

Chapter Three

Peter stopped at the nurses' station to check on progress. There was no one there, so he waited, examining a painting of a jungle that hung on the wall. The hospice often displayed work from the local art college. This one was rather good. It had a certain depth to it. Peter moved closer and was so engrossed in the greens and blacks that he jumped when someone said, 'Hello Peter.'

He turned to find one of the nurses wheeling the medicine trolley to the back of the nurses' bay, which was set up half way down the corridor. Apart from the trolley and the apron, the only thing that marked her out as a nurse was the big badge, which declared her name to be Maria. She put the trolley away and returned, minus the apron. 'Have you been to see her yet?' She smiled at him and pulled Sally's notes up on the computer.

'Not yet.' He looked down at the flowers.

'She's doing well. No change.' They always said that. As though 'no change' and 'doing well' were the same thing.

'Has she said anything?'

'She's been whispering again. We still can't make out any words though.'

He had sat with Sally night after night, talking to her, reading to her, listening to her. She hadn't whispered anything. 'Is there a pattern? Maybe something triggers it?'

'Not that we can figure out, apart from it's normally in the day time.'

'I'll spend the whole day here on Saturday,' he said. 'Maybe I'll be able to see if there's anything that stimulates the whispering.'

'Did Dr Harris call you? She was going to call you about a change in medication.' Maria pulled open a drawer and looked through the files.

'She did.'

'I have a consent form for you to sign, right … here.' She pulled the document out and laid it on the counter for him. She handed him a pen. 'Are you okay with it? Do you have any questions?'

'No. I think Dr Harris covered everything. She's trying to get Sally to a higher level of alertness … if she can. That's fine with me.' He scanned the document and signed. 'What's the date?'

'Twenty-third,' said Maria. She watched him sign and took the papers from him. 'And how are you doing? Are you okay?' She had that concerned voice that people did.

Peter forced a smile. 'Yes. I'm doing okay. Just, you know, tired.' He knew better than to say how he really felt. The last time he'd done that various people had pestered him until he agreed to see a counsellor. It was nice that they cared, but really, the only thing that would help was Sally coming out of her coma. Unless they could do that for him, they were just wasting his time.

'Okay. If you need anything, just say. We are here to look after the relatives as well. Not just Sally.'

'I know. Thank you.' He held the smile as he turned and went into Sally's room.

Sally had been here for months now and it still hurt him to come in. This room was much better than the one she'd had in the hospital. It was almost worth the price he paid to keep her here to have a private room with pretty wallpaper and rugs instead of clinical walls and moppable lino. He had even brought in Sally's bed linen from when she lived

17

alone. It shouldn't make a difference, but it did. Sally would have preferred it.

She was lying on the bed, covered by a bedspread with blue flowers on it. It looked like it had been washed many, many times. It may well have been a favourite of hers. But Sally couldn't see it, so what did it matter? He approached her, searching for signs of change, but there were none. Her hair had been neatly combed and gathered so that it fell over one shoulder. The blonde had grown out of it almost completely now, leaving it heavy and brown. The nurses made sure it always looked clean and brushed, for which Peter was grateful. Sally would have appreciated that.

'Hello Darling.' He leaned over and kissed the top of her head, careful not to disturb the NG tube that ran into her nose. She didn't look like Sally. She was just a woman, pale and still and covered in tubes and pads and things. A mock person. The only movement was her chest going slowly up and down. Up and down.

'I've brought you some red roses again,' Peter said. He took the old flowers out of the vase. 'I thought these ones needed changing.' He spoke loudly, in case she could hear. 'They're not quite the same bright red as the ones before. The man in the shop has changed supplier.' He was talking nonsense. It was hard to keep a conversation going when the other person didn't respond. He changed the water in the vase, pitched the old flowers in the bin, bit the edge of the packet of flower food to open it. 'I really should bring a pair of scissors,' he said to Sally. 'I keep meaning to.' He put the flower food in and arranged the fresh roses in the vase. 'There.' He moved it to where her eyeline would be, if her eyes had been open. 'Do you like them?'

In and out. In and out. Nothing more.

He sat in the chair, close enough to the bed that he could hold her hand. Her wedding ring was on her hand. She'd been wearing it when the crash happened. He'd asked if she could keep it on. The chart at the end of the bed said Mrs Sally Wesley. Not Sally Cummings. It seemed the right thing to do when admitting a bride.

He told her about his day, about the new client who wanted a database setting up to manage his documents. He mentioned that Steve was being a pain, but he couldn't let him go because he couldn't manage the back office stuff and go out to client meetings by himself. After some time he ran out of things to say.

He pulled out a Reader's Digest. He'd known Sally for nearly two years now and the only things he'd seen her read were self help books and decorating magazines. Reading self help books made him want to scream and he didn't know or care about the celebrities in Sally's favourite magazines, so he read the Reader's Digest to her instead. At least it was relatively interesting and the articles were short.

A different nurse popped her head in. 'Hello Peter, I'm just going to do her readings.'

'Okay.' He pushed his chair back, torn between being annoyed and glad for the interruption.

'How are you?' She stood in front of Sally's monitor and wrote things down.

'I'm alright, thanks.'

'Doing anything this weekend? Apart from visiting us obviously.'

'Not really.' He put the book down on his lap. 'I've got to go to my mum's for a family lunch on Sunday.'

'That's nice.' The nurse straightened a crease out of the bedclothes. 'Sally has such lovely bedding. I love the little blue flowers. Were they her favourite?'

'Pardon?' He looked up in confusion. What was this woman going on about?

'I just wondered, because she has so many sheets with forget-me-nots on them ...'

He shook his head. 'I think her favourite flowers were roses. I don't know why those sheets have blue on them.'

'Ah, well they're very pretty anyway.' The nurse leaned across and checked Sally's drip. 'I reckon that drip's going to need changing in about an hour.' She made a note. She stood back and looked down at Sally's prone figure. 'I'll come back and sort that out for you in a bit Sally, okay?' she said, as though speaking to a child. 'You said something earlier to me. Are you going to repeat it for Peter?'

Breathing. In and out. In and out.

Peter perked up. 'What did she say?'

'I'm not sure.' The nurse sighed. 'It sounded like "far". Or could've been "car".'

It wasn't much help, but it was nice to know. Sally had been whispering things for a few weeks now. Not loudly or clearly enough for anyone to hear. But it was movement. Something beyond a simple cough and a twitch. A sign that his Sally was in there. Somewhere.

When the nurse left, Peter stood up and leaned closer. 'Darling, can you hear me? Sally?'

Nothing.

'If you can hear me, cough.'

Nothing.

Peter sighed and sat back down. 'Oh Sally.' He rubbed his face. His eyes rested on the bunch of flowers and for a moment, he had a flashback to the woman in the lift. 'There was a woman,' he said, still staring numbly at the flowers. 'In the lift. She said they were beautiful flowers. I said I bring them in in case you can smell them. Can you smell them, Sally?'

20

Nothing.

'I wish …' There were so many things he wished. He wished he'd never found that blasted lottery ticket. He wished he'd handled it differently. He wished he hadn't lost control of the car. But all the wishing in the world wouldn't change what happened. He lost control of the car. He swerved off the road. He pitched the car over the bank by the road. He'd survived with only a few broken bones and a leg that hurt in the mornings. He'd let her down.

He rubbed his face, digging his knuckles into his forehead. 'Who am I kidding? You can't hear me. It's all just random twitches. You're not there at all. It's just … your body.' He stood up. 'I'm going to get myself a coffee. I'll be right back.'

He didn't like being angry when he was in Sally's room. If she could hear him, it would only make her sad.

Grace stood next to her friend Harry and surveyed the common room on level three. To her it looked perfectly serviceable. 'I think it looks okay, I'm not sure what all the fuss is about?' she said.

Harry gave her a sidelong glance. 'Sometimes, we get so used to seeing something, we stop noticing it altogether.' He picked a vase of plastic flowers out of an alcove and rubbed a finger on the leaves. 'Ugh. These can go for a start.' He replaced them.

'Aren't you going to put them in the bin, then?' said Grace.

'Nah. Best to leave everything as it is until the weekend. We'll start with a good clear out first. Then we'll clear it section by section.' Harry strode across the room, warming to his theme. 'We'll start over there.'

Grace tuned him out as he planned things. Harry liked

to think out loud. She had known him for a while now. He visited daily too. His father had been in several times as his condition waxed and waned. Harry and Grace had got to know each other through bumping into each other so often that they'd started to chat.

She looked around the room and thought of what Margaret had said about doing something to get herself shaken out of her rut. Like what? Going out with her work colleagues wasn't an option. She worked as an R&D biochemist in a small start-up company. Most of her colleagues were new graduates whose idea of fun involved clubbing and drinking and going on the pull. She couldn't remember the last time she'd been out on the pull.

'Penny for them?' Harry came up beside her and made her jump.

'Oh, just thinking about something Margaret said.' She told him the gist of the conversation.

'She's got a point, my darling,' said Harry. 'You're too young and too pretty to be wasting your life coming here and hanging out with crumblies.'

She didn't much like being called 'my darling', but she took it from Harry. Partly because he called everyone 'my darling' and partly because she couldn't stop him anyway.

'But Margaret hasn't got anyone else. She needs me.'

Harry gave her a knowing look. 'Are you sure it's not the other way around?'

Grace opened her mouth to argue, then thought of her silent, empty house and what was left of her life now that her mother's death had robbed her not only of a parent, but of a major purpose. If it weren't for work and Margaret, she would see no one. She looked away.

'It's hard to move on,' said Harry. He put a hand on her

shoulder. 'But you need to, Grace. You don't want to end up haunting this place like a lost soul because you can't face real life any more.'

Grace said nothing. She moved over to a table and straightened out the magazines on it.

'You need to do something big and bold and out of character,' said Harry, waving his hands expansively. He was getting into it now. 'Something that will lift you out of the doldrums.'

Grace shook her head. 'I don't think I'm ready for that sort of thing yet.'

Harry gave a theatrical sigh. 'Oh okay then. We'll just have to start small. Maybe with redecorating this room and making it a fun place for the patients and families to hang out, eh?'

Grace smiled. 'That sounds like a plan. What do you need me to sort out before Saturday?'

Harry pulled a notebook out of his back pocket. 'I have a list.'

Grace laughed. 'You always do.'

Sally tried to sniff. She had a nose, she knew she did. She breathed in. Nothing. There was no smell in the nothingness.

Peter had said something about flowers. Smelling flowers. He'd said roses. Did she like roses? She was sure it wasn't that. What did she like? In the comforting darkness, Sally thought of forget-me-nots. She liked forget-me-nots. Little sprays of blue. So, why did she tell Peter she liked roses? And then, out of the nothingness, a memory surfaced.

'Look, Daddy, roses, aren't they beautiful?' Sally looked up. She was small. Her little fist clutched her father's forefinger. There were people about. A market. 'Mummy would love some roses Daddy. Shall we get her some?'

Her father smiled down at her. He had a charming smile. Vivid green eyes and brown hair. Sally had inherited them both. 'I'm not sure we can afford them, Princess.'

'I'm sure we can Daddy. I'm sure we can.' She pulled him towards the buckets set out at small child level on the floor.

'How much are they?' Her father asked the seller. When he heard the response, his face fell. Even from that angle, Sally could tell. He crouched down until he was level with her. 'I'm sorry Princess, we can't afford those.'

She wanted them. She wanted her mummy to have the pretty flowers. She wanted to see the smile spread across her face when she came in from her cleaning job. Daddy would get her a cup of tea and she, Sally, would present her with a beautiful bunch of roses. And now that couldn't happen. Daddy had ruined it all. Hot tears gathered. 'You always say that!' She stamped her foot and tried to pull away from his hand. 'You never do anything nice for me and Mummy.'

Her father pulled her closer to him and hugged her. 'I know, sweetheart, I know. I've let you down.' He held her, stroking her hair. 'Tell you what, we'll find some different flowers for Mummy on the way home, okay?'

Eventually, Sally nodded. She wiped a little palm across her eyes and drew away from her Daddy. As he stood up, she thought his face was wet.

Later, when Mummy came home, Sally was bursting to tell her what they'd found. She hurtled into Glenda as soon as she came in the door.

'Hello darling,' said Daddy, following his daughter out of the kitchen. He kissed his wife. 'Sally, let Mummy get her coat off.' He bent forward. 'I'll get Mummy into the living room, you go get the surprise.'

Sally zoomed off into the kitchen. The posy of forget-me-nots was in a small glass, with one of Sally's hair ribbons tied round it. It was in the middle of the table, Sally had to drag a chair across so that she could reach. Daddy came in and made a cup of tea. He set a tray, with tea and a small cake they'd bought. 'Okay Sal? Ready?'

Sally nodded and went into the living room where her mother was sitting in an armchair, rubbing her temples. 'Happy Birthday Mummy.' She presented her with the posy.

'Oh Sally, they're beautiful. Did you pick them? How lovely.'

'We got them from the park. We would have got a gooder bunch, but the man came and shouted and we had to run away. It was such fun.'

Her mother glanced up at her father. 'Really? From the park? What an adventure.'

'Happy Birthday darling.' He kissed the top of her head. 'I'm sorry we couldn't get you the special things you deserve. But ...'

Her mother gathered him and Sally to her. 'I have all I need, right here.' She kissed them both. Sally snuggled up on her lap. She looked up and caught the expression on her father's face. Even at that age, she could see the despair in his features. But she couldn't understand why it frightened her.

Chapter Four

Peter woke up when a nurse shook him gently by the shoulder. 'Peter, it's nearly 9.30. Would you like us to make up a camp bed for you?'

He sat up and rubbed his eyes. He had been watching Sally. He couldn't believe he'd nodded off. What if Sally had whispered something? He'd have missed it. 'No. I'll be off in a minute.' The book had fallen on the floor. He retrieved it. Sally lay in exactly the same position as before, her chest rising and falling peacefully. 'Did she say anything while I was asleep?'

There were CCTV cameras in all the rooms and Sally was hooked up to so many monitors that something would have gone off.

The nurse shook her head. 'I'm sorry.' She put her head to one side in a concerned manner. 'Are you sure you don't want to me to set up the bed for you?'

Peter covered up a yawn and stretched. 'No. You will call me though, won't you? If she says or does anything.'

'Of course.' She turned back to look at Sally for a moment, before giving Peter a smile. 'I'll leave you to it, then. I'm sorry to have woken you.'

'No, no. That's fine. I didn't mean to fall asleep. It defeats the object of my being here.'

'I'm sure Sally was grateful for the company,' said the nurse.

Peter thought that was a ridiculous thing to say, but didn't respond. What was the point? People needed to say something.

He pulled on his coat and tucked the book back into his

pocket. 'Bye, bye darling. I'll come see you again tomorrow.' He kissed her forehead and stroked her hair. 'Maybe tomorrow you'll talk to me.' Another kiss. He turned back at the door to look at her lying there like a rag doll. 'Night.' He left the room, closing the door carefully behind him.

Someone was walking past and he almost walked into them when he started towards the lift. 'Oh.' It was the woman from earlier. They walked along the corridor, both heading for the same place, but not wanting to talk to each other. Peter looked at the ground as he walked. Well, this was awkward.

When the lift arrived, he let her go in first. She cleared her throat. 'I was just at a meeting with the fundraising committee. We're redecorating the common room on this floor this weekend. Would you like to help?'

Peter blinked. He hadn't been expecting that. 'Fundraising? Whatever for? This is a private hospice, surely the extortionate fees cover everything.' Oh bugger. That made him sound tight. The place was expensive. He didn't mind. He wanted his Sally to have the best care and comfort available.

She smiled. She was tall and had smooth skin the colour of latte. Her features were a delicate mix of Asian and Caucasian – high cheekbones, big eyes, wide mouth, sharp chin. It was her hair that caught his attention. It gleamed.

It occurred to him that she was quite beautiful, if a little grave. He wondered where that thought had come from.

'Actually, it's a social enterprise,' she said. 'The fee paying part of the hospital subsidises the West Wing.'

'West wing?' He was aware that there was another wing to the place. He had assumed it was more of the same.

'Hedgehog House. Children's Palliative and Respite care. It's funded by the charity. The hospice donates all profits.'

Peter ran the words past his internal dictionary. Children. Palliative. Respite. 'Oh.' More of the same, yes, but sadder, somehow. 'I hadn't realised.'

'I didn't either when I started coming here. I used to wheel Mum out into the garden sometimes when the weather was nice, just so that she got to see the sun. We used to meet the families then.'

There was an awkward silence.

'I'm Grace, by the way,' she said

'Peter.'

The lift door opened and they stepped out into the lobby. They walked out to the door together, Grace giving the security guard a wave as they passed.

'So, what about it?' she said as they reached the doors. 'Will you help?'

Peter hesitated. He didn't want to help. He wanted to be left alone. He was busy. He had a business to run. His wife was in a coma. Life was a ridiculous circus of work meetings, medical meetings and long, pointless evenings sitting next to Sally's bed, waiting for her to wake up. It was exhausting. He didn't have anything left to give anyone. 'I don't …'

Her disappointment showed on her face. It was as though she had a personal investment in making him join the cause. 'I understand,' she said. Her face resumed its stoical expression. 'Well, it was nice to talk to you Peter. I hope … things get better.'

He felt like a selfish wanker, but he'd done the right thing. He was walking such a tightrope between coping and going mad with worry that he had to be careful. Too much stress and things could go very wrong. Sally was an orphan. She had no one else to depend on. He had to be there and be fit to look after her when she came round. He couldn't make commitments he couldn't keep.

He watched Grace walk, her plait swinging, across the car park. Yes. He had done the right thing. He sighed and went to his own car. So why did he feel like such a git?

Grace threw her keys into the little pot on the shelf that was there specifically for that purpose. It had once held the whole family's keys, but now there were just hers. She hung her coat up and thought for the umpteenth time that she really should get round to throwing away her mother's scarves that hung on the other pegs in the downstairs loo. It was on her list of things to tackle. She'd get round to it at some point.

It didn't take her long to defrost a meal that she'd batch cooked at the weekend. It was so much nicer to have meals already done when she got home. When the microwave pinged, the soup was too hot. She left it to cool and put a sliced bagel in to toast. Watching the toaster, she thought about her encounter with Peter. Hah. So much for doing something bold and out of character. Well, she'd tried that and look how that turned out. Take that, Harry!

Walking around the common room had made her look at the familiar room in a different way. Suddenly, things that she'd never noticed before jumped out at her. The carpet showed tracks where feet and wheelchairs had rolled over it every day. The comfy chairs in front of the TV were worn from many different bottoms and knees and heads. The wallpaper and curtains were faded where the sun caught them. All this had always been there for her to see, yet she'd never noticed. It was as though she'd been walking through the area with blinkers on.

The sudden feeling that this wasn't just about a common room hit her. This could just as well apply to her life. She'd been a carer for so long, first helping her mother with looking after her father, and then by herself, looking after her mother. When she'd finally allowed herself to put her mother into a hospice, she'd felt so bad that she'd spent every spare minute visiting. Somewhere in amongst all that she'd forgotten how to be young. Now it was almost too late to learn again.

The toaster popped. She gathered her food and sat at the table. As she ate her soup and bagel, she let her attention roam around the kitchen. This was another place that she'd got so used to that she'd stopped really seeing it. The walls were exactly as her mother had left them. The same cookbooks on the same shelves, sitting next to the same twee little tins.

Grace twisted around in her chair and surveyed the whole room. It could do with a repaint. Maybe a declutter. She thought about the terribly difficult to use knives and the wooden spoons so old they were starting to dissolve at the ends. She could do with a new set of cutlery too. She smiled to herself. She could go on a shopping spree. Now that sounded like so much more fun than dusting around knick-knacks that meant nothing to her anymore.

She finished her soup, washed up the bowl and spoon and left them drying next to her mug on the draining board. Her mother would have made her dry them up and put them away. It suddenly occurred to her that she only ever used one set of crockery. The same mug, bowl and spoon, the same one plate. She shook her head. How had she let this happen?

Photos of her at various ages hung on the wall along the stairs. Her parents had already been old when she arrived. Her mother in her forties, her father just past fifty. To them, she had been a late given gift. They had tried to document every bit of their happiness that they could. She had taken it for granted that everyone's parents kept every single school photo and a folder full of every appearance in the nativity play, school poetry competition, whatever. They were a family. Wasn't that what families did?

Normally, she would have gone straight to her room, had a shower and gone to bed. Today, she paused. The door to her parents' room was shut. She rarely went in there, apart from to clean it when it came up on her cleaning routine. She opened the door and turned on the light. She had cleared her father's wardrobe out after his funeral, so that her mother didn't have to do it, but there were still photos and bits and bobs of his around the room. There was a photo of him as a young man, skinny and fresh off the boat from Sri Lanka. A photo of him, much older, standing next to his pretty English wife, both laughing. Grace picked up the photo of the three of them, her parents beaming, despite the shadows under their eyes, and herself; a tiny bundle in her mother's arms. She sank down onto the bed.

She missed them. It was natural. Those last years had been such an endless treadmill of meals, medications, appointments, tantrums and frustrations, but she'd got used to that. So used to it, that she'd almost forgotten what it had been like before, when her parents were able. How sad to have lost all those trips to museums, bedtime stories, games of chase, where Daddy could never catch her because he was too wheezy after a few steps. Grace smiled. She missed them, but she didn't have to preserve them in their old age. It wasn't fair to any of them.

She was about to replace the photo back on the dressing table, where it had always lived, when she decided against it. Instead, she took it with her. She would put it somewhere in her room and remember them as they were then.

Later, in bed, she could just make out the shape of the photo on her bedside table. It made her feel better, somehow, as though a tiny parcel of weight had lifted. Grace smiled and closed her eyes.

Sally remembered a party. The room had been decorated in rich reds and creams. There were chandeliers hanging from the ceiling. She had to persuade a man to give her a ticket and had to pay a fortune to buy the dress, even second-hand. Charity shop? Hah. Rip-off merchants more like. The prices they charged for something they'd been given for free! Sally had haggled, but that bitch that ran the shop had stood firm. Charitable? Bollocks.

She checked the dress was clinging to her in all the right places and gave a little wiggle to make sure it swished properly. Excellent. Designer wear at high street prices. She supposed she couldn't really complain. It was an investment. If tonight paid off, she could afford the real thing. She swept into the room and was marginally pissed off when heads did not turn instantly in her direction.

She grabbed a glass of orange juice off the tray as the waiter went past. Sipping it delicately, she scanned the room. The trouble with rich men was that most of them didn't make it big until they were middle-aged. She could do the sugar daddy thing again, she supposed, but really, if she had to sleep with a man, it would be a massive help if he was attractive. She spotted Maurice Kemp, the securities guy. Too old. Jeremy Traynor, whole food retail – nearly bald. Seth Bridley ... not bad looking. Decent value too, but suspiciously quiet. Rumour had it, he was gay but not out. Sally didn't understand why he didn't just come out and be done with it. Seth was talking to a tall, blond man in glasses. Sally narrowed her eyes. If Seth was flirting with this guy, he was certainly not responding. He seemed to be listening and smiling though.

Sally slinked a little closer. The man laughed at something Seth said. His face creased lightly at the eyes. His attention was on Seth, giving Sally ample time to study him. He was tall and handsome in a clean-cut sort of a way. Short blond hair, blue-grey eyes, chiselled jaw. It was the smile that was interesting. Smile lines that deep must mean that he did it a lot. She drained her glass, set it down and waited until there was another waiter bearing a tray near the man. She stood where the man could see and hear her, then pretended to try and fail to catch the attention of the waiter. A flicker on the eyes told her he'd spotted her. She ignored him for a moment before making eye contact.

'Hi.' She gave him her best smile. 'I'm dying for a drink, but I can't seem to catch the waiter's attention. Could you …' She looked up at him, pleading.

'Oh, of course.' He turned, raised a hand, and waved to the waiter. 'Here you go.' He handed a glass of champagne to Sally.

'Thank you so much,' she said.

'No problem.' There was that smile again. She found herself smiling back. It came naturally. She liked this man.

'I'm Sally, Sally Cummings.' She held out her hand. Hopefully the manner in which she said it would encourage him to introduce himself in the same way.

He shook it. 'I'm Peter Wesley.'

'And what do you do Peter Wesley?' Her mind churned through her internal who's who file. Wesley. Something to do with IT. Not hugely wealthy, but had potential. Besides, she thought, taking in the broad shoulders and lack of paunch, he's nice to look at. A quick glance at his left hand to double check he was single. Married men were lucrative, but she was twenty-five now. She needed to find someone before she had to start worrying about the aging process. Yes. He would do nicely.

'I'm an IT consultant. I do mostly knowledge management.' His gaze skimmed over her, resting fractionally on her hair when she flicked it over her shoulder. 'How about you?'

'I'm an estate agent,' she said. By this time, Peter's former companion had wandered off. They were standing together in a crowd. Perfect.

'How funny,' he said. 'I'm looking for a house to buy at the moment.'

'Fate.'

He seemed amused.

She gave him her most dazzling smile. 'So, tell me, what sort of thing are you looking for?'

He explained what he was after. She translated in her head – a house big enough to leave his options open, but not so big that it suggested a family. Good money, but nothing ostentatious. He seemed to be looking at moving along the ladder from a bachelor pad to something more grown up. This all sounded very promising.

'I believe I can help you with that,' she said. 'I can think of a couple of places on our books that might interest you. Here, let me give you my card.' She pulled a card out of her clutch bag and scribbled her phone number on the back. 'I've put my personal mobile on the back. You know … in case …' She lowered her eyes.

'Yes,' he said. He took the card. She looked back up in time to see the flicker in his eyes when their hands touched.

Someone else touched his arm and Sally left him alone. He would be in touch. She could tell. She knew just the houses to show him. The first would be exactly what he thought he wanted. The second would be different, but she would sell him the dream. The third would be perfect for the new dream. By the time they'd seen the third house, she would have him.

The next morning Peter woke up to the sound of a car crunching up the gravel drive. A car door slammed. He groaned and pushed himself out of bed. He had just got to the landing, pulling his dressing gown over his pyjamas when his mother let herself in through the front door. 'Peter, darling. It's only me,' she shouted. She looked up and spotted him. 'Hello darling. Did we wake you?'

As Peter limped down the stairs, the door opened again to admit his father. 'You did, but that's okay. I said I'd sit with Sally all day today.'

His parents exchanged a glance. His father carried some carrier bags into the kitchen while his mother removed her coat and scarf, still watching Peter.

He ignored them and went into the kitchen. 'Coffee?'

'Hmm,' said his father, as he deposited the bags on the surface and then sat down. Peter put the kettle on and put on a round of toast. His leg was particularly painful today. He moved it around, trying to warm up the muscles so that the pain eased.

'I've brought you some cottage pie, which can go in the freezer, and some bolognaise sauce for today. You'll have to make yourself some pasta to go with it. I was going to make some this morning but I didn't have time.' Diane Wesley was a small, tidy woman. She moved around Peter's kitchen with the assurance of someone who knew exactly where everything was. Peter noticed that she'd moved a few things from the places Sally had allocated for them. Sally was going to be really pissed off when she came back.

Diane unpacked a load of Tupperware containers from the bags. The kettle boiled. Peter started making drinks.

'Oh Peter. You haven't eaten half the meals I left for you.'

Peter ran a hand through his hair. 'Uh … I got home late the past few nights and I wasn't hungry.'

'I know you come in late. That's why I leave these meals for you. Darling, you have to eat.' She came over and put a hand over his. 'Look at you. You're so thin. And you need a haircut.'

He moved his hand away. He'd had this lecture before. 'I can look after myself. Don't worry.'

His father made a noise. Peter looked up. 'What?'

His father was frowning. 'Don't talk to your mother like that,' he said. 'And we're not so sure you can look after yourself.'

'Frank …' There was warning in his mother's tone.

'No love. We can't keep pretending that things are going fine. We're worried about you, Peter. We think you need to see a doctor.'

His mother gasped. 'Frank!'

Peter scowled. 'A doctor? I see doctors every day. Why do you think I need another one?'

Frank shot a quick glance at Diane, before he said, 'We think you might be depressed. Just a bit. We could be wrong.'

'Yeah? Well, let me see. I was in a car crash on my wedding day. I have a scar the size of Berkshire from my car keys cutting into my leg. I live in a house with more rooms than I know what to do with. I spend my days either working or in a hospital room because my wife, the person I was supposed to be sharing the rest of my life with, is in a fucking coma.' He slammed the kettle back onto its base. 'Excuse me if I'm not bursting into song!'

'It's hardly surprising, given what you've been through,' said Frank. 'There's no shame in admitting …'

'I'm not depressed.'

'You're showing all the signs—'

'Frank,' his mother cut in. 'See, he's not ready. Stop pestering him.'

'No, wait. What signs?' Peter glared at his father. His mother said nothing.

'Dad?'

'You've been really distant. We expected to you be sad and angry, but we didn't expect you to stop noticing the world around you. You spend all your time at work or with Sally ...' His father ticked things off his fingers, as though running through a list. He had come prepared for an argument.

'Your sister had a baby, you haven't even been to see him,' his mother added. 'This isn't like you, Peter.'

'Val's baby?' He'd sent a card and a present. He intended to go and visit. Soon. Sometime soon.

'Jacob. He's six months old.' His mother fetched her handbag and dug around. Pulling out her phone, she tapped through and turned it to face him. There was a photo of his nephews with a chubby, smiling baby nestled between them. 'There. That's him.'

Six months? No, it couldn't have been. He'd got the text only a few weeks ... he frowned. Maybe it had been more than a few weeks. But six months? Christ. Where had the time gone? He reached out for the phone and studied the picture. 'The boys look so big.'

'Yes. Having a baby brother meant they grew up a lot. Terry's a bit jealous about not being the baby of the family any more, but he loves his baby brother.' His mother's eyes glowed with grandmotherly pride.

He looked back at the photo. His nephews who had got bigger without him noticing and a baby he'd never met.

Maybe his father had a point. He looked up and caught his father's eye. Understanding dawned, unwelcome. He had been so busy feeling sorry for himself and worrying about Sally that he'd forgotten the rest of the world carried on.

Peter opened his mouth to speak, but his mother held up a hand. 'I know what you're going to say, and I do understand. It's been a really horrible year. You've had unrelenting stress and worry. But darling, you need to think of yourself too. If you carry on like this, you're going to find that if Sally dies, you won't have anyone to support you.'

A moment of silence followed. His parents watched him, cautiously, as though they were bracing themselves. His mother was standing next his father. Peter could see her hand gripping Frank's shoulder. He looked up to her face, and felt as though he were seeing her for the first time in ages. She looked tired and ragged with worry. Her eyes were trained on his face, as though waiting to see if her words would make him crumble. His father seemed outwardly calm, but Peter could see the tension in his shoulders and in the pinched brows. It had taken a lot for his parents to say that to him. They must have worried for ages.

'Oh, just leave me alone.' He abandoned his coffee and stalked out of the room.

'Where are you going?'

'To have a shower and shave. Or would you rather I didn't go near a razor?' He heard the intake of breath behind him. He got as far as the bottom of the stairs before his conscience kicked him. He shouldn't have said that. They meant well. They worried about him. It's what they always did. He sighed and leaned his head against the wall. He should go back and apologise, but he didn't want to move. It was all so … difficult.

He wasn't sure how long he stood there. He started when his heard his mother say, 'Peter?'

He pushed himself away from the wall. 'I'm sorry Mum. I shouldn't have said that.'

She reached up and touched his face. 'You can't help it.'

Peter sank down onto the bottom step and his mother sat next to him.

'I know you're stressed, sweetheart, and that you're hurting and missing Sally. But beating yourself up like this isn't going to help anyone. You need to stay strong and healthy. If Sally wakes up, she'll need you.'

'If Sally wakes up ... and I want her to wake up, Mum. So desperately. But what if ...' he couldn't say it. 'If ...'

'If she's damaged?' See. She couldn't say it either. It was too horrible to contemplate. Sally without the ability to walk. Or speak. Or bowel control or whatever. He would have to look after her like she was a child. He'd do it, but she would hate that. Or what if she didn't remember him when she woke up? Or her personality had changed? The thing he loved most about Sally was her enthusiasm for life. It was her energy that dragged him out of his dull grey comfort zone and showed him this wonderful future where they brought the best out of each other. What if she woke up without it? What if she blamed him as much as he blamed himself?

'It's my fault,' he said. 'I was driving.' He closed his eyes and saw Sally, in her wedding dress, her eyes big and piercing green. The concern on her face as she said, 'Don't you trust me?' That was the last thing she had said to him. 'Don't you trust me?' And he'd tried to throw the lottery ticket away. Because he didn't. If he'd had faith in her, if he hadn't had the moment of doubt, she would still be here. 'I let her down.'

'Oh Peter.' Diane put her arms around him. 'Oh my boy. My poor darling boy. You can't blame yourself. It's not your fault. It was an accident. No one knew it was going to happen. No one could have prevented it.'

He turned to look at her worried face. She was wrong. But he nodded. 'I'm going to get ready.' He stood up, and climbed the stairs, leaving his mother sitting at the bottom.

By the time he'd had a shower and dressed, Peter felt better. He sat on the edge of his bed and stared at the wedding photo on his bedside.

His parents' concern for him had shifted everything slightly. It was as though he had gained some sort of clarity compared to before. Something needed to change. The phrase 'parallel planning' popped into his mind. It was what he'd been told he had to do. Live life with two parallel futures – one where Sally woke up and needed help and one where things stayed as they were. The idea of either was too horrendous to contemplate, so he'd avoided thinking about either; tackling each day as it came. He realised that this was an exhausting way to live. He couldn't plan anything and he kept putting everything non-essential on hold.

Well, something was going to have to change. He wasn't sure how he was going to achieve that. The memory of the woman from the lift, Grace, popped into his mind. She had asked him to help with redecorating the hospice. It was happening that day and it wasn't exactly out of his way … perhaps doing a spot of volunteering with a bunch of people he didn't know wasn't as silly an idea as he'd originally thought.

When he got back downstairs, his father was outside cutting the grass and his mother had restocked his fridge with food.

'Mum,' he said. 'I just wanted to tell you that I'm

volunteering to help refurbish one of the sitting rooms at the hospice this weekend.' Now that he'd made up his mind to go, it seemed the perfect solution. It would put his mother's mind at rest. He could always retreat to Sally's bedside after a short while. So long as he could honestly say he'd tried it.

Diane shut the fridge door and looked at him seriously for a moment. 'I'm glad to hear that,' she said. From the caution in her voice, he knew she didn't believe him. Now that he took the time to observe her properly, he could see that she had worry lines on her forehead and she seemed older than he remembered. Perhaps Sally's coma had affected more than just him. He hadn't thought of it that way.

He went up to his mother and gave her a quick hug. To his surprise, she wrapped her arms around him and held him, her cheek pressed against his. 'We love you, Peter.'

'I know Mum,' he said. 'I sometimes forget, that's all.'

Sally was floating in her tranquillity. It was daytime, she could tell from the routine noises that came in through her door. She didn't know what day it was, but she knew that Peter would come. He had mentioned something about his mother the day before. Sally couldn't remember what, but she wouldn't be surprised if it was something unpleasant. The old bat didn't like her anyway. She remembered all too well the sniffy look Diane had given her when Peter introduced her. And the involuntary gasp when she'd realised that, two months after getting together, they were engaged.

Sally felt a stab of satisfaction. It had been fast work, that. She'd known, from the minute she kissed him and dragged him to the floor in the empty house, that she wanted to have him for herself. She'd always known she wanted the good life. To live in middle class comfort. Peter, bless him, was sweet and caring and so beautifully impressionable. He would give her everything she wanted, provided she didn't push her luck. He wanted a family, that was obvious. Sally wasn't sure how she felt about kids, apart from that she didn't like them. Other people, usually ones with kids running round their ankles, had told her that there was a biological clock that somehow drove them to reproduce. If that happened, then well and good. Otherwise, there were ways she could keep safe. So long as he got a decent amount of sex, he would think she was actually trying.

Now that she had a sense of time, she was beginning to realise that she'd been in hospital for more than just a day or two. Weeks probably. With nothing to do but listen, she was hearing more about Peter's business than she had ever done before. She still wasn't desperately interested, but it was better than listening to the radio that was interrupted by nurses talking to each other.

She had looked Peter's company up at Companies House the day after they'd met, just to check before she hitched herself to him, but she hadn't really understood the work behind it. She also realised that she'd never really paid attention to Peter himself. Physically, of course she did, but she'd never taken the time to get to know him as a person. His hopes, his dreams. To an extent, he'd never made an effort to talk to her about that sort of thing either, what with the whirlwind romance and the wedding planning, there just hadn't been time. Now time was all she had.

She discovered that her husband worked too hard. He treated his work with the same level of seriousness that he showed when slicing onions, working with steady concentration to produce fine, even slices. She remembered him smiling a lot, but he didn't sound very smiley these days.

In fact, he sounded heavy and tired. She briefly wondered if he'd changed, or whether it was just the fact that she was ill that was making him a bit down. Not surprising really, she herself would have been pretty sad if she was married to someone who was in hospital. Or rather, she would have been annoyed. It was a sign of what a nice guy Peter was that he chose to see it as sad, not just a bloody nuisance.

'Hello, Peter,' came the voice of a nurse. 'How are you today?'

'I'm good thanks, Judy. You?'

Sally's spirits rose. Oh good. Peter was here. At least things would be interesting. He'd talk and maybe read her something from those books he seemed to always have with him. Sometimes they were boring, but mostly, they were okay.

There was a pause and Peter said, 'How is she?'

'You're doing okay, aren't you Sally,' said the nurse, loudly. Sally hated that patronising tone. If she were really doing okay, she wouldn't be lying here unable to feel anything, would she?

'Has she said anything?'

'Let me check … no, nothing last night.'

'Oh. Okay. Thanks.' There was another pause. Presumably the nurse was leaving the room. When Peter spoke again, his voice was closer.

'Hello darling,' he said. His voice was normal, not slightly raised as the nurse's had been when she visited. She wished she could say hello back. The tranquillity held her, not restrained, just unable to struggle. She had a vague feeling that she should be able to do something with her body, but had no idea what that might be or how to do it. She would have checked what her body looked like, but in the tranquillity there was nothing to see. Sound was all there was.

'I'm only here for a bit today,' he said, his tone apologetic. 'I said I'd help out with preparing the common room on the third floor for redecoration. They needed volunteers.'

Well that sounded tedious. What did he want to do that for?

'Mum and Dad came round the other day,' Peter carried on. 'We talked. They... seemed to think I need to get out more.'

Ah well, that explained it. She wondered what that old cow had said to Peter. Having that dry old witch for a mother-in-law was going to be one of the few downsides to being married to Peter. Of course, Peter always thought the best of his mum. It was probably a mother-son thing. She thought, fleetingly, about her own waste-of-space mother. Mothers and daughters saw each other more clearly.

'Sally,' said Peter suddenly. 'Do you think I'm selfish?'

What? Where the buggering hell had that come from? His mother, probably. That woman knew no shame. The fact that Sally couldn't actually communicate with Peter wasn't good enough for her. Noooo. She had to make him feel bad about coming to visit too. Bitch.

Sally wanted to say 'No! I don't think you're selfish. I think you're the kindest man I've ever met. You come here every day. You talk to me, not even knowing if I can hear you.' She wanted to hold his hand, feel his skin against her palms and look into his face and say 'I think you're the most amazing man I've ever met', or some other platitude to make him feel better. But of course, she couldn't. She had no hands to hold him with. No eyes to see him with. No voice to tell him. For the first time since waking up in the tranquillity, she was annoyed. She hadn't wanted out before. Now she did. And it made her angry.

'Val had a baby six months ago. I meant to go and see her,

I honestly did. But stuff got in the way and I kept putting it off.' Peter sounded miserable now. 'Then I forgot. Now the baby is six months old and Val thinks I don't care. Worse still, Alex and little Terry think I don't care. That makes me the worst uncle ever.'

Wait, Val had another baby? Sally thought back to her wedding. There had been no bump on Val. Sally had only met Val a couple of times, but she was sure that Val was the sort of odious yummy mummy that would tell everyone about how wonderfully fertile she was. Definitely. She hadn't mentioned anything at the wedding, so maybe she was still only in the early stages then ... and the baby was six months old. So ... the wedding had been at least ten months ago, if not longer. Bloody hell. How long had she been in this place for then?

Chapter Five

Peter almost chickened out before he entered the third floor common room. The furniture had been removed, leaving an enormous space. There were people everywhere, sanding skirting boards and painting walls. That jovial man that seemed to bounce around everywhere putting up posters spotted him hovering by the door and bounced up to him.

'Hello, I'm Harry,' he said, offering Peter a chubby hand to shake. 'Are you coming to join us?'

'I am.' There, he was committed now. 'I'm Peter Wesley. Someone said you needed volunteers …'

'Brilliant. Come on in and we'll find you something to do.' Harry led him to the other side of the room. A few people looked up from their work to smile or nod at him. Mostly the conversations didn't cease. There was a smattering of laughter from a group who were busy stripping wallpaper from the far wall.

Grace waved to him from across the room. She was wearing a paint spattered shirt meant for someone much wider than her and a pair of worn jeans. Her hair was pulled back and the plait tucked into the back of her shirt so that it didn't get paint on it. The plait pulled the collar of her shirt askew slightly, revealing a glimpse of collarbone. It was the most unflirtatious outfit Peter had ever seen. Yet, the oversized shirt only served to highlight how slim she was underneath it. He tried to imagine Sally wearing anything so unaffected. No, he decided. Sally would never be seen so plain and unadorned. In the few months that he'd lived with her, he hadn't seen her without make-up for more than a few minutes.

Thinking of Sally drove a splinter of sadness into his thoughts. This was closely followed by guilt. He shouldn't be looking at another woman. His wife was down the corridor. He quietly took the paint brush Harry gave him and got to work.

Grace risked glancing across the room to where Peter was on his knees, painting the skirting boards. If she'd known he was going to be there, she would have worn something a bit more flattering than her father's old shirt and jeans that she'd had since uni. Next to him, Harry was telling him one of his interminable jokes. Peter seemed to be listening and smiling. He seemed less bowed down by life already. Harry had that effect on people. Good old Harry.

The redecorating was going well. Grace had been sandpapering the old wooden window frames all morning. Her arm was starting to ache. After the tea break, she'd swap with someone. She stopped to drag a forearm across her forehead and lowered the paper mask that was keeping the dust out. The air that rushed through was surprisingly cool. She stood up and inhaled deeply. These masks certainly retained the heat. She thought about her mother in the last few weeks of her life. How uncomfortable she must have been with the mask over her face and the tube down her throat. The memory squeezed her heart. She had done what was best for her mother, for as long as she could. When her mother died, there had been a lot to do — the funeral to organise, the various people to be informed, so many people to thank. She had handled it all by herself, just as she handled everything that went before. She was used to having no extended family to lean on, but seeing the small gathering at the funeral, which consisted of mostly nursing staff and a few old colleagues of her mother's, had saddened her. Still, that was the price of independence. Grace pulled the mask on and got back to scrubbing.

She was so focused on her task that she didn't notice Harry until he tapped her on the shoulder.

'Time for tea my darling,' he said.

'Oh, cheers.' Grace removed her mask again and let it hang around her neck. 'Give me a minute, I'll go wash my hands before I take that.'

When she got back, Harry was inspecting her window frame. 'Good job there, Grace.'

'Thank you.' It was satisfying seeing the old wood clear from the horrible lumpy varnish that had been on before. A feeling of accomplishment. It made a change to do something which bore such immediate effects. She gratefully took the cup of tea and biscuits that Harry gave her, and sat down on the floor. 'I wouldn't mind a change of job though,' she said.

'I thought you liked being a scientist.'

'Ha, ha, very funny. I meant, my arm's aching from sandpapering.'

'I'll swap with you,' he said. 'The view's better over there.' He nodded over to Peter.

'Harry!' said Grace, in a shocked whisper. 'You're a taken man and so is he.'

Harry grinned. 'He keeps glancing at you, you know. When he thinks no one's watching him. I think he might have a thing for you, my darling.'

Grace felt her heart thump louder. 'Don't be silly,' she said. 'He just doesn't know anyone else, that's all.'

'Well, the elusive Peter Wesley, never comes to any events, until *you* ask him and suddenly, there he is. The man's wife's been out of action for a while now ...'

'Don't be horrible.'

They both turned to look at Peter, who seemed to sense being stared at and looked up.

'Tea break,' Harry called over. 'Want one?'

'Oh, yes please.' Peter stood up and dusted himself off. He took his glasses off and blew on them to get the dust off. He looked different to normal. Grace realised it was the first time she'd seen him without a preoccupied frown on his forehead.

Peter walked across to her, stretching his arms as he walked. 'How's it going?'

'Not bad. You?' She gave him a smile, hoping it came across as relaxed and friendly, rather than nervous and slightly embarrassed. 'Glad you came?'

'I am actually.' He sounded almost surprised. 'It's nice to do something physical. Something different.' He glanced around the room as people milled around with their mugs, inspecting each other's work and appreciating progress. 'It's nice to meet people too. I didn't expect everyone to be so …'

'Friendly?' Grace finished the sentence for him. 'I know what you mean. I thought it's such a sad place, it must be hard to laugh here. But this is different from a hospital, I guess. When something's for the long term, you just have to accept it. It's a different sort of normal.'

Peter gave her a sidelong look. 'Yes … I suppose that's true.'

'It's nice to talk to people in the same position, isn't it?'

'Yes. It definitely is.' He hesitated. 'Thank you. For asking me to help. I wouldn't have thought to come otherwise.'

Grace waved his thanks away. 'I'm glad you changed your mind and came along after all.'

They took their teas to the window. Peter looked out and saw a lovely view of the walled garden behind. The view from Sally's window was narrow and showed mostly the car park. This was clearly the better side of the building to be on.

Outside people pushed patients around in wheelchairs. A couple of families were sitting on the grass near the mini orchard, one of the children nestled next to his mother, who was carrying his catheter bag in one hand and cuddling her son with the other.

'Did she like the flowers?' Grace said, making him jump.

He turned around and leaned against the sill, turning his back on the scenes below. 'Pardon?'

'The person you visit in the hospice. Did she like the roses?' She leaned on the wall next to him, cradling her mug in both hands. She had a dust mask slung around her neck and there was a smudge across her nose. Peter decided not to mention it.

'I don't know,' he said. 'She doesn't say much.'

She raised a questioning eyebrow.

'Coma.'

'Ah.' She nodded, as though he'd just said his wife was at the supermarket. He was used to the sudden intake of breath and the awkward pause while people frantically tried to think of what they should say. This was usually followed by profuse outpourings of sympathy or worse, pity. But Grace took it as though it were perfectly commonplace.

'I'm sorry,' she said after a moment. 'That's harsh.' There was still no pity. No concerned voice. 'At least you know she'll be well looked after here.'

'Yes.' It was strangely comforting that she just took his revelation at face value. No questions. 'She's my wife,' he added.

This seemed to be of more interest. 'You must miss her terribly. How long have you been married?'

Did he miss her terribly? Yes. He did. 'We've been married about eleven months.'

'How long has she been comatose?'

'About eleven months.'

She looked him full in the face. 'Oh, that's heartbreaking,' she said, and this time there was sadness. 'Did it happen on your honeymoon?'

'Something like that.'

'I'm sorry.' She sounded genuinely sad about it.

They sat in silence for a bit. Peter felt his head churning with a mix of emotions. He would normally be angry at this point, but he wasn't now. Maybe it was being here, in this convivial atmosphere. Maybe it was Grace and the way she accepted his pain without commenting on it. Whatever it was, he felt normal here. It was … nice. Comforting even.

'So, who do you go to visit?' he asked. 'I see you around quite a lot.'

'Margaret. She's a friend of my mother's. Or rather *was* a friend, when my mother was alive.'

So the mother was dead. Peter sifted through the implications and tried to find the right thing to say. There wasn't one. 'I'm sorry for your loss.'

Grace shrugged.

'Do you miss her?'

Grace looked up and met his gaze with her frank brown eyes. 'Yes,' she said. 'I do. But I'm glad for her sake that she died. She was in pain.'

Right. Well, that put him in his place then. In the pause that followed, he studied her. He had a sudden image of that thick black hair spread out around her face, rather than lying sensibly plaited down her back. How wonderful to feel those thick strands sliding through his fingers. The erotic nature of the thought startled him. He hadn't thought about a woman like that in two years. Not since he met Sally. He looked away quickly.

'I'm sorry,' Grace said suddenly. 'That was a bit of a

51

conversation killer. I'm not very good at this social situation stuff. I've forgotten how to do small talk.'

'Don't worry about it. I'm not exactly Mr Conversation either.' Peter turned his head to look at her. 'Shall we have another go?' he said. 'Let's see. What's a good conversation gambit? What do normal people talk about?'

'I can't remember. I told you I wasn't very good at this.'

'Right ... let's see ... what are you doing next weekend? Anything exciting?'

'Oh yes,' she said. 'I'm clearing my house.'

'Really? Why? Are you moving?'

'No. I've just decided it's time I did it. I live in a three bedroomed house and sleep in the tiny little room I grew up in. When there's a perfectly good master bedroom next door. How silly is that?'

'I can top that,' said Peter. 'I live in my own house, which has four bedrooms and I sleep in the spare room. In my own home.'

'Okay. You win. You're more pathetic than I am.'

Peter did a mock punch in the air. 'Yes. Result.'

'Now you're just taking the mick.'

They both laughed. Another feeling that was almost forgotten. How long had it been since he'd laughed? Beside him, Grace drained her tea. 'I suppose I should get back to work,' she said. 'Harry's a difficult task master to please.' She raised her mug to Harry. 'I'll go see what he wants me to do next,' she said. 'It was nice talking to you Peter.'

With a smile in his direction, she was gone. Peter felt her absence next to him. When had he last had a conversation that wasn't about work or Sally? Probably not since the accident. Or even, slightly before that. Most wedding related conversations had been based around Sally too. He allowed himself a small smile before finishing off his drink.

* * *

52

The redecorating took three weekends. Grace ended up working next to Peter most days, thanks to Harry stirring. They settled into a comfortable level of friendship. Grace found that talking to Peter came easily to her. Harry often accused her of flirting with him, but she had never done that. Not consciously anyway.

Peter didn't seem to mind either. As the days went on, he seemed to unwind more and more, until it seemed almost commonplace for him to smile and laugh at Harry's jokes. The only problem was, the more she learned about him, the more she liked him. She would catch herself thinking about him when she was meant to be concentrating on something else. Each day she came in to help with the redecorating, she would feel a flutter of anticipation in her stomach at the thought of seeing him. She told herself it was something she could control. She wasn't a teenager. She was perfectly capable of noting someone was attractive and still keeping a healthy distance.

When Harry announced it was time to call it a day, people downed tools and started to clear up. Some people drifted off to go and see their loved ones while others lingered, talking and laughing as they finished off small jobs.

'Thanks for coming today,' Harry said, ambling up to where Grace was. He said that every day. To everyone.

Grace paused in the middle of rubbing her nails to get the paint off them. 'It was fun.'

'And we got quite a lot done.'

They surveyed the room. It still looked untidy, but the work was nearly finished. The walls and woodwork had been repainted in tranquil green. The floor was covered in paint and footprints, but that was to be replaced soon. The room looked brighter and bigger than before.

'I think we've done a good job,' said Harry. 'We've got

some photos from before and once everything's done, I should be able to do some nice before and after slides for the presentation at the fundraiser dinner next month. You coming to the fundraiser Peter?'

Grace turned to see Peter strolling up, drying his hands on a rag. 'Sure. Why not? When is it?' When Harry told him, he said, 'Put me down for a ticket.'

Harry grinned. 'Excellent.' He pulled a notebook out of his pocket and wrote something down. 'You know,' he said, still busily scribbling, 'I was just trying to persuade Grace to do the charity abseil down the side of the hospital building.'

'What?' Grace stared at him. He'd mentioned it before, and she'd said no. What was Harry talking about?

'It's a great cause, obviously, and it'll be a great adventure for her.' Harry put his hands on Grace's shoulders. 'It's a shame you're too scared, Grace.'

Grace shrugged off his hands. 'Damned right I'm too scared.'

'Abseiling's not scary,' said Peter. 'It's quite exhilarating, in fact. I used to do that sort of thing a lot.'

'Really?' said Harry. 'Would you consider signing up to do the abseil?'

Peter shrugged. 'I can, but where's the challenge in a climber doing an abseil? I'd do that for fun. It's not exactly worth sponsoring me to do that.'

Grace took a step back, wondering if she could just sidle out while Harry was distracted by Peter.

'He's got a point,' Harry said, turning to her. 'I wouldn't sponsor him. But I'd sponsor you.'

A couple of the other volunteers chimed in with their support.

'Go on,' said Harry. 'It'll be fun.'

'Throwing myself off a building? I don't think so,' said Grace.

'It'd be a great way to raise money for the hospice …'

'If it's such a good idea, maybe *you* should do it?'

Harry shook his head. 'Sadly, I can't. Not with my back. You on the other hand, would be great. And much more photogenic than I am.'

'I … I've never done anything like that before. I'd be petrified.' The words 'something out of your comfort zone' floated into her mind. Was this the sort of thing Margaret was talking about? Climbing up the biggest building she knew and chucking herself off it like some sort of crazy Bond girl was pretty much as far outside her comfort zone as it got.

'Seriously. The thing that's scaring you is the IDEA of going over the side of building. The actual abseil itself will be amazing. Trust me,' said Peter.

Peter's intervention made Grace pause. She had this immediate urge to agree with him. What was wrong with her? Just because she liked him, didn't mean she had to jump at trying to impress him. She wasn't a teenager. Grace shook her head. 'Still not making it sound appealing.'

'And we'd all be there to support you,' said Harry. 'We'll have a stall selling tea and cake and make up a little cheering squad for you at the bottom.' He thrust the sponsorship form at her. 'Go on. If you won't do it for yourself, do it for us. We need the money to buy new stuff for this place.' He gestured to the newly painted room. 'Please?'

Grace looked around. The new paint did make the place brighter. With a few hundred pounds they could replace that sagging sofa and maybe re-upholster some of the other chairs. A quick glance at the poster that was now lying on the table showed that she'd be expected to raise at least £250. The place could certainly do with some new stuff … Grace sighed. 'I'm not sure I can raise that much in the time left, anyway.'

'Of course you can. We'd all be supporting you. I'll take a spare form and take it around my work.' Harry's eyes were sparkling now.

'My company will sponsor you,' said Peter. 'I can pledge, say a hundred quid, right now. I'll even give you a lift there, if you like. So that you can ask me any questions about abseils that are bothering you.'

'And,' said Harry, giving her a meaningful look. 'It would be really bold of you … And daring.'

A few of the others piped up their support. Maybe Peter was right. The idea of getting back out there was scarier than the actual thing. Time to do something dramatic. Grab life by the throat. Something out of her comfort zone. Peter was watching her expectantly, as though willing her to say yes. If she backed down would he think less of her? Was she really so childish that she would do something so crazy just to impress a guy? Her eyes met Peter's. He gave her a small smile. Yes. She would.

Around her, the noise level had risen. She threw her hands up. 'Fine,' she said. 'Fine. I'll do it.' The grin that Peter gave her made her feel effervescent. She took the paper off Harry, who was beaming now. 'But you have to all sponsor me. Guilt rates, okay?'

There was a flurry of agreement and the paper was passed round so that people could put their names on the list. Grace looked up and caught Peter's eye.

'If this goes wrong, I'm holding you responsible.' She pointed at him.

His eyes widened a bit with mock alarm.

'And Harry,' Grace added.

Harry gave her a mock bow. 'You can. I think you'll be great. I'm so proud of you my darling. Margaret will be too.'

Chapter Six

By the time Peter came to visit her that day, Sally was annoyed at how late he was. She knew because she'd heard Coronation Street start and end. If he didn't get a move on, he'd run out of visiting hours.

When he finally arrived, he sounded completely unlike his usual self. He told her he'd been helping out with the redecorating again. She still couldn't figure out what that was all about.

'It's quite nice just working alongside people,' he said. 'I'd forgotten what it was like to just do stuff and chat to people.'

Well he could have fooled her. He did nothing BUT chat when he was visiting. She supposed she should be grateful, but something was niggling her. Peter seemed different for no reason. It couldn't just be the fact that he was talking to people that was cheering him up. She listened carefully, in case he said something that gave her a clue.

'There's going to be a charity abseil down the side of the new hospital tower. You know, the one where ICU is …' He paused. 'Anyway, Grace, she's one of the other people volunteering today, is going to do the abseil to raise money for the hospice.' Another pause. 'I don't think she's totally happy with the idea, but I think it's very brave of her to take up the challenge.'

It was the pauses that gave away the significance.

Sally's attention heightened. There was something else about this woman. He'd mentioned her, and then justified having spoken to her. It had occurred to her that if *she* had been looking for a man to invest in, other women might too. In fact, she knew a few who were. Most of them were too old and witchy now to attract a man as young as Peter, but it didn't do to get complacent.

'And I met a potential client. He runs a logistics business and sorting out systems for him could be quite interesting,' said Peter.

He was talking about work again. Sally stopped listening. She wanted to find out about this woman, Grace. But he didn't mention her again. Sally could feel that there was something important happening. Perhaps Peter fancied this Grace. She would have to remember that name. She'd have to keep an eye on things. In case this Grace creature turned out to be a husband grabbing harpy.

Sitting by himself in his kitchen, Peter wondered if offering to drive Grace to the abseil had been the wisest thing to do. She was an attractive woman and they got on very well. He considered her a friend. But lately, he had been thinking of her more often than he should. Out and about in the day, he would see things that reminded him of her. Sometimes, he daydreamed about what it would be like to kiss her.

Being in a car with her for any length of time would not be a great idea. He loved Sally. He had no intention of throwing that away. He knew he couldn't trust his own emotions these days. He probably didn't even fancy Grace that much. It was just that he'd lost his sense of perspective. Not for the first time, he wondered if he should take his mother's advice and go see a doctor. No. Things weren't that bad. He could handle it.

He wondered whether he should call Harry and ask him to swap lifts. Harry was giving some other guy a lift and they'd all agreed that people driving in a state of high nerves was a bad idea. Harry had suggested that Peter might be able to help calm Grace's fears. After all, he knew about climbing and abseiling, whereas Harry would just wind her up more.

He convinced himself that he was doing it out of friendship and common sense and not because he found Grace attractive.

He had finished having an early breakfast when there was a banging on the door. Odd. His mother didn't usually show up until much later in the morning. Besides, she knew he was going to be out most of that day.

Frowning, he opened the front door to find a man with spiky hair and a tattoo of a starburst on the side of his neck, standing outside, brandishing a letter.

The man jabbed his finger at the letter in his hand. It had something red on the top of it. 'Where's Sally Cummings? I need to talk to her.'

'She's ... not here. I'm her husband.'

'Well where is she? Tell her we're not having this. We've had the bloody bailiffs round again, threatening to take our stuff away. I told them she didn't live there no more, but they came again anyway. Scared the crap out of my girlfriend. She's in her third trimester you know. It's not good to scare pregnant women like that.'

Peter put his hands up defensively. 'Wait. Slow down. What are you talking about?'

The man shoved the letter at him. 'We've been getting these for ages. We kept sending them back to sender. Then the bailiffs started to show up. It's taken me bloody ages to find out where she went to. I've had enough of this. Here. It's your problem now. I'll be passing this address on to the bailiffs when they next come round.'

Peter stared at him for a moment and took the letter. He

had paid all of Sally's debts off ages ago. 'Okay. I'll see if I can sort things out. I had no idea she owed any money to anyone.'

'Oh.' The man seemed surprised. The bluster seemed to drop out of him. 'Oh, okay mate. That would be great. Er. Thank you.'

Peter smiled. 'No problem. I hope everything goes well with the baby.'

'Cheers. Me too.' He took a step back. 'I guess I'll be off then.'

'Bye.' Peter retreated back into the house and shut the door. He skimmed the letter and spotted the address of the collection service. Sally had assured him that she had no more debts. Perhaps this was an old one that she had forgotten about. He scanned down to the details of when the loan was taken out and did a double take. The date was two weeks before the wedding. That was strange. By then he had paid off all of Sally's gambling debts and if she needed money, all she would have had to do was ask. What did she need money for that was so secret she couldn't tell him about it? Five hundred pounds.

He frowned. Perhaps she had been gambling again. An uneasy vision of the lottery ticket crossed his mind. She'd said 'don't you trust me', but he'd seen the temptation in her eyes. Perhaps he had been right not to trust her.

He dismissed the thought as unworthy. Sally had been going to Gamblers Anonymous for two months before this loan was taken out. He would have known if she had a relapse. Wouldn't he?

He sighed. It didn't matter anyway. Sally wasn't around to answer his questions and he didn't have the energy to fight a legal battle. All he could do was pay the debt.

He put the letter on top of his briefcase so that he didn't

forget it and went back into the kitchen to wash up his breakfast things.

Grace waited by the window, watching for Peter. She hadn't slept the night before and her eyes felt red and raw. She hadn't had breakfast either, because she felt too sick. The more people talked about the abseil, the worse it got. Now, with only hours to go, she felt as though something was crawling around in her stomach. This was a bad idea. She should call and say she couldn't do it.

She reached for the phone and hesitated. She was supposed to be moving out of her comfort zone and doing something to show herself that she could do it. Quitting now would be an admission that she couldn't and she may as well stay trapped in her rut forever.

A car drew up outside and Peter got out. He was only helping her because he thought she was doing something brave. If it hadn't been for this, she would never have seen him once the common room was finished. Was she only doing the abseil so that she could see Peter again? She decided she wasn't that crazy. Depressed maybe, but not that far gone. She left the phone alone and opened the door before Peter knocked.

'Hello. Your chauffeur, reporting for duty,' he said.

'I'm ready,' she said, more to convince herself than anything else.

He stepped inside. 'Are you okay?'

She tried to smile and managed a tight grimace. 'I'm petrified, actually.'

He gave her a look full of concern. 'You don't have to do it, you know. You can always pull out. People will understand. Even Harry.'

For a split second she wanted to take him up on that.

Then her pride broke through. She lifted her chin and stood up, taller. 'I can't back out now. I won't let everyone down. Come on.' She grabbed her coat and a small backpack. 'Let's go.'

He opened the car door for her. She got in and sat bolt upright in her seat, staring straight out of the window. She could feel the tension in her shoulders, but was powerless to do anything about it.

'Are you sure about this?' said Peter, when he got into the driver's seat. 'You really don't look happy.'

'I'm not.'

'But you're going through with it anyway?'

'Yes.'

He pulled the car out. 'Why? Why put yourself through something if you know you're not going like it?'

She gave him a sidelong glare. 'I thought you said it was going to be amazing and exhilarating.'

He looked a little sheepish. 'I did, because I genuinely believe it is, but I hadn't realised you had vertigo.'

'What makes you think I have vertigo?'

He gave her a look that bordered on pity. 'Because you look like you have.'

'You know what? Vertigo and all the other phobias – they're all just chemistry. I can beat chemistry. I'm not going to let my body get one over on me. I'd be an idiot to let it stop me from doing something I want to do.'

There was silence for a moment. 'But that's true of just about anything. You'll break yourself if you carry on like that.'

'Yes, well I didn't think I could write up my PhD and look after two sick parents either. But I did it.' It came out too sharp, as though she were snapping at him.

'O-kay.'

'I'm sorry. I didn't mean to snap. I'm just a bit highly strung. Which, I should think is normal for someone who is about to throw themselves off a building.'

Peter shot her another glance. They passed a road sign with a big H written on it. The tower was visible at the other side of the site.

'It is perfectly safe, you know,' he said. 'There's a safety rope and a harness. One of the safety crew will be ready to come down after you if you get stuck. It's all very well thought out.'

'I know.' She forced the words out through her clenched teeth. 'Can we not talk about it for a minute?'

'Okay.' He turned into the hospital site and they drove in silence for the rest of the way.

Harry, wearing a T-shirt with the hospice logo on it, met her at the entrance to the building.

'Hello my darling. All ready for our little adventure?'

Grace didn't reply.

'She's a bit nervous,' Peter said.

Grace shot him a glare. He raised his hands up in front of his chest as though in surrender. 'Sorry.' He smiled. 'Just remember to focus on your hands and don't look down. So long as you feed the rope steadily through your hands, all you have to do is walk backwards.'

She nodded.

'Come along my darling.' Harry put an arm around her and ushered her inside. He kept up a cheerful chatter all the way up in the lift, but Grace was too nervous to hear a word he said. She forced herself to concentrate on her breathing. She tried to imagine the lift was a bubble in a tranquil ocean. It didn't work.

The topmost floor of the hospital held a nondescript lobby with wards leading off left and right.

'This is our stop,' Harry stepped out of the lift and waited for Grace to follow him. 'This way.' He led the way to a side door, set next to the lifts, that she hadn't noticed before.

The door led to small stairwell, with concrete stairs that went upwards. A cheerful lady with a clipboard was waiting, leaning against the door. 'Hello? Are you one of our brave abseilers? What's your name please?'

'Grace Guneratne.' Her voice sounded far away, even to her. At least her heart had stopped trying to climb out through her mouth

'That's lovely, thank you,' said the lady. 'Come with me and I'll help you get kitted up.'

'I've got to leave you here, Grace.' Harry gave her a warm hug. 'Good luck. Enjoy it. I'll see you at the bottom.'

Grace managed a weak smile, hugged Harry back and followed the lady in the high visibility jacket into what appeared to be a small maintenance room which had been taken over by climbing harnesses and other equipment. She was given a helmet and gloves.

Calm. She had to remain calm. The lady was talking to her, her voice level and soothing as though she were speaking to a skittish animal.

'These go round your legs.' She helped her into it. 'You need it snug around you, with the chest strap—'

'At my chest?' She couldn't help herself. The nerves were making her head pound. It was either sarcasm or burst into tears.

The lady glanced up, a brief flash of humour sparkled before she was serious again. 'That's right.'

'Sorry.' She stood there, her arms held out to the side, feeling awkward whilst the woman expertly threaded straps through buckles, pulling here, fastening there. Her hands moved over Grace's body with firm purpose. It was closest physical contact she'd had in a long time. She should be finding this amusing. Or at the very least embarrassing. But there was no room for any emotion other than fear.

'Let's just check that that's snug and closed.' The woman's voice was still calm, which was starting to feel reassuring. She clearly didn't see anything as dangerous.

'Ready?' said the lady.

'No.'

The lady laughed. 'You all say that. You'll be fine. It's the ones who are too cocky that we worry about.'

Chapter Seven

The bald stairs led up to a rectangle of daylight. Grace tramped up them, like a prisoner being taken to execution. Did she really want to do this? Perhaps it was just a matter of adjusting her expectations so that she was happy with her rut. After all, there was nothing WRONG with her life as it had been. What had all this fuss about change really brought to her? Not a lot. She stopped, a few steps from the top.

'Not having second thoughts, are you Grace?' an amused voice said from behind her. This woman had clearly seen it all before. 'Don't worry, everyone feels nervous. It's healthy. You'll be fine. We'll take very good care of you.'

If she went back now, what would she say to people? She was sure most would understand, but they would think she was a wuss and couldn't handle the pressure. They'd be right, but that still didn't mean she wanted to hear it. Margaret would never let her live it down. Besides, how could she face Peter again? Looking over her shoulder, she could see the woman smiling encouragingly at her. So she took a deep breath and stepped out into the light.

The first thing that hit was the wind. It whooshed around her head and pressed clothes against her body. She felt as though she were swaying. She grabbed hold of a railing, hoping it wasn't in fact the building swaying. Logic told her it wasn't tall enough for that. Panic told her otherwise.

There were three men at the top of the platform. Two of them were looking over the side watching the previous person go down the side.

'This is Grace,' the woman hollered above the wind. The third man nodded. He gave her a twinkly smile from under his hard hat and Grace warmed to him immediately.

'I'm just going to check your harness.' He tugged and checked buckles and gave her the thumbs up. 'Shake your head for me?'

She shook her head, and he touched the helmet. 'Nice and snug. Good.'

There was a cheer from below. The other two men turned around. 'He's down,' one said. 'Next please.'

'That's you love,' He guided her hand and helped her step towards the small platform that had been rigged up for the abseil. 'Let's get you hooked up.'

Grace's pulse pounded, she could feel the heat rising in her face. 'I'm scared,' she said.

He looked up. 'Now, take your time and go slow. Sit back in your harness. Focus on your hands. Keep it controlled and you'll be fine.' He gave her another smile.

The men helped her step over the low railing and stand with her back to the drop. She could feel the tug of the empty space behind her. She tried to focus on what the man was saying. It was hard to hear above the blood roar in her ears. She gulped and leaned back as she was told. For a split second she thought her heart stopped. The rope held her, sitting on nothing. She leaned further. Panic swirled. She couldn't do this.

From somewhere behind the chaos in her mind, she recalled Peter saying, 'Focus on your hands.' She opened her eyes and glared at her gloved hands clutching the abseil rope.

'Step back, like you're backing away from something. That's it.'

Concentrating hard, she did this. Step, by step, by step,

for what seemed like forever. A bird flew past, making her jump. The movement dislodged the thick plait of hair that she'd tucked into her shirt to keep out of the way. Her hair fell behind her, dragging her head back momentarily. She turned her head and saw the enormous drop behind her. It was only a split second, but it was enough for her to misplace her feet. Panic burned through her stomach. She twisted to the side and hit the building side on. Shit. Focus. Focus.

She swung herself back, trying to work out how to steady herself with gravity behind her rather than below. She got purchase with one foot and bent her knees to stop herself swinging round. Then she was squatting on the side of a building. Above her she could see heads peering down. Someone clipped on and prepared to follow her.

She slowly extended her legs, stable now and resumed her descent, concentrating fiercely on keeping her movements smooth and steady. She had no idea how long she went on like that.

'Nearly there,' said a voice.

She turned her head to see the top of someone's hard hat. Immediately, she looked down. The ground was blessedly close. A hand touched her back. She reached down with her foot and made contact with the ground. Gratefully, she got into a standing position and stood stock still while someone unclipped her and congratulated her. She was dimly aware of applause.

Grace resisted the urge to throw herself on the ground and kiss it.

Relief flushed through her veins, exhilarating and exhausting. She took a few steps away to where she could see people coming towards her. Suddenly the world was spinning and she folded over gently and ended up sitting on the ground. Everything narrowed until she could only make out a small space in front of her. Faint. She was going to faint. How embarrassing. She drew her knees up and stuck her head between them. Couldn't faint now. Not now she'd actually made it down.

'You okay love?' A voice came from far away. 'Can we have some help here please!'

The tightening in her ribs brought with it the familiar fear that she was having a heart attack. The thought 'who will look after Mum?' was swiftly followed by the realisation that no one needed her now. If she were to die in a humiliating heap at the bottom of the building, there was no one left to care.

She opened her eyes and focused on her hands, which were gripping her knees. This wasn't a heart attack. This was an anxiety attack. It was only adrenaline. She knew how to deal with that. She released her grip on her knees and clenched her fists hard, as hard as she could. She could feel the tendons straining in her wrists. She clenched until she could feel the pain in her forearms. And release. The sudden release seemed to scatter the panic through her fingertips. The roar in her ears lessened, only a little, but enough to remind her how to control it. She concentrated on breathing. Someone put a paper bag in front of her face. Good. Hands gently lowered her back until she was lying down.

It took her a few minutes for her anxiety to recede. When her vision cleared, she realised there were people clustered around her. They were in the process of rolling her into the recovery position. Peter was holding the paper bag over her nose. She reached up and pushed it away.

'Don't sit up until you're comfortable,' said a woman in a St John's ambulance uniform. 'Take it easy.'

She said, 'I'm okay,' and immediately realised she wasn't

fooling anyone. She lifted up a hand. It trembled. 'A bit shaky.' She laid her head back. The roar in her ears was dying down now and she could breathe normally, more or less. The anxiety attack would ebb away in a few minutes, but after it she would be completely drained. She needed to get home before the dizziness hit.

She took a deep breath. 'I'm okay. Really, I am.' She pushed herself into a sitting position, ignoring the attempts to keep her lying down. 'It's just an anxiety attack.'

'You have anxiety attacks?' Peter said quietly. 'Why didn't you tell someone?'

There had been some paperwork to sign at the start. Vertigo, mental illness, that sort of thing. Bugger. She'd forgotten about the anxiety. 'I haven't had one in ages. I weaned off the drugs ages ago. I didn't think to mention it. Sorry.'

There was some concern from the other two. She could still feel her pulse in her ears. 'I would really like to go home, please.'

'Maybe we could get you a drink?' said the first aider, taking Grace's wrist in her fingers and eyeing her watch. 'You're getting some colour back in your face now.'

'Yes,' said Grace.

'I'll get it.' Harry shot off.

By the time he returned with a KitKat and two cups of squash, Grace was feeling a lot steadier. 'I'm sorry,' she said. 'I didn't mean for there to be so much fuss.'

'No problem at all,' said the first aider. 'Are you feeling better now?'

'Yes thanks. I'll be fine. This happens sometimes. I'll be all right now.' Grace smiled.

It took a bit of persuading to get the first aider to leave. The two men watched her as she finished the second cup of squash. 'Stop it,' she said. 'It's embarrassing enough being all shaky without you two staring at me.'

'Are you sure you're okay?' said Harry. 'I feel terrible. I pushed you to do it and you said you were afraid of heights.'

'Don't. No need to feel bad. I'm a big girl. I could have ducked out of it.'

'But you didn't,' said Peter. 'And you did the abseil brilliantly. It's a tall building. You did great.'

She looked past him to the building where some other poor sod was coming down the ropes. It was tall. Massive, in fact. And she'd done it. The most terrifying thing she could have thought of and she'd done it. 'I did, didn't I?'

'You certainly did,' said Harry. 'I'm so proud of you, I could burst.'

'Me too,' said Peter softly.

She caught his gaze briefly and felt warmer instantly.

'I think we should get you home,' said Peter.

'How are you getting back? You can't drive in this state,' said Harry.

'I'll give her a lift.'

Harry's gaze flitted from Grace to Peter and back again. He gave her a knowing smirk. 'Oh. Right. Well, I'll see you kids later, I guess.'

Grace didn't have the energy to glare at Harry for stirring so obviously. Thankfully, Peter didn't seem to notice. He helped her to her feet. It was strange having someone to lean on. She took the support gratefully.

In the car, Grace slumped in her seat as the last of the adrenaline drained away, leaving her hollowed with exhaustion. The roar in her ears had subsided now, but her vision was still clouded at the edges, like she was looking down a microscope. She focused on taking deep breaths to keep on top of the nausea that was sweeping the other way.

Peter said nothing, but he kept casting anxious glances at her. Finally, when she felt better, she turned her head to the side and said, 'Don't worry. I'll be back on my feet in a bit.'

'Does this happen often?' He was looking at the road.

'No.' She would have shaken her head, but the effort seemed like too much. 'It used to, when Mum first fell ill. Dad was still alive then and I had to take care of them both. The GP put me on anti-anxiety drugs, but I hadn't had an attack in ages, so I weaned off them about a year ago. I haven't had an attack since.'

'You should have mentioned it.'

'I know. It's been so long, I forgot.' When he didn't say anything, she added, 'I'd convinced myself it wasn't a problem anymore.'

'I can understand that.' He turned his head to give a small smile. 'You sound a bit better. I was starting to really worry.'

'I'm sorry.'

He nodded, as though acknowledging her apology.

After a few minutes of silence, he said, 'I guess moving out of your comfort zone wasn't such a great idea.'

Grace managed a small laugh. 'I was so far from my comfort zone, I think it had disappeared over the horizon. I was petrified. If it wasn't for the safety rope, I'd have just fallen off the wall.'

'That's why you have a safety harness,' said Peter. 'You know, for safety.'

She managed a weak chuckle, quickly followed by a sigh. 'It's just embarrassing. I hate that I flaked out when other people were around.'

'You mean you'd rather flake out when there's no one to help?'

'Wouldn't you?'

Peter gave this more thought than she'd expected. The silence was pulling at her, forcing her to say more. 'When my father fell ill and my mum asked for help, it was okay. There were two of us. I was supporting her. Then slowly the balance tipped and when she fell ill, suddenly there was just me looking after them both. Oh, there was lots of help – carers, respite, whatever, but it was still my responsibility to make sure they got to their appointments and their prescriptions got picked up. All that sort of thing. I got an extension on my PhD to finish writing up, which helped, but it was still a heck of a thing. When I finally got put on anti-depressants, I decided that if it didn't kill me, it would make me stronger. Some days were awful and I wondered how on earth I'd get through it. Other days were fine. On those good days I felt almost invincible.'

Peter frowned. 'Some might say that was a bit … bi-polar.'

'They might. I don't.'

There was more silence. Grace watched the clouds through the windscreen. It was almost hypnotic.

'Are you glad you did it?' Peter said, suddenly. 'The abseil, I mean.'

Was she? She looked at her hands which were still unsteady. She felt clammy and exhausted and dizzy. She was glad it was over, but was she glad she'd done it in the first place? 'I guess so. I raised a lot of money for the hospice and … yes. I'm glad.'

By the time the car pulled up outside Grace's house, she was feeling better, but still weak. 'Thank you,' she said, leaning forward to pick up her bag from the footwell. 'I'm sorry to have caused so much bother.'

'Are you sure you're going to be okay? You still don't

look a hundred per cent.' He pushed his glasses up a bit and peered at her.

'I just need some sugar and a cup of tea. I'll be okay.'

Peter nodded. 'I'll wait until you've got to the door.'

Grace grinned. 'How old-fashioned.'

'I'm just that sort of guy.'

It sounded like the end of a date, Grace thought. Embarrassed by the thought, she said, 'I guess I'll see you around at the hospice. Thanks again.'

'No problem. It was … interesting.'

She smiled and got out of the car. Despite her assurances to Peter, she still felt woozy. She really, really needed to start carrying sweets in her bag again. She managed to get through the gate at a fairly normal pace, focusing intently on her destination, but she missed the doorstep and stumbled, landing with her hands against the door. There were footsteps and Peter was beside her.

'I think I should see you in,' he said, taking her elbow.

Grace didn't argue. Despite her light-headedness, she was suddenly very aware of how close he was. She could smell his aftershave and a hint of sweat. His hand on her arm felt hot. If she closed her eyes now she could lean against him and pretend he was always there for her. She took a deep breath and forced herself to concentrate on opening her own front door. She felt an irrational spark of relief when Peter stepped in behind her.

Chapter Eight

Peter shut the door behind them, his arm still around Grace. She was trying to keep upright, but he could feel her weight against his shoulder. How strange to feel another human being lean against him again. Her hair brushed against his jaw, making him experience a thrill of contact. He pulled his concentration back to the problem at hand. 'What do you need?'

'Cup of tea and something sugary,' she said.

He led her into the living room and helped her sit down on one of the big armchairs. 'And your kitchen is?'

'That way,' she pointed through the linking doorway. Her hand was still shaking, she pulled it back and cradled it defensively against her chest. 'It's the sugar low. The adrenaline takes it out of you. I'm so sorry.'

'You sit down and direct me,' said Peter. 'I'll make the tea.' Before she could protest, he said, 'No arguing.'

'Kettle, teabags. Biscuits in the cupboard,' she said, pointing.

Peter busied himself making tea. It was strange doing something so domestic in someone else's kitchen. When he turned around, he could see her watching him through the open doorway. She looked floppy somehow, as though all tension had drained out of her. 'What would you have done if I hadn't waited?' he said, a little more sharply than he'd intended. 'If you'd collapsed and been alone.'

'I'd have managed. I always do.'

He found a packet of biscuits and took them through to her.

'It's not been this bad before.' She devoured two biscuits in quick succession and closed her eyes. Her honey-toned skin was grey and two islands of colour stood out on her cheeks.

Her head tilted back and Peter had a momentary fear that she'd fainted. He was about to move, when she sighed. He watched her and caught himself admiring her long, slim neck. Her hands lay flat on the arms of the chair, she had delicate fingers … He tore himself away from looking at her and returned to the kitchen and to making tea. 'How do you take your tea?' he asked, over his shoulder.

'Milk,' she said. She didn't open her eyes.

Even pale and unwell, she was entrancing. The whole abseiling experience had hit her really hard. But he had no doubt that she could handle it. She probably didn't need him there. Except, he wanted to be there. He told himself it was the novelty of being needed by someone who could open their eyes and respond. Part of him knew he wasn't fooling anyone. 'Tea, madam.' He put it down on the coffee table between them.

She opened her eyes and smiled at him. 'You are an angel.'

'So I've been told.' He grinned and plonked himself on the sofa opposite her.

Grace took a sip and visibly improved. 'That's better,' she said. 'I really needed that. Thank you.' Her eyes were clear and brown. Peter caught her gaze. They stared at each other for a moment until Grace looked down. Peter felt a flush of embarrassment. He should be careful. This woman was beautiful, but he had a wife. He forced an image of Sally into his mind, trying to picture the happy-go-lucky blonde that had whisked him off his feet. He kept seeing the pallid figure in the hospital bed instead.

Grace didn't seem to notice anything amiss, so that was okay. She held the packet of biscuits out to him, no plates, nothing. Sally would have insisted on having the proper equipment. He remembered her digging out an old dinner service that his mother had pressed on him and dusting off the delicate plates, exclaiming that she couldn't believe he'd never used them. He took a couple of biscuits, smiling faintly to himself.

'What?' said Grace. 'Did I say something odd?'

'I was just thinking that Sally would have insisted on side plates.'

Grace frowned. 'I suppose I should use them. I broke a couple of my mum's ones, so now I don't dare. I just use the Hoover on the sofa every few weeks.' She seemed to be recovering with each passing minute. She sat up straighter and tucked her feet under her. The open packet of biscuits went on the table between them. 'Silly really. It's not like Mum's going to complain.'

'Sally wanted white calf skin sofas. I wasn't allowed to eat anything messy on them anyway.' He was still smiling at the memory of it. At the time he'd found it endearing that she made such a fuss of his house. He barely went into the living room these days, let alone sat on the expensive sofa. He preferred to gulp down his reheated meals at the kitchen table.

There was a moment of silence as they both munched on their biscuits. Finally, Grace said, 'It looks weird in here without mum's knickknacks.'

Peter looked round and saw the patches on the walls from where pictures had been removed. The mantelpiece was bare. The mirror above the fireplace was yellowing slightly at the rim, and reflected a bright square of wallpaper that had been protected by a picture.

'I've been clearing out mum's things, bit by bit. It's a bit sad, really,' said Grace. 'But not as hard as I expected.'

'Really?' He thought she looked melancholy. 'I'd have thought it would be quite a wrench.'

She shrugged. 'The things don't make the place theirs. The memories do. All the things were doing was reminding me of them so that I couldn't let go.' She gave a small smile that only accentuated how full her lips were. 'I guess it was a bit like being haunted.'

Peter stared at the patch of wallpaper reflected in the mirror. One thing removed to leave something bright that had been hidden. 'When Sally first ... after the accident, I used to sometimes wish she could haunt me. Just so that I could hear her voice again. Except ... of course, she isn't dead.' He shook his head. 'Sorry. Don't mind me. I'm talking crap.'

'I think I see what you mean.' Grace dunked her biscuit in her tea. 'She's not technically dead, but to all intents and purposes ...'

'It feels like she is,' he finished the sentence for her. 'People always say, "where there's life there's hope" and "you've got to keep on keeping on" and "have faith." I guess they're right.'

'You need to grieve,' said Grace, matter-of-factly.

He stared at her. He'd thought she understood. 'But she's not dead,' he said slowly, as though she were an idiot.

Grace met his gaze. 'I mean you need to grieve the future you lost. You were married, you were going to have a life together and now it's gone. We all have a mental picture of the perfect future. You've lost yours. You need to let yourself grieve for that.'

Peter frowned. Was that what he had been doing over the past year? Snatching emotions from the dead weight of weariness? Anger, denial, fear, despair. But not acceptance. Never acceptance. How could you accept something when you didn't know what it was? Sally could wake up. Or she could die. Until she did one or the other he was stuck in this limbo. Not widowed. Not married. Not anything.

'If she wakes up,' said Grace, 'what damage is there likely to be?' She didn't skirt around the issue. Again, it was refreshing. Why did no one else talk to him about it like this? As though it was something that could be identified and sorted out efficiently and calmly, rather than a monumental calamity that invoked only pity.

'Don't know. She had a lot of trauma to the head, which is why they kept her in a medically induced coma for so long, to help her recover. They said she had healed better than they expected … but then they phased out the drugs and … she didn't wake up. Until she wakes up, there's no way of knowing how badly her brain was affected.' He sighed. 'I'm told it's very unlikely she'll be the person she was before.'

'Oh. That sucks.' Grace made a little movement as though she was thinking of getting out of her chair and coming towards him, but then she seemed to change her mind and settle back down again. 'I'm sorry.'

Peter shrugged. 'Shit happens.'

'Certainly does.'

'The worst is not being able to prepare for it. If I knew … I could start getting ready. But all I can do is carry on day after day, not knowing.'

Grace nodded. 'The dreaded parallel planning.'

Peter said, 'Exactly.'

Grace said, 'It makes it sound like there's a parallel universe running alongside doesn't it? One where they're dead.' She looked up, her gaze travelling to the spaces where the knickknacks had been again. 'Or still alive.'

There was silence as they both retreated into their own thoughts.

'When you were looking after your parents ... Did you ever have ... thoughts,' said Peter suddenly.

'Er ... yeah.' Grace looked amused. 'I have thoughts.'

'Sorry, that's not how I meant it. I meant ... thoughts you weren't ... proud of.' It was a question he'd wanted to ask a lot of people. Something he hadn't dared voice in front of counsellors. He hated that the thoughts even entered his head, but they were always there, in the background. 'I wish Sally would die, so that I can be free.'

This time Grace's smile had no mirth to it. Her eyes lost focus, as though she were looking at something he couldn't see. 'When my Dad was having a crappy day and was angry and hurting, I used to wish it would end ... one way or another. I was younger then ... I wanted my life to be normal. Like other people's. You know, go out, get drunk, meet friends, maybe meet someone ...' She didn't look up. She tapped her mug with a fingernail, the light pinging noise seemed to fill the room. 'After he died, I tried to get back into it, but by then my Mum was ill.' She looked down at her hands. 'It was different with her. She ... wanted to die. I wanted her to stay alive because otherwise there would be just me. It's bad enough being lonely. I didn't want to be alone as well.' She stopped talking and sniffed.

He could see that her eyes had filled up with tears. Looking around, he spotted a box of tissues and got up to hand them to her.

She wiped her eyes with ferocity, leaving a red mark on her cheek. Peter fought the urge to step across and hug her. He sat back down, allowing himself to sink into the sofa again. He had to think of Sally. Sally always cried tidily. Sniffs, dabs, tears. None of this noisy nose blowing, make-up running stuff.

'Sorry about that. It's the combination of throwing stuff

out and talking about depressing things.' Grace crumpled up the tissue, took aim at the bin … and missed. She stood up, took a moment to steady herself and strode to the bin to put the tissue in. 'All better now, see,' she said. 'More tea?'

'Yes please.' He was grateful for the break in the conversation. Grace seemed surer on her feet now. So another cuppa and he would go. He leaned back against the squashy sofa. It was surprisingly warm and comfortable. It didn't squeak when he moved either, which was a bonus. He felt some tension drain out of him, as though someone had lifted a weight from his shoulders. Unburdened. Is this what people meant when they said that? He was supposed to lighten his worries by talking to therapists, but none of them had made him comfortable enough for him to ask them the questions that worried him most. In one afternoon, Grace had got under his defences with seemingly no effort. He leaned his head back against the cushions and confessed to himself that perhaps it had something to do with the fact that he wanted her to get under his defences.

It was odd to be attracted to someone again. In a way it was nice to know that he could still feel something other than tired and miserable. But it was dangerous to indulge. He was a married man. His wife was in a coma. What if she stayed in her coma? Would he have to be celibate forever?

Grace watched the steam rising as the kettle boiled. She was still feeling weak, but she could hide it better now. All she had to do was persuade Peter it was fine and he would leave. It had been embarrassing enough when she collapsed like that at the abseil, but what happened at the front door was just silly. She should have braced herself against the door, so that he could drive off. She would only have had to hold up for a few more seconds. She sighed and threw teabags into fresh mugs. The mugs were a random assortment of branded freebies that she'd found at the back of a cupboard. Forgotten relics from her days at university. Looking at them reminded her of being younger.

The kitchen looked different now that she'd started giving stuff away. She'd left a few photos up, but most of the cookbooks were gone, along with the teapots that used to live on the windowsill and her father's paperback collection. It was a wrench, but cathartic too. She had found a few things that she knew she could never part with. A drawing of an aeroplane wing that her father had sketched on the back of a shopping list; she remembered his voice, patiently explaining about air speeds and lift. A photo of her mother laughing that she'd taken when she was twelve, which had a thumb shadowing the corner, so that it never made it into an album. These she knew she would keep. Maybe even frame them. It was as though she was purging the house of the unhappy memories of her parents in their old age and rediscovering them as they had been when she was a child.

If she were superstitious, she would have said it was her parents trying to tell her to move on. She smiled. Moving on was good.

She hadn't expected the abseil to stress her out like that. It wasn't as though it had been really dangerous. How stupid to forget that she might have an anxiety attack. If she'd been expecting it, she would have been able to prepare for it. Thank goodness for Peter for giving her a lift. She poured water into the mugs and prodded the tea bags, making the tea seep out.

Peter seemed to be helping her move on in more ways than one. She couldn't remember the last time she'd felt this way about a man. But he was married. He saw her as just some woman he'd befriended at the hospice. There was no chance of her getting any nearer to him than that.

She reflected that she shouldn't want to anyway. Sneaking off with someone whilst his wife was in a coma was just a bit too sordid for her. That wasn't the sort of person she was. But it didn't stop her wanting him.

'Do you want more biscuits?' she said, over her shoulder. There was no response. Wondering whether he'd somehow slipped out to get away from her, she went back to the living room to find him asleep on the sofa, head flung back against the cushions. The late afternoon sun cast his face in planes of light and dark. She snatched a moment of indulgence and took in the perfection of his profile, the hint of gold on his long eyelashes, the little worry lines that were in sharp contrast to the crow's feet at the sides of his eyes.

Her hands flexed with the urge to touch him and stroke the ridge of his cheekbone and feel the evening stubble. To run her fingers through his sensible blonde hair. But that was an indulgence too far. She clenched her fists and turned away. Peter was not for her. She may as well enjoy being his friend. It was the best she was going to get.

Peter had no idea how long he'd been asleep. He woke up to find the room in semi darkness. For a moment he wondered where he was. The sofa was hot and embracing. That might explain the dream. He'd had dreams like that when he'd first met Sally. This time they featured Grace. He rubbed a hand over his face and slowly sat up.

He was still in Grace's living room. The light was on in the kitchen and he could see Grace moving around. The radio was on. She was dancing a little as she leaned against the counter, reading something. She seemed to glow in the yellow light of the kitchen. He watched her for a moment, trapped between reality and the dream of a few moments ago, when she'd been wrapped around him. She was beautiful and he wanted her so much it was almost a physical ache now. He squeezed his eyes shut. This had to stop. It was lust, that was all. The best thing he could do was get away.

He made his way to the kitchen, feeling bleary from afternoon sleep. 'I should head off.'

Grace turned. A bit of his dream sprang back into his mind. He tried to focus on something else. Anything.

'Stay for dinner?' She pointed at a pan on the hob. 'I've made enough for two.'

He hesitated.

'It's only pasta and pesto,' she said, misunderstanding. 'Nothing special. So, don't feel you have to.'

'Excuse me a minute. I really need to wake up properly.' He hurried off to the bathroom where he splashed his face with cold water. He glared at himself in the mirror and told himself to pull himself together. He liked Grace and found her attractive. Fine. He was allowed to look. But he couldn't put himself in the position that he felt anything more than a passing attraction. He had to think of Sally. A small voice pointed out that he rarely thought about anything BUT Sally, but he squashed the thought. He should go home. Staying for tea until she recovered was acceptable. Dinner, probably not. He nodded at his reflection. 'Go home Peter.'

When he returned to the kitchen, he could smell the pesto. His stomach rumbled. It was such a clean basil smell. But he had to be strong. 'Thanks for the offer of dinner, but I really had better head off,' he said. He picked up his jacket, which he'd slung over the back of the chair.

Her face fell. Even if he'd had a heart of stone, he would have felt her disappointment. As it was, he wanted to change his mind and stay. He told himself to stand firm. 'I've got some work to do before bed. I'm sorry.'

Grace nodded. She sucked in her lower lip and let it go. Her composure returned and she smiled. 'Well, thank you for all your help. I don't know what I'd have done without you.' She followed him out into the hall.

'Thanks for the tea. I enjoyed it.' He was surprised at how true this was. He paused, one hand on the door handle. 'I'm sorry I got a bit deep on you at the end. And then fell asleep.'

'Don't worry about it.' She touched his arm. He felt the thrill of her touch zing though his body. She looked up, brow furrowed. 'I know how exhausting it is to be a carer. You take sleep where you can.'

He couldn't concentrate on what she was saying. All he could focus on was her lips. Moving. Time seemed to slow down. He raised his eyes to meet hers and saw them widen. The lips stopped moving, slightly parted. The realisation that she wanted him as much as he wanted her almost made him stop breathing. He managed to say, 'I should go.' It came out in a hoarse gasp.

She nodded. 'Yes.' Her eyes remained on his. 'I'll see you around at the hospice, I guess.'

He appreciated the effort to lighten the mood. 'I guess so.'

'Thanks again for helping me,' she leaned forward and placed a kiss on his cheek. The touch of lips on his face was too much. He turned his face as she was drawing away and kissed her back.

He hadn't intended to kiss her like that. It was meant to be a peck on the lips. But as soon as his lips touched hers, his mind went blank and his body took over, kissing her fiercely like he'd wanted to do all afternoon. She drew a sharp breath and then kissed him back. She tasted of pesto and lemonade and her smell was deliciously human, not flowery, not musky, but so very real. He wanted her so much he felt his blood fizzing in his veins. He wrapped his arms around her waist and pulled her tight against him. He wanted her with every cell in his body. Her hands in his hair sent thrills though him. When she finally drew away from him, he didn't want to let her go.

They stared at each other, both breathing hard. His hands were still on her hips. Hers rested on his chest. Her eyes were wide as though she were surprised with herself. The moment hung between them, a line beyond which there was no turning back. All Peter could feel was the pounding of need in him. She never broke eye contact with him. Slowly, she drew her fingers into a fist. He felt the path of each fingertip scorching him through his T-shirt and there was no more doubt. They were kissing again. Hungry and needing each other. He walked her backwards and pressed her against the wall.

They ended up on the sofa. He kneeled over her and stroked the side of her face. When he pulled the band out of her hair, she ran her fingers through it, so that it lay long and loose over her shoulder. He stopped for a minute, stunned by how beautiful she was. He wanted her so much. Her hair slipped, thick and silky, through his fingers. So dark, so heavy. Completely unlike Sally's whispy blonde.

'Sally.' The thought of Sally froze him. Dear god, what was he *doing*?

He looked up at Grace and saw the shock on her face too. She wriggled out from between his knees and drew her knees up, as though trying to hide from him.

'I should go.' He pulled his T-shirt straight and looked around for his glasses.

She handed them to him, as though she'd read his mind. When he saw her face, his heart cracked. 'I'm sorry. I'm so sorry.'

She looked away, hugging her knees closer. 'Me too.'

He grabbed his keys and fled. There was no goodbye. No empty promises to call her. Nothing. Just the memory of her lips on his. And guilt.

Chapter Nine

Grace locked the door and went back to the kitchen where her pasta was a soggy mess. She stared at it. She picked up the pan, then put it down again. The thoughts that she was avoiding came crowding in. She sank into a chair.

She could still feel his lips on hers. The warm slide of his fingertips against her skin. Her body felt as though it had woken up, as though his touch had turned something insubstantial into something real. She had seen the need in his eyes and sensed the connection between them. But she had also seen the guilt and panic just after.

She'd only known Peter a short time, but she knew him well enough to know that the guilt would eat away at him. He would blame himself, but it was her fault, really. She would have to catch him and let him know that she understood he didn't mean it. It was a momentary lapse that happened because they'd been through something out of the ordinary together, or because they were both so lonely.

All these things, she could say to him, but she knew that really there were no excuses for what happened. They had both wanted more, she was sure of it. But Peter had been sensible enough to stop things before they went too far. She should be grateful. The trouble was she still wanted him. She would give almost anything to feel the melting warmth of his mouth on hers again. In a moment of clarity she realised that there was more to it than that. She had wanted Peter with every level of her being. She wanted to be his – mind, body and soul. At some point in the past few weeks, she'd fallen in love with Peter Wesley.

Grace sighed. Sally may be in a coma, but she was still

his wife. Grace had no right to make any claims on him. He was married. That made her some sort of harlot. Or a hypocrite at the very least.

She poured the overdone pasta into the bin and tried not to cry. All this time alone and she'd finally fallen for someone. Why did it have to be someone she couldn't have?

Peter couldn't sleep. Whenever he closed his eyes he saw Grace. God, she was beautiful. He'd felt so relaxed in her company, something he hadn't felt in a long time. But there was Sally. His wife. He loved Sally. How could he even *think* of sleeping with someone else? What was wrong with him? He had never, ever thought he'd be capable of cheating on a woman. Never. And yet he almost had. He couldn't figure out where he'd gone wrong. When had he taken a turning that meant he could lose his self-control?

He threw off the covers and sat up. The clock by his bed showed it was nearly 3 a.m. Peter sighed and got out of bed.

He padded downstairs and into the kitchen. A night cap would help him sleep. Did he have any alcohol? A quick search through the cupboards revealed a complete lack of booze. He would normally have had wine, but his mother had started making sure he never had much in the house. He had no idea where she hid it, or even if she took it away with her. Part of him resented that she trespassed on his life like that. Part of him was amused and grateful.

'Desperate times,' he said to the empty kitchen. Talking to himself had started to feel normal too. First that, then adultery. Maybe he did need help. He shook his head as he crossed the hall to the living room and paused at the door. He hadn't been in there for months. He took a deep breath and let himself in.

Flicking on the light switch revealed a room that looked

just like it had done before the wedding. There were pictures of him and Sally. There were bridal magazines in a rack, next to where Sally usually sat. The table had the pale blue and lemon table cloth that Sally had brought with her. His own table cloths tended to be bold checks and blocks of colour. The pastel walls, the wallpapered 'feature wall' at the end, the creamy white sofas that felt soft enough to melt under your weight, the cushions that provided splashes of colour, were all Sally's choices. Sally had known exactly what she wanted. Peter, smitten and slightly relieved not to have to think about sofas and curtains, had let her have free rein over decorating the house. He had to admit she'd done a great job. The room looked like it had been crafted by an interior designer.

He picked up a photo in a silver frame from the side table. He and Sally had gone to Brighton for the weekend. He had his arm around her waist and was grinning like a nutter. Sally, her golden ponytail flying in the breeze was leaning her head against his shoulder and smiling to the camera. He remembered the Chinese students that had taken the photo for them. Sally, with smiles and gestures, had shown them what she wanted. It was a nice picture. Sally's eyes looked bright and sparkling. He didn't deserve a woman as beautiful and lively as that. So full of life.

The irony of the description made him snort. Full of life. Hah.

Peter took the photo with him and went to the sideboard. Inside were a number of bottles that had been intended for when they got back from honeymoon. He pulled out a bottle of whiskey and a glass. He put the photograph on the table and the tumbler in front of it. 'Here's to you, Sally,' he said, as he poured himself a small measure.

Grace's phrase 'like being haunted by someone' came

back to him. He swallowed the shot in one go. It burned, not unpleasantly, down his throat. 'I'm sorry, darling,' he said to the girl in the photo. 'I'm so, so sorry. I didn't mean for things to go that far. I just …' He poured himself another shot. 'It was all my fault. I've been missing you so much, Sally. There's no excuse really. It was stupid. I'm so very sorry.'

The second glass went down more smoothly than the one before. He looked at the bottle thoughtfully. Sally had always watched what she drank. Since meeting her, Peter himself drank much less. She said that alcohol was a great way to unwind, but too much and you start to unravel. Funny, for someone who was normally willing to grab life by the balls, alcohol was one of the few things she was scrupulous about. He wondered if she'd known an alcoholic in the past. She'd implied that once.

Peter sank into the softness of the white sofa, careful not to spill anything. It occurred to him that he didn't know much about Sally, really. All he knew was that both her parents had died when she was young and she was determined to make her way in the world by herself. Everything she had, she'd earned. That stubborn determination to make it to her dreams, no matter what, was one of the things Peter loved about her. They had so much in common. They both loved the same sort of bold, geometric art prints, the same music (although she had a tangential love of Brit Pop, which he couldn't really fathom), the same films. He had initially thought that cop movies was a bit of an odd thing for a girl to like, but she threw herself into them, fidgeting with tension during the chase scenes, just like she did with everything else.

Peter poured himself another glass. Last one, he promised her. Looking into the glass, he was surprised to realise it was crystal. He didn't remember having any proper cut glass.

The wedding presents. He had a distant memory of his mother saying 'Don't worry about that darling, I've asked people if they wanted them back, and most people wanted you to keep them for when Sally comes out of hospital'. It was a nice glass. Sally had chosen well for the wedding list. He'd trusted her with all that. She had clearly done a good job.

He took his time with the third glass. Of course, Sally wasn't perfect. Who was? The thing with the gambling addiction was a big one. He was glad she'd told him about the debts. Paying them off for her wasn't so much of a problem, he had the money, but it was persuading her to go to Gamblers Anonymous that was hard. For a long time she'd insisted that it was just a slip. She could control it. She would never go to a casino again. Didn't he trust her? In the end, she'd woken him up one morning and told him that yes, she wanted to go to GA. She wanted to kick this thing for good. Because she loved him and for him, she would do anything.

Peter smiled at the memory. It had taken a lot for her to face up to her own addiction. He remembered her sitting there, hugging her knees, her eyes full of unshed tears. He remembered his own sense of relief. He'd held her close and hugged her. He could support her through all of that. And they would get through it. Because they loved each other.

But then there was that letter, sitting on top of his briefcase.

'What were you doing, Sally?' he said. 'Why did you need money? And why didn't you just ask me for it?'

Had Sally been in some sort of trouble? How could he find out, if she had? Perhaps the debt collection company could give him more information. He couldn't confront Sally to ask.

If he could confront Sally, would he then confess what had just happened with Grace?

Kissing Grace was a mistake caused by his loneliness. It wouldn't happen again. He finished off his whiskey. He thought again of Grace and the vulnerability of her. She had made him feel … corrected. As though he'd been away for a long time and finally got back to where he belonged. He had never felt like that with Sally. Exhilarated, exhausted, but not that deep-seated satisfaction. He remembered her moan when he kissed her breast and his body thrummed at the mere memory. He had a special connection with Grace, but he could never feel it again.

'Oh Grace,' he whispered. 'I'm so, so, sorry.'

He had managed to be unfaithful to his wife and alienate the one person that made him feel human. 'Peter, you are a complete fuckwit,' he said. 'First you've got Mum and Dad thinking you're depressed and now you've screwed up your marriage as well. Great work, bud.'

He groaned and let his head slump back onto the sofa. Then there was his sister, who thought he no longer cared. Well, at least he could do something about that. He would call her as soon as he could the next morning.

Peter felt the terrible push pull of both wanting and not wanting to see Grace again. The text he had sent her had been simply worded and awkward. The whole situation was awkward. He'd asked her to meet him, at a coffee shop near the science park where she worked, in her lunch hour so that he wasn't putting her to too much trouble. What he had to say was sad enough without adding inconvenience to insult.

He got there five minutes early and got himself a coffee. He spotted her out of the window. Exactly on time, as he'd known she would be. She walked with a hand clutching her coat at the throat, as though she were cold. It made her look skinny and vulnerable. When she came in, she spotted him and she came over without a smile. Her whole demeanour was wary, like she knew what was coming. Perhaps she did know. She was a clever woman.

Peter rose, awkwardly, behind the table. 'Thanks for coming. What can I get you? Tea? Coffee?'

'Nothing, thanks.'

Peter sat back down and fiddled with his coffee cup.

Grace sat down, her hands clasped on her knees, her back rigid. So formal. So unlike the Grace he'd got to know. 'So …?'

Peter shook his head. 'I'm so sorry, Grace. I … it shouldn't have happened.'

She nodded. 'I know.'

'I'm sorry.'

'That it happened at all? Or …'

And there it was. He wasn't sorry it had happened at all. He had been prepared to say he didn't know what had come over him, but seeing her, he knew he couldn't do that to her. He had wanted her. He still wanted her. But what was the point of telling her that? It wasn't going to make anything better.

'I'm married. To Sally …' He looked at his coffee.

'I understand.'

'She's my wife. And I love her.'

He looked up. She hadn't moved. Her eyes seemed to glisten slightly. She blinked and drew herself up, stiff. 'I understand,' she repeated. 'And you're right. It can't happen again.'

He should have felt relief, but all he felt was sadness. No, more than sadness. Hollow. Emptied.

Grace drew a long breath, seeming almost to gather herself. 'Sally is your wife. She's very ill. To be unfaithful to her would be … wrong. And, I'm sorry too. I'm just as much to blame as you are.' She finally met his eyes. 'I'll miss you.'

He could see the effort it took her to say that and he was grateful. 'I'll miss you too.'

She held out a hand. He shook it and dropped it quickly. 'I guess I'll see you at the hospice?'

She stood up and it was as though a shutter had come down. 'I guess so,' she said, for all the world as though they'd never touched. 'I hope things go well and Sally recovers.'

'Thank you.'

Grace turned to leave. 'Look after yourself,' she said, over her shoulder.

'You too.'

After she'd gone, Peter sat in a trance-like hush, his coffee untouched in front of him. He had done the right thing. Except it didn't feel like it. It felt like he'd lost something important. He fought the urge to go back and throw his arms around Grace, to press his head against her and hear her heart beat, to feel her, taste her and, more than anything, just to talk to her. For a few weeks he'd found someone with whom he was comfortable. Now he was alone again. It was just him and Sally.

'Grace! I heard all about what happened at the abseil. Are you okay?' Margaret had clearly been tapping into the gossip.

Grace kissed Margaret's cheek. 'I'm fine.' She turned and drew the curtains shut against the gathering dark outside. The rain that had been looming all day finally broke out and smattered against the pane. In the distance, lightning flickered. 'It's pretty horrible out there. I just missed getting soaked.'

'Grace.' Margaret eyed her. 'Come here a minute. Let me see your face.'

When Grace stepped closer she exclaimed, 'My goodness child, you look like you haven't slept in days! Just how bad was this little fainting fit you had?'

Grace took a moment to reply. Margaret was right that she hadn't slept, but the reason wasn't the abseil. It was Peter. She had lain awake thinking about him. When she drifted off to sleep, she dreamt of him.

'Grace?' Margaret frowned. 'What's wrong? Is it the anxiety attacks coming back?'

Should she confide in Margaret? Would telling one person release the secret so that everyone knew? She was tired of watching the same thoughts go round and round in her head. She had to tell someone. Margaret was the only person she could trust.

'It's not the anxiety attack,' she said. 'Well, it was, but that was over pretty quickly. I think I just pushed myself a little bit too far then. I'll have to be more careful in the future.'

'Are you sure? Did you come off the medication before you were ready?'

Grace shook her head. The anti-depressants had made her tired and given her headaches. She was in no hurry to try them again. 'No.'

'Well something's clearly bothering you. What is it?' Margaret reached over with her good hand.

Grace sat on the side of the bed, taking Margaret's hand in hers. 'I'm not sure ...'

Margaret fixed her with a thoughtful stare. 'It may help to talk to someone. Pretend you're telling your mother.'

'I think my mother is the last person I'd want to talk

to.' She had always thought of herself as against adultery and now she'd nearly been complicit in it. She wondered what her mother would have said. Her mother, despite her rebellious marriage, had been very straight laced in some ways. Grace knew she would have been horrified.

Grace looked at Margaret's brittle hand resting in hers. Perhaps it would help to share. There was no one else she could talk to, really. Apart from a counsellor. She realised she'd let herself drift out of wavelength with her friends. It had been imperceptibly slow at first. But over the years … She looked up. 'I'm not sure where to start.'

'How about the beginning? I hear that's a very good place to start.'

She started with the meeting in the lift, where he'd turned down her request for help. When she'd finished Margaret said, 'Phew. That's the most exciting story I've heard all week. It's better than all these soaps they keep showing on the television.'

Grace sniffed. 'Thanks. I think.'

'What I don't understand,' said Margaret, 'is why you're so upset about it. Was it good?'

Grace was horrified and didn't answer, but she could feel her face radiating heat.

'I'll take that to be a yes,' said Margaret, in her matter of fact way. 'So, what's the problem?'

'He's married. I told you.'

'Yes, but his wife's as good as dead. He may as well have someone else in the meantime.'

'Margaret!'

'Besides, he's the one who's cheating on someone, not you. If he's okay with it, then I'd just go with it. Oh, unless you think he's just using you. What does he feel about it? Has he said anything?'

Grace shrugged. 'He says he's sorry.'

'Bastard,' said Margaret. 'I hope you told him to boil his head.'

'I don't know what to say.' Grace let go of Margaret's hand to rub her eyes. 'I suppose in a way, I'm glad that he's thinking of Sally. He'd be a horrible person if he didn't feel bad about cheating on her when she was lying there helpless. But ... I don't think I could see him again as just a friend. I can't possibly compete with his perfect wife. He lost her the day they got married. On the happiest day of their life. I can't compete with that.' She sighed. 'The worst of it is that I can't keep avoiding him all the time. We're both going to the fundraising ball in a few weeks. I'll be forced to see him then.'

'Oh Grace.' Margaret's thin hand clasped her shoulder. 'I'm sorry. I'm not surprised you're upset if he used you like that.'

'That's the thing, I don't think he used me.' Grace sighed. 'I think he was trying not to ... I think he's just trying to do the right thing. Whatever that is.'

'You're too good for him, darling,' said Margaret.

Grace smiled. 'It's sweet of you to say that.'

'Sweet, nothing. It's the truth. I've known you for some time now Grace, and I count your mother as one of the best friends I've had in my later life. If I had a daughter, I would be proud and honoured to have one like you. And I do not say that lightly.' For a moment Margaret's headmistress voice came through.

Grace laughed. 'Thank you. It means a lot.' She slid off the bed and delved into her bag. 'I've got a new book for you. Ready?'

'Of course,' said Margaret. She leaned back into her 'listening' pose. 'Read on McDuff.'

Chapter Ten

Grace stopped by the main entrance to the hospice and peered outside. Rain poured from the low sky. Lightning flashed somewhere close by, illuminating the parked cars in glaring white. The thunderclap that followed made her jump. She really didn't want to drive home in that. Turning around, she headed back into the hospice.

'Did you decide against going out in that?' asked the security guard as she went past. 'Can't say I blame you.'

'I'm going to leave it a bit, see if it eases up,' said Grace. She signed in again and took the lift, pressing Margaret's floor without thinking. As the doors closed, she thought of meeting Peter a few weeks ago. How long ago that seemed!

She wondered if he was still there, visiting Sally. She longed to talk to him. A glance at her watch told her that he'd probably gone home. It was nearly past visiting hours. Suddenly, she wanted to see the woman who had caught his heart. She could never compare to Sally, but she had to know whom she had lost out to. She jabbed the button for Sally's floor.

When the door opened, she stared at the lobby for a few seconds, psyching herself up to step through. As the doors started to close again, she leapt out. There was no point putting things off. If she chickened out now, she would spend the whole night thinking about it.

'I'm here to see Sally Wesley,' she said into the intercom. It sounded like a question, rather than a statement. There was a pause. Instead of buzzing her through, the nurse came to the door. She recognised her from when her father had been in intensive care.

'Oh, hi Grace,' she said. 'Sorry, didn't recognise you on the door cam.' She gestured towards the CCTV camera. 'What can we do for you?'

'I was hoping to catch Peter Wesley, if he's still around. It's about … the abseil. And sponsorship.' She wasn't sure why she was making up such an elaborate cover story. Now the nurse would go looking for Peter. What would she say then?

The nurse gave her a knowing nod. 'He's around somewhere,' she said. 'We know who you are, so you may as well come in.'

They reached the nurse's station and peered into Sally's room. It was empty apart from the patient.

'He's probably just nipped to the common room to grab a cup of coffee,' said the nurse.

A bell pinged and a red light came on above one of the rooms. The nurse sighed. 'I'd best go see what that's all about.'

'I'll wait here, until he comes back.'

The nurse bustled off, leaving Grace by herself at the nurse's station, looking at the door to Sally's room. There was no one around. She could go and have a look at Sally. Peering up and down the corridor and seeing no one, she quietly slipped inside.

Grace looked round the hospital room. It was gently lit with night lighting. You never got proper darkness in the hospital. This room had the same dimensions as the rooms in the floors above, but lacked a certain something. It looked more like a hospital room with the lino floor and a generic painting on the wall. This was a room for a patient. Not a resident. It smelled of disinfectant.

On the bed, Sally looked like she was sleeping. The sound of her breathing was just audible beneath the thrashing of rain on the window and the beep of the heart monitor. Grace peered at the dark hair, and the pale face under the tubing. So this was Peter's wife.

There was a wedding photo in a silver frame on the bedside trolley. Grace picked it up. Peter was beaming in it, his face radiating happiness. Sally was smiling. Her hair, which must have been bleached to be blonde, was twisted up into an elaborate tiara and veil arrangement. She looked delighted with life. It was hard to believe it was the same person as the woman on the bed.

There was something familiar about Sally's face. Grace frowned and tilted the photo toward the light to get a better look at it. She couldn't place where she might have known her from. She replaced the photo and went to look at the real Sally again. A hand lay limp on the bed, the veins showing up blue against the white skin.

Without really understanding why, Grace touched the hand with her fingertips, half expecting it to be cold, like it was made of marble. She was almost surprised to find it warm.

'Of course it's warm, you idiot,' she muttered to herself. 'She's not dead.' Then, feeling self-conscious, she said to Sally, 'Hi Sally. Peter's just gone out. He'll be back in a minute.'

There was no response. Poor Sally was lying there, unable to move, and she had almost slept with her husband. Guilt churned through her. She took Sally's hand in hers, feeling the weight of her palm against hers. A real weight, a real person. No longer just an abstract thought. 'You must love him very much.'

A flash of lightning from outside cast the room into stark monochrome. The thunder was almost instantaneous. Grace turned. 'That's really close.' They were the highest building in the area. 'Thank goodness for lightning conductors.'

The next flash was blinding. There was a loud crack and the lights went out. There was no dramatic sputtering. Just light and noises and then, total darkness. Grace, half blinded by the lightning, had a moment of disorientation. The only thing real around her was Sally's hand, held in hers. There was a sudden drop in temperature. She shivered.

The emergency lights came on, accompanied by a cacophony of beeps and bings and buzzers as the equipment came back online. Sally's heart monitor started up again, the alarm keening urgently. Grace stepped towards the monitor. The trace had a short bit of flat line and was now back to normal. Grace turned back to the bed and gave a little shriek. There was someone standing right next to her. She dropped Sally's hand and jumped back.

In the dim light, it was hard to see any detail, but the person appeared to be wearing a lot of pale clothes. Grace's hand went to her mouth. The person said 'What the bloody hell was that?'

The backup generators kicked in and the lights came back on. Out in the corridor footsteps pounded as staff and visitors went into action.

Grace sidled to the wall nearest the bed and turned on the light.

There was a woman, in full bridal dress, standing in the room. The woman looked around. 'What the hell is this?' She caught sight of Grace. 'Who are you?'

Grace's glance fell on the photo by the bed. Sally. She looked at the bride in the photo and the one standing there glaring at her. The dress was the same.

'Sally?'

Sally took a step forward. 'Look, who are you? Do I know you?'

Grace glanced at the area around Sally's lap. Sally looked just like any other person, apart from the bride theme, except that she was standing in the middle of the bed. Not on the bed. In the middle of it. Grace leaned to the side to look underneath. The rest of the dress and Sally's feet were there. She and the bed were occupying the same space.

Sally looked down too and let loose a string of expletives. She sprang away from the bed, patting her legs as though to check they were solid. 'What the buggering hell is going on?' When she looked up she looked frightened.

Grace steadied herself with her hands on the back of the chair. 'I think,' she said, carefully, 'you're a ghost of some sort.' She didn't believe in the supernatural. But it was hard to not believe in someone who was standing right in front of her, whilst lying in a coma at the same time. Ghost was the best explanation she could come up with.

'A ghost? Don't take the piss. I'm not dead.' Sally looked around the room. 'Where is this place? And who is that poor cow in … the …' The sentence ground to a halt as she realised the implications. She walked over to the side of the bed and glared at the patient. 'That's not me.'

A thousand questions clamoured in Grace's head. What had just happened? How was it possible? Was this woman dangerous? But as she watched Sally's stricken face, she felt sorry for her. Seeing a ghost was probably nothing compared to the shock of thinking you were at your wedding and suddenly discovering that you were really in hospital in a coma.

'You could check the chart at the end of the bed …' she suggested.

Sally gave her a short glare and walked over to the end of the bed. 'Sally Wesley?' She opened her mouth.

'You're married to Peter Wesley,' Grace said, partly for her own benefit.

The frown on Sally's forehead deepened. She lowered herself into a chair on the other side of the room. Grace wondered if she would fall through it, but she didn't. She put her head in her hand and was quiet for a moment.

'So all that stuff, in the … nothingness. It was real. And now I'm here.' Sally looked up. She gestured towards the silent figure on the bed. 'But I'm also over there.'

Grace had to admire the way Sally was dealing with this. No tears. No hysterics. A bit of swearing, obviously, that was excusable in the circumstances. 'Yes.' After a moment she added. 'I'm sorry.'

'Why? Is it your fault?' The eyes narrowed. Suddenly the face wasn't so much pretty as scary. This was not a ghost to be on the wrong side of.

'No. I'm just … sorry. It can't be nice for you.'

'No love, I'm in coma. Of course it's not bloody nice for me.'

'No need to snap at me. I just happened to be here when whatever just happened … happened.'

Sally paced back to the bed. 'Shit. Where's my hair gone?' She reached up to touch her own blonde hair. 'It looks like crap. All the blonde's grown out. How did it get like that?' She leaned forward. 'And what the hell is going on with my skin. Jesus wept, it looks awful. Don't they moisturise people in here?'

While Sally was examining her comatose self, Grace sidled to the door. She felt bad leaving Sally by herself, but the whole situation was just too weird. She didn't believe in ghosts, but Sally appeared to be just that. There would be a rational explanation. Perhaps an electric shock from the lightning was making her hallucinate things.

'And the eyebrows haven't been done. Bloody hell.'

For a hallucination, Sally was certainly swearing a lot. Grace reached the door. Just as she was reaching for it, Peter flung it open, almost squashing her.

'Is she okay?' Peter rushed to the side of the bed. Sally looked up in surprise. Grace stood by the door and watched.

'The alarm's going off.' He stared at the monitor. 'Why is the alarm going off?' He looked back at the pale figure on the bed. 'She's breathing. The heart rate looks fine. Why is the alarm going off?' He looked straight at Grace, his eyes wide.

'Probably because of the gap in the signal ...' said Grace. She hadn't even noticed the alarm. Seeing a ghost would probably do that to a person. 'You could press reset and see if it goes off again.'

'Peter?' said the other Sally. Her whole demeanour changed. Gone was the scowling angry woman. 'Peter! Darling.' She launched herself at him, running through the bed as though it wasn't there. She flung her arms around Peter and fell right through him.

Peter gasped and shuddered. 'Did the heating go down too?' he said. 'It's freezing in here.' Again, he looked at Grace.

Grace shook her head, not trusting herself to speak. It seems that Peter could not see Sally. Which made it even more likely that she was just imagining the ghost. What did she do about that? Would it go away once she'd had some sleep? Should she get psychiatric help? Perhaps the stresses of the past were catching up with her.

Peter seemed to register Grace's presence for the first time. He frowned. 'Grace? What are you doing here?'

Behind him Sally got to her feet. Her eyes were fixed on

Grace. 'Grace? So you're Grace.' She looked her up and down as though assessing her.

Grace opened the door and backed out. What had Peter said in front of Sally? Had he confessed what had happened?

Peter took a step towards her. 'Grace? Are you okay?'

Sally moved forward too. Grace fled. A couple of nurses were rushing a bed towards the lift, so Grace ran in the other direction, down the corridor towards the stairs. At the door to the stairwell, she turned. Sally was standing outside her room, hammering on an invisible wall shouting. 'Come back!' Peter was behind her, standing in the door to Sally's room, torn between confusion and concern for his comatose wife.

Grace raced down the stairs and out into the rain. When she got to her car, her hands shook so badly, it took her several goes to get the key in the lock. She got into the car and locked the door. Looking out into the rain, she couldn't see anything. Grace sat rigid in her seat. She checked the rear view mirror. Nothing. Did figments of imagination have reflections? Slowly, she turned round in her seat and looked in the back. No one. She breathed out. Her heart was still pounding. She put her hands on the steering wheel. She had to calm down. A few more deep breaths and she felt steady enough to drive. She checked behind her one more time, flicked the wipers on to max speed and set off.

The car park was in front of the hospice. To leave, she had to pass by the entrance. Someone was standing there in the light. Grace's heart picked up again when she spotted the white dress and the veil streaming out behind it. She would have to go past Sally. There was nothing for it. Hopefully, she'd get past before Sally realised it was her.

She neared the hospice, a cold sweat crept down her

back. Sally's head snapped up. Just as Grace's car went past the entrance, Sally leapt into the road. There was no time to stop. Grace hit the brakes, but the car slid on the wet surface and right through Sally. Grace screamed. A blast of cold hit her as Sally passed through her. She looked over her shoulder to see Sally spin round and start after her. Grace put her foot back on the accelerator and sped away.

Chapter Eleven

Sally tried to take the lift back up, but she couldn't seem to press the button hard enough to get it to go anywhere. She looked hopefully out into the foyer, in case there was anyone else wanting to go up. No luck. The only person there was a security guard who was reading a book and occasionally looking at the CCTV screens. She tried the lift buttons again.

'Aargh. What the hell is going on?' She stamped her foot. 'Bloody work you bloody thing. I just want to go back upstairs and talk to Peter.' She pictured the room, with its waxy, doll like figure in the bed.

She wasn't sure what happened. One minute she was in the lift. The next she was back in the room, next to the poor cow in the bed. She hadn't even blinked. 'Shit. What just—'

Peter was standing next to the bed, holding the sick woman's hand. 'All up and running again now, darling,' he said, looking down at the bed. 'It was only a short power outage. Everything is back on properly now. It's okay.'

'Peter.' Sally composed herself. 'Peter, darling. I'm so glad you're here.'

He didn't seem to hear her. She went up to him. 'Peter? Can you hear me?'

Peter continued to gaze at the woman in the bed, stroking the limp hand that rested in his.

Sally put her mouth next to his ear. 'Oi. Peter!'

Peter shuddered and looked over his shoulder. He looked right through her.

She waved a hand in front of his face. 'What do I have to do to get you to notice me? Flash my knickers?' She tried it. He just turned back to gaze insipidly at the plastic woman.

Sally thrust her hand into his midriff. It went straight through.

Peter shivered. 'It really is cold in here darling. Let me just check the temperature.' He laid the lifeless hand back on the covers and crossed over to a thermostat by the door. He looked at the reading and shrugged.

Sally watched as he went back towards the bed and pulled up a chair. He took a small book out of his pocket and started to look through it. 'Where did we get to yesterday?' he said. 'Did I finish the short story?'

'Yes,' Sally replied automatically. 'Yes you did. He came back from the Middle East and decided to work in London.'

'I think I stopped at the bit where he left to go to his new job,' said Peter, frowning.

'No, you read it.'

Peter started to read. Sally rolled her eyes. 'You've already read that bit, you doofus.' When he didn't stop, she sat on the bed and watched him. The cadences of his voice washed over her, familiar and somehow comforting. It calmed her enough for her to be able to think about what had happened.

So, that woman, Grace, could see her. Peter couldn't. Okay. That was weird. The poor cow with the brown hair in the bed was her ... she took a quick glance across at the figure and looked away. She didn't want to think about that. She looked back at Peter. He had aged. How long had it been since the accident? She hopped off the bed and checked the chart at the end for the date. Holy shit. Just under a year. Bloody hell. No wonder her hair had grown out. She wondered who had cut it. Letting it grow out was one thing, but cutting it so badly, that was just cruel.

She looked closely at Peter, who shivered and zipped his fleece up to his neck. There were lines on his forehead that hadn't been there before and she was sure she could see some grey hairs at his temples. Bags under the eyes, okay, temporary, but that scar wasn't going to fade. There was something else about him, a heaviness that she didn't remember seeing before. It was as though her handsome, dynamic Peter had suddenly been replaced with an older, more tired version of him. She pulled herself back onto the bed and fretted about with the skirts until she realised that they would probably always look just the way she remembered them.

She muttered 'sod it' and sat cross-legged. Looking down, she realised she was sitting on the sleeping woman's feet and shuffled out of the way. 'Sorry love.'

Peter carried on reading. He didn't do the voices or anything, which was sad in some ways, but quite nice in others. She didn't think Peter would be that good at voices.

'What to do, what to do,' she said. She drummed her fingers on her knee. The cloth, a heavy silk, should have felt rough under her fingertips, but she could barely feel it at all. She wondered if she could feel anything else. She touched her face. She tried to pinch the coverlet on the bed. Nothing. She couldn't feel her own fingertips against each other. Oookay. Her breathing quickened. She couldn't touch anything around her. How was she going to eat? What if she needed the loo? What if … She put her hands to her head. 'Don't panic, Sally. Don't panic. Don't panic. There has to be a way out of this.'

There was a knock at the door and a nurse looked in. 'I'll just check her stats are still okay,' she said.

Peter stopped reading and nodded. He moved out of the way while the nurse checked dials and displays. Sally had another go at trying to get him to notice her. She passed through him twice, making him shiver violently.

'Are you sure the thermostat's okay?' Peter walked to the side of the room to look at it. 'I'm freezing.'

'It's not cold,' said the nurse, not looking up from the notes she was jotting down. 'If anything, Sally's temp is a bit high. Nothing major, but we'll keep an eye on it.'

'Do you think she's caught something? A virus or something?' There was genuine worry in Peter's voice. Sally saw his frown lines leap into focus. Had they come just from worrying about her? Ah, that was sweet. She would have rewarded his devotion with a hug and kiss ... except she couldn't touch him.

Sally sat back down on the bed and watched as the nurse messed around with the chart and Peter stood there gazing worriedly at the bint in the bed.

'Peter. My Peter.' She reached up to stroke his face.

'I must be coming down with something,' Peter said. 'I can't stop shivering.'

'Oh dear, I hope it's nothing nasty.' The nurse's eyes darted from Peter back to the woman in the bed.

Peter looked shocked. 'I hope I didn't pass whatever it is on to her. I washed my hands on the way in and everything.' He looked plaintively at the nurse, who gave him a sympathetic smile and said, 'Maybe you'd better get yourself to bed.'

Peter grabbed his coat and stood a small distance away from the bed. 'I'm leaving now, darling,' he said.

Sitting in the middle of the bed, Sally felt as though he really was talking to her. 'Peter, babe, you're not ill. It's just me touching you ...'

'I'll see if Mum will come and visit you while I'm ill,' said Peter. 'I'll be back as soon as it's safe, okay?'

'Oh no. Not Diane. She just sits here and knits. I know you can't visit me, but please don't inflict your mother on me! You know she doesn't like me.'

'I won't kiss you. I don't want to give you my germs.' He blew her a kiss and practically fled from the room.

'Don't leave me, Peter.' Her voice sounded desperate, even to her.

The nurse dimmed the lights and left the room, leaving Sally alone with her own still breathing body.

It was peculiar being in the hospital at night. The machines purred and blipped quietly. Sally tried lying down and sinking back into her body. That did nothing other than make her feel slightly repulsed. Sally slumped in the chair feeling the world spin. She was a ghost. There was no getting around that. She could walk through furniture. She was a ghost, except she wasn't dead. She looked up at the figure on the bed. The only movement was a slight rise and fall of her chest.

Peter couldn't see her. She felt the fear rise and breathed in deeply to squash it. The hospital room was so bloody depressing. 'I want to go home,' she whispered into the darkness. Suddenly, she was standing in her last flat. She recognised the room and the view over next door's roof. She would know that skyline anywhere, she'd lived in that poky little place for six years. But she didn't recognise the stuff in the room. She had proper curtains, for a start. There was a couple asleep on a futon on the floor. Sally looked around. A cot frame without a mattress was pushed against the wall. She'd left this flat well over a year ago. Why was she there now?

'Home.' She'd thought of home and ended up here. She shrugged. For the best part of her life this flat had been her home. She'd decorated it just the way she'd wanted it. She'd lived her life exactly the way she'd wanted to. She put her hands on her hips. At her feet the woman on the bed shivered and huddled into her partner.

Sally had moved out of this place to move in with Peter. 'Home,' she said, scornfully. 'Not this.' She pictured her hallway in the house she'd so memorably persuaded Peter to buy. And, somehow, she was there. It was as though she could move from one place to another, just by picturing it. She tried out a few other places – her work, the hospital, a pub and back to her house again. Amazing.

'I could get used to this way of travelling.' If she'd been able to zap herself about like this, there would never have been a car accident. Again, she wondered what happened to the lottery ticket. Peter probably didn't bother checking it. Sally clicked her tongue.

The hall was dark, save for a little light coming in through the glass panels on the front door. Sally tried to switch on a light and swore as her hand went through the switch without flicking it. Never mind. She could walk in the dark. It's not like she was going to bump into anything. She checked out the living room, as much as she could see in that light, anyway. It looked pretty much the way she'd left it. Good.

The kitchen was tidy. There was a single plate, a fork and a mug, upside down on the draining board. Sally wished she could open the cupboards and look inside. She tried sticking her head in through the door and saw nothing but dark inside. She stalked around the table, noticing things that were in the wrong place. Finally, she psyched herself up and went upstairs.

Light from the streetlamp outside illuminated the master bedroom. The curtains were wide open and the bed was empty. Sally did a double take. 'Where is he?'

Looking around the room, she saw all her stuff still on the dressing table. Her iPad was still plugged in next to her side of the bed. All good, so far, but where was Peter?

Could it be that he hadn't come home yet? It had been several hours since he left the hospital …

Sally frowned. Could it be that he was sleeping somewhere else? With someone else? That Grace creature …

There was a sound from one of the other rooms. Sally jumped before she remembered that SHE was the ghost. 'I AM the thing that goes bump in the night,' she said out loud. The idea made her laugh. Her voice seemed to echo in the dark house.

There was a mumble from another room. Stepping back onto the landing Sally tracked the noise to the spare room. It was dark in there and it took a few minutes for her to be able to see. Someone groaned and rolled over in the bed. Sally tiptoed forward and peered at the sleeping man.

'Peter?' She stood straight and frowned. 'Why are you in the spare room?'

Peter mumbled something. Leaning closer, she caught a few words. 'Won't do it again' was repeated among the jumble. 'Won't do what again?' she demanded. There was no response. Not one that made sense anyway.

She wondered if he would be able to hear her in his sleep. She leaned forward and spoke in his ear.

'Peter. It's me. Sally. I'm alive. I can hear you when you talk to me. Please. Come and find me.'

But all Peter did was shiver violently and curl up into a ball, bunching the duvet around him.

Sally ended up back in the hospital room. There was nothing she could do in her house and it was too strange being there, watching Peter in an almost delirious sleep. This was all wrong. She looked miserably at the body on the bed. 'This isn't how it's supposed to go. I'm supposed to be married and living happily ever after. Maybe even have won the lottery. I can't be lying in a hospital bed with bloody awful hair. I just can't.' She wanted to cry, but there were no tears. Maybe ghosts couldn't do tears. She pulled up her knees, not caring about what it did to the dress, and hugged herself tight. 'This is all wrong,' she said. 'All wrong.'

It took a while for her to finish feeling sorry for herself. She had never been one to hang around worrying about what couldn't be changed. Soon, she was back on her feet. Ready for another fight.

'Come on Sally,' she told herself. 'Don't get sad. Get mad.' She'd handled worse than this before. Finding her father, hanging from the bannisters, for one. She remembered the horror and the screaming. She had run away from the grotesque, distorted face and gone next door. The neighbour had calmed her down and called the police. By the time Glenda came home, the body had been taken down and Sally had subsided from hysterical to distressed. Sally, only fourteen years old, then watched her mum take in the news and saw her crumble.

Glenda's inability to deal with the news had been Sally's salvation. There was only room for one emotional wreck in the family. Sally had to save the day. She did this by replacing her grief with anger. She got angry, then she got organised. She would never, ever let herself be so poor that she would be driven to hang herself from the bannisters so that her teenage daughter would find her. No way. She had a plan. When her mother started drinking, the plan wobbled off track. So Sally, who was sixteen by then, packed her bags one night and walked out. Easy as.

If she could deal with that, she could deal with this crock of weirdness now. She just needed a plan. She jumped to her feet. 'Okay. What have we got …' She paced around the bed, talking to the person in the bed. 'I'm a ghost. I'm married to Peter.' She stopped to allow herself a little smile of satisfaction. That part of the plan had worked. She was married to Peter, which meant that she was now rich. 'Not much use if I can't get near it to spend it. I need to get back to being properly alive for that.' She resumed her pacing. 'So I've been married to Peter for a while. The accident happened when I was still in The Dress. Peter's put me in this hospital type place and he visits me every day ... and reads to me. He can't hear me.'

She looked at the waxy woman with the travesty of a haircut, who was lying on the bed. 'He still comes to see *you*,' she corrected herself. 'And he still loves *you*. I can hear it in his voice. He still loves you, even when you look like that.' She remembered the way he used to look at her. Did he still look at her like that? She doubted it. But that look would be back again soon. She was sure.

'Focus, Sally, focus. You've been in a coma for nearly a year. His attention is starting to wander. Understandable, in some ways. So the first thing to do is to get Peter's attention.' She paused at the window and tried to drum her fingers on the windowsill. They didn't make a sound. She gave an annoyed 'tsch'. 'But Peter can't see me,' she continued. 'So I can't work on him.'

'The only one who can see me, is that husband tempter, Grace. At least she's not in my house.' Sally frowned. Something pinged in her memory. She knew Grace from somewhere before. Where did she know her from?

Chapter Twelve

Sally sat in her own kitchen, with her feet up on the table. She'd watched Peter shuffle around making himself toast. She took a chance to examine the rest of him while he had a shower. Not much change there, thank goodness. He was still hot, even if he did keep yawning all the time. He had started shivering violently and turned the heat up in the shower, so she'd ducked out before he boiled himself alive.

She decided not to sit with him in the car when he went to work. She didn't want him to have another accident trying to heat the car up. Instead she hung around the house, checking everything out in the daylight. As far as she could tell, Peter had changed very little, but everything was spotlessly clean. She wondered if he'd hired a cleaner. It was something they hadn't got around to doing after they moved. It wasn't like he could clean the place himself. He spent all his time at work.

There was the sound of a key in the lock. Sally took her feet off the table, wondering if Peter had forgotten something. The door slammed and Diane came in, carrying a heavy looking cool bag. Why did his mother have a key? Sally cursed Peter. She would have to have a word with him about that.

Diane stopped and surveyed the scene, as though looking for something. She put the bags on the table, rubbed her arms and turned the thermostat controller up.

'You seem to know your way around my house,' said Sally.

Diane, of course, didn't hear her. She opened the fridge and started pulling out Tupperware containers. For the first time, Sally noticed the neat stack of containers, washed and dried, that were next to the fridge. Diane shook her head and removed a few tubs. Opening the cool bag, she took out fresh boxes and restocked the fridge. Sally took the opportunity to examine the boxes she was getting rid of.

Each was neatly labelled with the meal description and the date it had to be eaten by. It seemed that Diane was bringing Peter's meals. Hmmm. That was strange. Peter hadn't been so dependent on his mother when Sally married him. But maybe that was just a front he put on for the girlfriend. Or maybe his mother was taking back the opportunity to care for her boy. In Sally's experience, no man refused free meals. Least of all meals that were cooked by his mother. This was interesting to know before she woke up. She added Diane to her list of things she needed to tackle.

Diane stacked the containers she was throwing away and spent a moment staring at them. She pulled out her phone and called someone.

'He's only eaten one of the meals from this week,' she said into the phone, without even bothering to say hello first.

Sally leaned forward to see if she could hear the other half of the conversation. She assumed Diane was talking to Frank. She wouldn't be that rude to anyone else.

'Yes, but I don't think he eats much at lunchtime. I'm not sure he eats at all, in fact. I was hoping he was having at least one good meal a day, but he's just leaving them.'

Sally could hear Frank saying something in a reassuring voice.

Diane gave an impatient flick of the head. 'I know he's an adult, but he's not exactly got a normal life at the moment, has he? I'm worried about him, Frank. I really am. There's something bothering him, I can tell. More than the usual, I mean. He keeps insisting that he's fine but ...'

More babble from the phone.

'I'll try,' said Diane. 'I don't think he really wants to talk about it ... no, you're right. I'll try at the weekend.'

Sally put her head next to Diane's, trying to hear Frank's half of the conversation. Diane gave a little shiver.

'I think there's something wrong with the heating too,' she said. 'I keep feeling a draught. And there's this weird ...' she looked around, almost furtive in her movements. '... I don't know, darling, it's a strange feeling.' She turned her head so she was looking straight through Sally. 'I think I'll leave the cleaning today and just get home. You're right. Yes ... Okay. I'll see you in a bit.'

Diane hung up and looked over her shoulder again. Then she shuddered and shook her head. 'Imagining things again,' she muttered to herself. She picked up the bag, grabbed her coat, and started out of the kitchen. At the door, she paused. After a few minutes, she shook her head again and left.

Interesting. So Diane could sense someone there, but still couldn't see or hear her. Very interesting. Sally already had an idea of how to get rid of Diane from the house. That should be easy.

Working out what to do about Grace was harder. From what she could tell, Grace was the only one who could see her. If she wanted to get an avenue to Peter, she would have to keep Grace on side.

Sally sighed and stood up. 'Oh well,' she said. 'It's time to go and make friends with the husband tempter.'

It was dark when Grace got home after visiting Margaret. She had been jumpy, but no ghost had materialised. It was a relief to know that the night before had been a one off.

Grace vowed to take it easy that weekend and maybe force herself to have a lie in. Hallucinations were not something to be taken lightly. She let herself in and turned on the light.

There was soup in the fridge. She had forgotten to pick up any bread. Oh well, just soup then. Grace stretched her arms above her head as she strode to the kitchen. She turned to flick on the light switch, turned back and yelped. Sally was standing in the kitchen, arms folded, leaning against the wall as though she were quite at home. 'I figured out where I knew you from, see?'

Something clicked into place in Grace's mind. The familiar face. Of course. Sally was one of the estate agents that came round to value the house. She had, now that Grace recalled, been quite candid about how much work the place needed if she were to get an asking price that was anywhere near the other ones in the neighbourhood. That was nearly two years ago. She was surprised either of them remembered. Sally had been in a coma for … She was overthinking this. Sally wasn't here. It was just a manifestation of Grace's own imagination.

Grace closed her eyes. 'Not real,' she said, to reassure herself, and opened them.

'Still here,' said Sally. 'Sorry.'

'But I don't believe in ghosts,' said Grace. She immediately felt silly. If she didn't believe in ghosts, then she was talking to herself. She ignored Sally and helped herself to her soup.

'Look, I know this is weird for you,' said Sally. 'Try and see it from my point of view, it's pretty bloody weird too. One minute I'm getting married and the next thing I know, I'm walking through furniture.'

This was insane. How did one interact with a ghost? Even if there were such a thing. Grace shook her head. 'I really need to get some sleep.'

'Grace, listen to me.' Sally stood right in front of her.

Grace reached across for the microwave. Sally didn't move, so Grace's arm went through Sally. Watching her arm disappearing into someone's ribs was nauseating. She felt a stab of intense cold. Grace gasped and pulled her arm back.

'I'm not going to hurt you. You're the only one that can see me. I'm invisible to everyone else.' Sally looked up, her expression pleading. 'Please. I just want to hang around with someone who can hear me.'

The look on Sally's face was so plaintive that Grace felt a rush of sympathy. How horrible it must be to have so much to say to people and not be able to communicate. She wondered if Sally had been locked into her body for all those months. She couldn't think of anything worse. She felt a stab of guilt. The least she could do was listen to her.

'What do you do of an evening?' said Sally, peering at the kitchen calendar which was more or less clear.

When Grace's parents had been alive, the calendar had been covered with appointments. Now, since her mum's funeral … nothing. The first time she'd turned over a page for a new month and seen it clear of appointments, Grace had burst into tears. She still didn't know if it was with sorrow or relief.

'I'll do stuff with you, then,' said Sally. 'It's just nice to, you know, exist. It'd probably be good for you to do that too.' She nodded meaningfully at the empty calendar.

'Right.' Grace gave up arguing against the evidence of her own eyes. If Sally was going to stand here and be rude about her social life, she may as well talk back. She went to the fridge and put away the remaining half carton of soup. 'Do you … want something to eat?'

'No point. Ghost, remember. Besides, my body's being given everything through a tube. I'm good thanks.'

'Oh yes. Sorry.'

'No need to apologise. Look, don't let me stop you.'

Sally started talking when Grace was eating. She talked about all sorts of random things, asked about what was happening in soap operas, various celebrities, local businesses.

Grace couldn't answer any of those questions. She tried to puzzle her way round the situation. Assuming Sally was a 'real' ghost, why was she there? Why haunt Grace and not Peter? Was Grace part of her unfinished business? Was that stuff about unfinished business real or just a construct of the movie industry?

The scientist in her came up with a load more questions – why was Sally sucking the heat out of her immediate surroundings? Did she need the energy to be visible? If she stood next to a big enough energy source, would she become solid? Could she move things? Could she feel emotions without hormones or a nervous system? How close was her connection to her body? If she felt fear, did her body's heart rate increase?

'Oh come on,' said Sally. 'You own a TV. Don't you ever watch it?'

'Actually, no. Not really. When Mum was alive, I didn't have time.'

'And now?' She had her hands on her hips again. Sally really was very bossy. Grace wondered what Peter saw in her.

'I guess I've got out of the habit.' She crossed over to the sink and started to wash the bowl. 'I can turn the TV on for you, if you'd like.' What was she doing? She didn't know if this whole ridiculous situation was real. And even if it was, she didn't want to encourage Sally.

Sally walked through the kitchen table to come and stand next to her. It was creepy when she did that.

'I'd be stuck watching the same channel. Besides, I just want to do something normal. Sit around with a mate watching telly.'

A 'mate'. Was that what Sally was expecting her to become? A friend. Grace thought of Peter. What would Sally say if she knew? Immediately, Grace felt guilty. Sally was trapped in a limbo all alone and she, Grace, had nearly slept with Sally's husband. What kind of a monster did that? On the other hand, this whole situation was too weird and she wasn't totally convinced it wasn't all in her head. Maybe it was her mind working out her feelings of guilt? Either way, she was pretty much obliged to be nice to Sally. 'I understand what you mean, but I need some time to get my head round this,' she said, carefully. 'If you don't mind, I'd like some time to myself.' She turned her back on Sally and left the room.

The hairs on the back of her neck prickled. There was a chill. Sally had followed her. It was like being shadowed by an iceberg.

She had intended to go to bed, but there was no way she was doing that with Sally following her. Grace went into the sitting room instead and pulled out the DVDs she'd bought but never got around to watching. Hopefully, an hour or so of being ignored would send Sally away. It was easier to ignore an unwanted guest if there was something she could watch.

'DVDs. Brilliant. Let's do that.' Sally swept through the sofa and leaned forward to read the box, which Grace had left blurb side up by mistake. 'Being Human? What's that?'

Grace said nothing.

'Ghost, Vampire, Werewolf, living together.' Sally laughed. 'How appropriate.'

Grace refrained from pointing out that she was neither a vampire nor a werewolf. And, since Sally herself was not dead, she didn't actually qualify as a proper ghost either. More an ... avatar. *Athma*; the word popped into her head out of nowhere. Her parents hadn't been big on religion, but she'd read enough books to know Buddhist vocabulary. *Athma*. The manifestation of you in each life.

'Just me who finds it funny, then.' Sally threw herself onto the sofa. She sank a little too far in and it took a few seconds for her to work out the right depth.

Grace watched her and was interested, in spite of herself. 'How come you don't just go through that sofa?'

'Don't know. Habit, I guess. It's easier to walk through something if I've not noticed it, I find.'

'I guess that makes sense.' She turned on the TV and DVD player using the various remotes. 'You've become accustomed to instinctively walking around obstacles, so you'd have to reprogram yourself to walk through them. Interesting.'

'I can't walk through walls though,' said Sally. 'Look.' She scrambled to her feet and walked, frowning at a wall. It stopped her, just as it would have stopped someone corporeal. 'But doors, no problem.' She went through the closed door and back in again. 'Weird huh?'

'Maybe your conviction that walls are solid is too strong.' Grace was getting interested now. It occurred to her that she knew very little about any research, if any, into the supernatural. She would have to look into it. She wondered which subject that came under. Not biology. Physics, perhaps, or psychiatry.

'What, like I think doors aren't solid?' Sally flopped back onto the sofa. 'I don't think that's it. There's places I just can't go.'

Grace loaded the DVD into the player. 'Like the other end of the hall in the hospital.'

'Exactly.' Sally grinned. Sally pulled her feet onto the sofa and snuggled down into the corner, her petite limbs settling in, making her look vulnerable and child like. If Grace tried to do that, she'd end up all elbows and knees. Maybe that was the attraction. Men liked small, pretty women.

Feeling huge and ungainly, Grace sat on the other end of the sofa. Normally, she would have stretched out on it, but didn't feel it was appropriate to do so now. She might end up sticking a foot through Sally by mistake.

They sat in silence through the ads.

'I hate these,' said Sally when the anti-piracy ad came on. 'Why put it on legal copies? We've paid for ours, so why ram this crap down our throats. Bloody morons.'

'Please don't swear,' said Grace, noting that it was 'our' DVD now. 'I don't really like swearing. Especially in the house.' She looked up to where her mother's room was above, out of habit. Her mother hated swearing and it still seemed wrong to swear in the house.

Sally muttered 'Sorry' and put her head to one side to watch as the programme started.

It took two consecutive episodes before the tension in the room waned. Sally watched Grace and she gradually unclenched herself and seemed to get absorbed by the story on screen. Studying her rival, she realised just how tall Grace was. She could see how Peter would find that combination of long limbs and softness appealing. But to her eyes, Grace's features were too large for her face and the chin would lead to chubbiness when she got older. She sucked in her own neat pout. Grace's hair was looped into a loose bun that was resting on the nape of her neck. It was nice hair, thick and glossy. Sally hated her own light feathery mane, but Peter loved running his fingers though it and playing with it. He said he felt like it was already spun into gold. Of course, now he knew that she dyed it. She wondered if it mattered to him. He had a thing about hair. Grace's hair was probably the major attraction for Peter. Well, she'd have to do something about that.

She wondered what exactly happened between Peter and Grace. Peter's voice had given away guilt, so did Grace's, so something must have. But how far had it gone? Had they slept together? Sally narrowed her eyes.

Grace smiled at something on screen. Her eyes moved towards Sally. Sally pretended to be really interested in the story. After a second or two, she sensed Grace's attention moving away. She remained, carefully watching until the episode finished and the credits started rolling.

'Well, it's getting better, isn't it?' she said. 'I could watch Aidan Turner all day. He could bite my neck anytime.'

Grace stretched her arms out. 'I suppose.'

'Which one's your favourite?' said Sally, in her best girl pal voice.

'George.'

'The goofy one?'

'He's not goofy. He's shy. And nice. I think he's quite sweet.' Grace said. 'I like that.'

Goofy and naive. Like Peter. Hmmm. 'Well, I prefer my men dark and dangerous.'

Grace raised her eyebrows.

'What?' said Sally.

'Peter isn't dark and dangerous.'

Bingo. 'Ah, but he's different. He's not an idealised fake man. He's my REAL man.' She looked at her hand. 'He's my husband.'

Grace looked away. Sally waited.

After a moment of staring out towards the window,

Grace said, 'He loves you very much, you know. Very much.' She still didn't turn around. There was something wistful about the slump of her shoulders.

Sally smiled. That was just what she'd been hoping to hear. He loved her and he'd told Grace that. Brilliant. He fancied this woman, but he wasn't doing anything because he was married to Sally. That's my boy, thought Sally.

'Yeah,' she said. Because she couldn't help rubbing it in, she said, 'I love the way he looks at me. Like I'm the most perfect woman in the world and he can't believe his luck.'

Grace turned to face her. There was sadness in the downturned corners of her mouth. 'He still thinks you're perfect. He's been holding on to that for all this time.'

'Really? A year is a long time. And I look ... different, lying in that bed.'

Grace nodded. 'He visits you every day. Reads to you. Talks to you. He's completely devoted to you.' She smiled in a grave sort of way. 'You're very lucky. To be loved that much.'

'Oh, I know,' said Sally, smiling gaily back. Her head hummed with triumph. Peter was still hers. He would still look at her like she was the best thing in the world. If only she could find a way for him to see her again. She would have to work on that slowly. For that, she'd need to keep Grace on side.

The programme came to an end. Grace wondered what to do. Sally was still there, showing no signs of leaving. She flicked the DVD back to the main screen to select another episode.

'I see you're redecorating,' said Sally.

Grace looked across. 'Um ... yes.'

Sally gave the room a once over and nodded. 'It needs it.'

'So you said, when you came round to value it.'

The glance that Sally threw at her looked slightly alarmed. 'Did I upset you when I said that? I didn't mean to.'

Grace shrugged. She hadn't been upset by the candid assessment. She knew it needed to be done. In fact, she'd felt that Sally's valuation had been more accurate and more informative than the rest. She had pointed out the things that could be improved and how much the changes would affect the asking price.

'I could help you with the redecorating, if you'd like,' said Sally. 'I love home décor.'

'Really?' She just viewed it as another job to do.

'Oh yeah.' Sally jumped to her feet. 'Come on then, what are you planning for this room?'

Grace hesitantly outlined her plans to paint it a pale green.

Sally listened to her, looking thoughtful. 'What's your budget?' she said. 'Can you replace this?' She waved to indicate the sofa.

Grace shook her head. Not because the budget didn't stretch, but because replacing the sofa was a step too far.

'If I remember rightly,' said Sally. 'This room gets light in the morning. You want to make the most of that.'

Sally talked enthusiastically about painting three walls one colour and making the further wall darker to make the room look bigger and about colour accents. As she spoke, her eyes shone and for a moment she looked radiant. The vision she painted was compelling. Grace found herself nodding, carried along by Sally's ideas.

'Show me round?' Sally suggested. 'I'd love to hear what you're doing with the rest of the place.'

For a moment, Grace wasn't sure, but then she had

nothing to lose. Sally was there anyway. She turned the DVD off and set off to show Sally around.

'I can't go into the garden, you know,' said Sally conversationally. 'I didn't go out there when I came to view the house. It was raining, remember.'

'So it was,' said Grace, looking at the rectangle of darkness that was the back window. 'So, you can only go to places where you've been when you were ... walking.'

'When I was properly alive,' Sally supplied. 'Yes. It's really weird. I think about a place I want to be and ... I'm there. Here. Watch.'

She disappeared. One minute she was there, the next, she wasn't. Grace stared at the empty spot. She waved a hand in it and immediately felt silly. Just as she withdrew her hand and shook her head, Sally reappeared.

'Not a lot happening in the hospital,' said Sally. 'I've just been there. All quiet.'

If Sally really could travel like that, it was incredible. 'How did you do that?'

'I don't know how it works. It just does. I think about a place, picture it ... and I'm there.'

'What if something's changed since you saw it?'

'Doesn't make a difference. I can see the small changes you've made here, can't I?'

'What if it's a big change? Like a wall being taken down or an extension or something.'

'Why are you so interested?'

'Because it's amazing,' said Grace. 'You're a ghost, but you've got a connection to the living world. The questions you could answer ...'

'I'm not someone's guinea pig,' said Sally. 'Anyway, I haven't come across anything that's changed in any major way.'

Grace wondered if that was true or because Sally just

couldn't see the new bit, but she refrained from saying so. 'Sorry.'

They went around the whole house, Sally pointing out features and furniture worth highlighting and suggesting ways that the rooms could be improved. When she got to Grace's room, she said, 'Why do you sleep in here? What's wrong with the main bedroom?'

Grace laughed. 'It's just habit. That's all. I think of the main bedroom as my mum and dad's.'

Sally looked at her thoughtfully. 'Sounds like you need to have a more dramatic change for that room. Something that will make it look completely different.'

The words were eerily similar to what Margaret had said about her life. Making a dramatic change there hadn't been such a great move.

They went back into the main bedroom. Sally stared thoughtfully at it for a moment. Grace sat on the bed. She wondered what Sally saw. With that changed perspective, the room looked hopelessly old-fashioned. Everything was decades old. Including the mattress, she realised. She needed to add that to the list of things to replace.

Sally started talking. Grace had intended to just get on with painting and not do much else, but Sally's enthusiasm was catching. Sally had a good eye for colour and light. In fact, the advice she'd dispensed so far would probably cost a fortune coming from an interior designer.

'You're really good at this,' Grace said, admiringly.

Sally looked surprised. Her forehead creased as she considered it, her head to one side. 'I suppose I am, really,' she said. She sat on the bed, beside Grace. 'I love this kind of thing. I used to read decorating magazines all the time. When Peter bought our house, it was terribly old and flaky. I had a brilliant time redecorating it.'

'I bet you did,' said Grace. 'I've not seen it, but I'm sure it's lovely.'

Sally shot her a quick glance. 'It is lovely,' she said. 'A great improvement, even if I do say so myself.'

'I remember you gave me advice when you came to view the house.' Not that she'd appreciated it at the time.

'Yeah. I do that. A lot of the clients take up my ideas and it does make a difference. People underestimate how much difference a good first impression can make.' She sounded more like an estate agent now.

Grace smiled. 'Is that why you're an estate agent? Do you like seeing places?'

'I hadn't thought of it like that, but yes. I guess it is. When I see a house, I can see its potential. D'you know what I mean? People live in their houses and mould it to themselves. They get so used to it, they can't see it any other way. When I show people round, I like to paint a picture of how the place could be. You know, show them the dream.' Sally's eyes sparkled, her expression intense.

'I see what you mean, I think.' Grace was starting to understand what drew Peter to this woman. When she talked about her passions, she changed. Her whole body seemed to vibrate with energy. It was fascinating to see.

Her gaze fell on her mother's clock, with the big digital display so that her mother could read it without her glasses. 'Oh my goodness, is that the time? I'm sorry, Sally. I'm going to have to go to bed. I've got work in the morning.'

'I didn't realise it had got so late. No body clock,' said Sally. 'I guess I'll head off. Thanks for … letting me hang out here.'

'You're welcome,' said Grace.

'Night,' said Sally. She vanished.

Grace stared at the space that Sally has vacated. That

evening had been more interesting and eventful than an evening spent by herself. If she wasn't careful, she might actually get to enjoy spending time with Sally. That would be so very wrong.

Peter got to his front door and realised that he'd left his briefcase in the car. Having retrieved it, he looked up as he closed the car door. A woman in a blue coat and sort of peculiar hat was standing by the streetlight on the corner, watching him. There was something familiar about that hat and coat combination. Where had he seen it before? Was it near work? He took a step towards the woman, but she turned and walked away. Odd. He must try and catch her the next time he saw her.

As he walked into the house, he checked the thermostat. After all the chills and shivers last night, he was convinced he was coming down with something, but he was feeling fine today. He'd even forced himself to go climbing after visiting Sally. If he really was ill, he'd be aching more than this by now. He shrugged. There was a post-it note with Val's number on. He still had to ring her. There was no point putting it off.

'Get a grip Peter,' he said out loud. It was past nine now, so his sister's children would be in bed. Hopefully, she hadn't fallen asleep on the sofa yet. The phone rang, far away in Val's comfortable suburban home.

'Hello?' She sounded tired.

'Val. It's me.' When she didn't respond immediately, he added, 'Peter.'

'I know. To what do I owe the pleasure?' Her answers were too curt and polite. She was annoyed with him.

'I'm just phoning to see how you are.'

'I'm okay thank you. We got your card and the gift voucher. Thanks for that.'

'Look, Val, I know I haven't come to see you. I'm really sorry, but time ran away with me, you know how it is.'

'Yes, Peter. I understand how it is.'

He could see her in his mind's eye, frowning while she fiddled with a lock of hair. Val had come to visit a couple of times while he was in hospital. He'd barely registered her presence, he'd been so worried about Sally. With a start, he realised he hadn't spoken to her since she and the premature baby came home.

'Val. I know I've been a crap brother and an even worse uncle. Can I come visit? I haven't seen you guys in ages. And I'd like to meet the new one, obviously.'

'Um ... okay. When did you have in mind?'

'This weekend? Sunday?'

'Okay.' Her tone lightened a little bit. 'It would be ... It will be nice to see you Peter. It's been a while and we've both had some tough times.'

Peter let out a breath. She was softening. That was Val all over – prickly but not able to hold a grudge for long. 'Yes. I'm sorry. It's been so long.'

Val sighed. 'It's my fault too. What with the kids and all.'

'There just aren't enough hours in the day, right?'

'Exactly.' Val's voice lightened again, as though she was smiling. 'How are you anyway?'

'I'm okay. Muddling along.'

'And Sally?'

'No change.' What else was there to say? He added conversationally, 'It's our wedding anniversary in a couple of weeks.'

There was a pause from the other end while Val thought of something suitable to say.

'We don't really have plans to celebrate,' said Peter. 'I

might get a takeaway. I asked Sally what she wanted to do, but she's giving me the silent treatment.'

'Peter ...'

'You have to laugh,' said Peter. 'Otherwise you can't carry on.'

To his surprise, Val laughed. 'I feel like that about my life too, sometimes.' When she continued, she sounded less weary and more like the sister he remembered. 'You should come for tea on Sunday. We can eat the same time as the kids then and we might even get a chance to chat after we've got them to bed.'

'That sounds great. I'll bring wine, then.'

'You read my mind.'

'I'll see you Sunday,' he said. 'I'm looking forward to it.'

There was a sound in the background. 'Shit. One of the kids is awake. I've got to go. I'll see you later.'

'Bye. Give the kids a kiss from me.'

'Will do. And Peter ...'

'Yes?'

'Thanks for calling. I really appreciate it.'

When he hung up, Peter felt better. He hadn't realised quite how guilty he'd felt about not visiting. Now that he was doing something about it, he felt happier already. He and Val were very different people, but they got on fairly well considering they were siblings. As for his nephews, he loved them more than he'd thought possible.

He let himself into the front room and poured himself a whiskey. He stood in the light of the standing lamp and examined a photo of himself and Sally. He had hoped to have children one day. His future as he'd imagined it had always involved a house, a wife and a family. He'd had a few girlfriends, but by the time he met Sally, he'd been single for so long that he'd lost hope of settling down for long enough to have a family. Sally had swept into his linear, database centred world and thrown it into a breathless whirl of light and colour. She had made him feel like anything was possible. And now she wasn't there anymore.

He had to make sure he bought something suitable for his nephews. Sally would have been able to help him with that. She was an excellent shopper.

'I wish you were here,' he said. 'I need help with some shopping.' He thought about Sally, arms laden with bags from clothes shops. Would she really know what to get for his baby nephew? He tried to remember how she'd responded to his nephews when she'd met them. He realised she'd only met his family once before the wedding and it had been an awkward affair. He'd apologised to her for the volume and pace of the kids as they ran around the house.

'Maybe not,' he said to the picture. 'I'm sure I can think of something.' He gulped down the rest of the drink, relishing the burn of it. 'It'll be nice to see Val again. Now that I've spoken to her, I've realised how much I missed her.' He remembered that Val didn't approve of Sally. How would they have got on eventually? Val would have made an effort to get on with his wife. Wouldn't she?

The hairs on the back of his neck prickled. He turned round. There was no one there. He turned the main light on. Still nothing. He looked at his glass.

He shouldn't have any more, especially as he wasn't feeling very well. He reached for the bottle to put it away and felt a chill so intense that he almost dropped it. He gasped. Once the bottle was back in its place, he waved his hand, trying to find the draught. Nothing. Strange.

He turned out the lights and left the living room, trying not to look behind him. Even in the kitchen, he felt as though someone were watching him. 'Get a grip, Peter.

You're just getting paranoid.' Nevertheless, he dumped his glass in the sink and hurried upstairs.

In his room, the feeling of being watched vanished. He took a couple of painkillers and went to bed. After a few minutes, the temperature in the room seemed to drop. He climbed out of bed to pull on a pair of socks and a T-shirt. He burrowed into the bed until only his face was exposed to the chilly room. The feeling of being watched was there again. He clamped his eyes shut and tried to sleep.

Eventually, he dreamed of being stalked by something he couldn't see.

Sally was bored. She'd never visited Peter at work, so she couldn't go watch him. Grace was at work too. The nurse's station was too busy for them to gossip and the TV in Mr Wright's room was off. There was one place where something was always going on. Sally whisked herself away.

There was no natural light in the inside of the casino. The bright lights looked the same day or night. Sally tried to breathe in the smell of the place before she remembered she couldn't. It always smelled the same. Carpet cleaner, air freshener at the start of the night, then alcohol, perfume and sweat by the evening.

It was still early for the punters, but there were a few people already at the slot machines. Sally spotted a woman who looked familiar from before. She was a tallish brunette dressed in Marks and Spencer's clothing who fed token after token to the garish machine, trying to work out the system. Sally stood behind the woman, a small distance away. The woman looked around, pulled her collar closed and went back to what she was doing. Soon she was preoccupied again, hypnotised by the machine.

Sally watched idly for a few minutes, then she too became interested. 'No, not that one,' she shouted. 'Green. Green.'

The woman's finger, which had been about to press the orange, stopped. After a moment's hesitation, she changed her mind and stabbed green. The lights whirred. Ding. One of the stars on the winner panel lit up. Ding, ding, ding. The woman's hands flew to her mouth and she watched for the last one. No, that was it. There was a cacophony of noise and coins crashed into the tray below. It wasn't the torrent of coins you saw in the movies, but it was enough to make the woman squeal with delight and scoop it all up. As she stood up to take the pile of tokens to the booth, she whispered, 'Thank you,' her eyes looking upwards as though talking to a guardian angel.

'You're welcome.' Sally herself was jumping up and down with excitement. Okay, it wasn't her win, but she'd helped. Without her the stupid woman would have pressed the wrong button and messed it all up. Next time ... well next time they'd do better. They could get that last star. There had to be a pattern to this. How had she missed these machines before? She'd always gone for the roulette table. Why? When this was so much more fun?

She looked around and noted that the carpet had been changed and there were new pictures on the walls. It had only been a year and they were already updating the place. Nice. She wondered if her favourite croupier was still there. She was always lucky when he was around.

She turned her attention back to the slot machine and tried to peer inside, but it remained solid to her. Never mind, she would just go look at the other players for a while, until her friend came back.

Chapter Thirteen

Peter checked through his bags. One present for each of the kids. A bunch of mixed flowers and a box of Guylian shell shapes for his sister. Nothing for the brother in law. He got out a bottle of red wine and added it to the pile. Hopefully that would be enough to buy his way back into Val's good books. He checked the time. Another half hour or so before he needed to set off. Time for a coffee.

He'd just poured his drink when the doorbell rang. Peter frowned. He wasn't expecting anyone and his mother didn't usually bother with the doorbell. Leaving his coffee, he answered the door.

The woman in a blue mac and feathery hat stood outside. So she had been looking for him. What did she want? Why was she following him? He kept the door open just a crack, ready to shut it at the first hint of trouble. 'Yes?'

'You're Peter, aren't you? Sally's husband.'

'Ye-es.'

'Can I speak to Sally please?' The woman's face, which would once have been beautiful, was red and weathered. There were blue thread veins and creases around her eyes. Yet there was something vaguely familiar about her. Something about the mouth and the flyaway grey hair.

'You are?'

The woman smiled. Again the tug of familiarity. 'I'm Glenda. Sally's mother.'

But Sally's mother was dead. The mention of Sally sent a stab of pain through him. It had hurt Sally when she lost her mother, so soon after her father's suicide. Whoever this woman was, she was playing a cruel game. He stepped back to shut the door.

Glenda stuck out a hand. 'I know she pretends I don't exist, but I worry. I'm her mother.' Her face was against the crack of the door now. 'Please. I just want to know she's okay.'

Peter hesitated. He had no reason to believe this was true, and every reason to slam the door in this woman's face. But there was something about her that made him pause. Either she was lying or Sally had been. He believed Sally, without question, but yet …

Seeing his hesitation, the woman carried on talking. 'I haven't seen her since her wedding and I've been watching out for her. She hasn't been to work. She hasn't walked by here. Her mobile is turned off … please? Tell her I won't be any bother. I … just …' There was fear in her eyes. And tears.

She didn't know. Peter took in the worried, aged face. She was just an old lady, who seemed to genuinely know and care about Sally. He should at least tell her what had happened. Maybe try and clear up this confusion. 'Okay,' he said. 'You'd better come in.'

'Thank you.' There was a waft of alcohol and the sour smell of someone who hadn't quite made it back to sobriety. She walked past him, steady and stiff.

'Down the hall and first left.' Peter directed her into the kitchen. She turned and gave him a smile. Sally's smile. It hit him like a thump in the chest. She was related to Sally alright. Judging by her age, she could very well be Sally's mother. Or an aunt. Either way, Sally had family she'd never mentioned.

He followed the woman into the kitchen. She was looking around approvingly. 'By the way, I'm Glenda, Glenda Cummings.'

Another jolt of familiarity. The way she said it sounded just like Sally. Peter stared at her, immobilised by the memory.

Glenda watched him for a second and sighed. 'Did she tell you I died?'

Unable to find a response, he nodded.

'She does that sometimes,' said Glenda, wearily. She frowned. 'Did she tell you about her father?'

Peter found his voice. 'She said he ... committed suicide.' Hanged himself, that was what Sally had said. He'd hanged himself from the bannister, so that Sally found him when she came home from school. He remembered Sally's whole body trembling when she told him. And then she'd told him about how her mother had just faded away and died of a broken heart soon after. She'd said she didn't want to talk about it ever again. He had respected that.

Glenda looked away. 'That's right,' she said. 'He did.' Another sigh. 'After that Sally and I fell out and we don't talk. Sometimes it's easier for her to pretend I'm dead too.'

Sally lied to him? Why would she do that? She'd done it before, with the gambling, but once he'd confronted her, she'd told him everything. All those debts and sorry secrets. About the affairs that had funded the gambling habit. It had been their first and only row. She had cried and begged another chance. He'd loved her so much that he'd agreed. On the proviso that she went to Gamblers Anonymous, which she had eventually done, never missing a single meeting. He'd thought she'd told him everything. He remembered the red letter he'd dealt with the week before. No, not everything. It was entirely possible this woman really was Sally's mother.

He made Glenda a coffee, which she took without comment. She sat at the table, still in her coat, and looked around. 'This is a nice place,' she said. 'She's done alright for herself, my Sally. Is she not in?'

Peter drew a breath. 'I don't know how to tell you this ...'

The watery eyes widened. 'She's dead? There was no ad in the paper. When? How?' The voice rose in pitch, also eerily like Sally's.

'No, no, no. She's not dead.' Peter held out his hands in a calming motion. 'I'm sorry, I didn't mean to scare you like that. She's alive. But she's not ... well.'

Glenda frowned. 'Not well? Is it serious? What is it? Is she in hospital? Is that why I haven't seen her?'

There was no painless way to explain it. 'She's in a coma. There was a car accident after the wedding. She was injured. She's been in a coma for nearly a year now. That's why she hasn't been ... anywhere.'

The blue eyes widened. Glenda looked down at her hands. She gave a small sob.

'Are you okay? Is there anything I can get you?' He'd just told this woman that her daughter was in a coma. It was bound to be a shock. He wished there had been another way to tell her, but there wasn't. 'I'm sorry.'

Glenda didn't look up. Her shoulders hunched in as though she were protecting herself. 'Tell me.'

He told her. About the accident, about the hours of operations, the medically-induced coma. About how Sally never woke up. About the hope of each slight change that might move her closer to consciousness. Partway through his explanation, Glenda started to rock. She whispered, 'My baby. My poor, poor baby.'

Peter stopped. What did he do now? He remembered all too well the feeling of being told all this about his wife. For him the news had come in bursts. Each new development punching into the ache left by the previous bit of bad news. Glenda was getting it all in one go. 'Glenda? I'm so sorry.'

After what seemed an age, Glenda looked up. 'I need a drink,' she said hoarsely.

Peter hesitated. Glenda had clearly been drinking already.

'Don't worry,' said Glenda. 'I'm not going to get mean and rowdy on you. Right now, I really, really need a drink. I'm begging you.' She looked up at him, her eyes hazy with tears. 'Please.'

Frankly, he could do with a drink himself. Peter fetched the whiskey and watched as Glenda knocked back the glass he poured her. The resemblance to Sally and the response to the news of Sally's coma was enough for him to believe that she was closely related to Sally. If she was her mother, she must have had Sally very late. Glenda closed her eyes briefly and Peter noticed that, despite the thin looking skin, Glenda's skin was not that wrinkled. Perhaps she just looked older than she was. As he watched, the alcohol seemed to chase away some of the defeat from Glenda. When she finally looked up, she seemed more collected.

'Did she tell you I died of a broken heart?' Her eyes met his for the first time.

'Yes.'

Glenda nodded and looked back at her hands. She rotated the glass, round and round. There was a thin layer of amber liquid at the bottom. 'She did that a lot.'

'Why? Why would she lie?' What he didn't say was 'why did she lie to me? I'm her husband.'

Glenda shrugged. 'She's ashamed of me. It was easier to have a mother who was dead than one who's an alcoholic who lives in a squat.'

'She didn't need to be ashamed. I would have helped. I

helped her with—' he stopped, wondering if Glenda knew about Sally's problem.

'With the gambling?' Glenda gave him an appraising look. 'She told you?'

Somehow that annoyed him. 'Yes, she told me. We were getting married. She didn't want to have secrets when we started our married life.'

'But only up to a point, eh?' There was something in the way that Glenda was staring at him, as though she were weighing him up. Something like sadness ... or pity. 'Don't judge my girl too harshly,' she said. 'She didn't have it easy in life.'

Peter folded his arms. 'No.'

'She found her father, you know. Hanging from the bannister.' Glenda took another sip of the whiskey and closed her eyes. 'She went to the neighbours. By the time I got home, she'd calmed down.' She pushed the glass across the table and looked pleadingly at him.

These were things Sally had never discussed. A side of Sally that he'd never seen. Peter poured another short measure. Glenda was clearly highly dependent on the stuff. He wondered if addictions ran in the family. He wondered if he should be feeding her addiction.

'Thanks.' She drew it back towards her, the glass rumbling against the table top. 'She handled it so much better than I did. And when I ... when I fell apart, she tried to help for a bit. But then she gave up and left.' Glenda sniffed and wiped a tear away with the back of her hand. 'She blamed me, you know. For her father taking his life. She thought it was my fault. But ...' She gave a loud hiccupy sob. 'I loved that man so much. I just couldn't face life without him.'

Shit. Peter looked around and spotted the roll of kitchen towel. 'Here.' He passed it to her. He patted her awkwardly on the shoulder.

Glenda blew her nose and managed a watery smile. 'I'm sorry. I'm sure you don't need this. Your wife's in a coma. You don't need a silly old woman crying in your kitchen.'

'It's okay.' What else could he say? He no longer doubted that she was telling the truth when she claimed to be Sally's mother. She looked too much like Sally to not be related to her. Sally had told him the story of her father's suicide. She'd also told him about her mother's subsequent pining and early death. Clearly, only half of the story had been true. Why would anyone deny the existence of their mother? Why, after all that song and dance about not having secrets, did Sally lie to him?

The chair scraped on the floor as Glenda stood up. 'I should go,' she said. 'Sally would be livid if she knew I'd spoken to you.'

She took a step closer and the smell of stale alcohol grew stronger. 'You're a good man, Peter. I can see that you'll do your best for my Sally. She's lucky to have you.'

Peter didn't know what to say. Glenda started towards the door. Peter put a hand on her arm. He couldn't just let Sally's mother disappear from his life, just like that.

'Can I help you with anything?' he said. 'Money?'

She gave a short laugh. 'I'll only drink it.'

'Something else then?'

'A sandwich?' she suggested, the smile pulling at her mouth making her look like Sally again.

Peter remembered the carefully labelled boxes of food in the fridge. 'Wait a minute.' He pulled the boxes out and stuffed them into a carrier bag. 'Here. Take these. There's food enough for a week.'

Glenda peered into the bag. 'Thank you.' She gave him the full benefit of her smile. 'Thank you, Peter.'

He nodded, awkward.

As Glenda reached the door he said, 'Wait. How can I contact you? If ... if I need to.' If the worst happens. If Sally dies. If Sally wakes up.

Glenda stopped. 'I read the Times every day, you know. Not Sundays, because the library's shut then, but otherwise. I read the classifieds and the births, deaths and marriages. So if anything happens to Sally, will you put a notice in the Times? So that I know.'

'Of course. I'll do that. If she wakes up, I'll put something in the classifieds. I promise.'

'Thank you.' She gave him another one of Sally's smiles and let herself out.

Peter went into the front room and watched her leave. Her step was a little quicker than when she'd arrived. Probably from the two glasses of whiskey she'd had. Poor woman. He wondered what she must have been like before the alcoholism had got its claws into her.

He thought of his own mother, who was so clean-cut and normal. Who cooked him meals that he gave away to strangers because he didn't appreciate that they were just what he needed. He'd been so busy feeling sorry for himself that he'd forgotten to appreciate his family.

Family. Oh shit. Val and the boys! He looked at his watch and realised that he'd spent longer talking to Glenda than he'd thought. It was too late to join them for tea now. Bollocks. He called Val.

'Val it's Peter. I'm very sorry—'

'But you're not coming? Fine Peter. I should have known.'

He had expected her anger, but he still felt wounded by it. 'I was all ready to go out but—'

'Is it Sally?' She sounded weary, as though she was just being polite.

'No.'

'In that case, I'm not interested in the excuse. I'll see you when I see you Peter. Bye.'

'No, wait! I'm still coming.' Val had every reason to be disappointed in him, but he didn't have to leave things like this. So what that he wouldn't see the kids? He could still go see his sister.

Val was dubious. 'It'll be gone 10 o'clock when you get here.'

'I could sleep over on the couch,' he said. 'I can be a couple of hours late for work tomorrow. It's my company. What am I going to do? Fire me?'

'I … okay. I'll see you in a few hours.' She still sounded unconvinced, as though she was still expecting him to cancel at the last minute.

He needed overnight things now, but apart from that, he was set to go. He felt much better. He needed to talk to someone and Val was one of the most blunt and down to earth people he knew. She was also the only person he could trust to keep a secret.

Chapter Fourteen

Peter was glad he'd made the effort to come to visit Val. He sat on her sofa, drinking a hot chocolate with a splash of whiskey in it. Val sat opposite him, telling him about the kids. She looked tired and puffy and much older than she had done before her son was born. Peter had just peeped in to have a look at the sleeping children. He couldn't believe he'd managed to miss his nephew's arrival so completely.

'So,' said Val, pulling a blanket around her knees. 'Tell me what's going on with you.'

'How much is mum telling you?'

Val rolled her eyes. 'You're not eating properly. She's worried you're withdrawing from the world.' She examined him for a moment. 'I thought she was exaggerating, but you are looking a bit scraggly and thin.'

Peter smiled. 'And I need a haircut. I know.'

'She says Sally's condition hasn't changed.'

'No.' He sipped his hot drink and felt the warmth burn down his throat. It reminded him of Glenda.

'So what has?'

'Pardon?'

'Why are you here, Peter? You haven't bothered to come and see us for nearly a year and suddenly, you turn up. You're so keen not to break your date that you turn up late. It must be something important. So what is it?' Ah, good old Val. Always to the point.

'I did want to see you, you know. And the kids. It's just that life got in the way.'

'Yeah, yeah. I get that. And ...'

Val knew him so well. He glanced at her over his mug and wondered how she would judge him if he told her.

'What have you done?' said Val. 'I know that look.'

He told her. About volunteering to help at the hospice just to get his parents off his back. About Grace. About what happened between them.

Val stared at him. 'Woah. Peter! I didn't think you had it in you. You were always the goody two shoes in the family.'

'Val ...'

'You were. It was all "why can't you be sensible, like Peter" when we were kids. Mum would have a fit if she knew you'd been shagging some woman from the hospice.'

'I'm not. It was only a kiss. I didn't sleep with her.' Just. 'And I feel terrible about it.'

'You didn't tell her that, did you?'

Had he? He thought about how he'd avoided Grace and how their last encounter had ended with her just running away. 'Not ... in so many words.'

'Poor girl. Imagine how she must feel. Married man leads her on, then goes back to his wife. Honestly.'

'I didn't mean ... I like Grace. I really like Grace. But I'm married to Sally and ...'

'And you're stuck with her,' Val finished off for him. 'Well, it was always going to be the way, wasn't it?'

'What do you mean by that?' He had assumed that Val would like Sally once she accepted that he was serious about her. Sally had certainly liked Val.

Val was quiet for a moment, frowning as though she were wrestling with some internal argument. Finally, she sighed. 'You know I never really thought she was very good for you. I figured you'd realise that eventually, but by then it would be too late.'

'Not good for me?' He thought of the gambling problem

and the lies that were slowly coming to light. Sally had her faults, but she had been working so hard on changing.

'I hate to say this, but I think she was after your money.'

Peter laughed. 'I don't have that kind of money.'

'No, but you were an investment. You've already done well with one company. You're well on your way to setting up another successful business. It was only a matter of time before you make a fortune.'

'I could get unlucky and lose everything.' It was a gamble. His heart dropped a little. Sally liked a gamble.

Val rolled her eyes. 'How likely is that? I know you, little brother. You will have carefully invested in a lot of different pots.'

She had a point. He took after his father when it came to money. Careful and measured. The only thing he'd ever done spontaneously was to fall in love with Sally. He looked at the floor. That and kissing Grace. Clearly spontaneous didn't always suit him.

Val changed tack. 'Tell me about this Grace woman.'

He told her. As he spoke, he felt a fresh wash of guilt and longing. He had messed things up with Grace and he should be ashamed of himself. The trouble was, he missed her. He missed talking to her and he kept daydreaming about her when he should be working. He longed to see her again, but wasn't sure he could trust himself to maintain his distance if he did. He'd thought life was at its worst six months ago, but he'd been wrong. The strain and the heartache was still there, but now he'd added extra guilt. He only had himself to blame.

Sally was leaning against the door frame, listening to the nurses gossiping, when Peter walked through her. He went straight to the thermostat and shook his head. She'd given up trying to speak to him, or even teasing him by blowing

149

cool air on his cheek. She waited for him to sit down, but he remained standing.

He went up to her bed and stared down at the sleeping woman. He looked ... strange. It wasn't an expression she'd seen on him before. She'd seen happy, confused, baffled, even ecstatic, but not this. If she didn't know better, she'd say he looked angry. Except her Peter never got angry. Certainly not with her.

Peter said nothing for the longest time. Sally sat in the middle of her comatose body and swung her legs over. 'So, Peter darling. What's new?' She lay next to her body and looked up at him. 'You never look at me the way you used to,' she said. 'In fact, it's like you look right through me.'

She examined him from her viewpoint. He looked even older today. She'd chosen to marry him because of his averageness. Attractive enough to sleep with, but not so devastatingly attractive that other women would fight her for him. Now he looked old. The scar on his forehead didn't do anything for his looks either. 'You've let yourself go, darling,' she said. 'When I come back, we're going to have to fix that. A bit of cover up on that scar would sort out the worst of it. And a decent haircut. Of course, I'd have to grow my hair back properly. We know how you like to run your fingers through it.' She touched the set in lacquer wedding hair-do she was still wearing. She couldn't feel it. 'Mind you, I'd quite like to run my fingers through my hair right now. It's very annoying having it up like this.' She reached up and tried to touch his hand.

Peter shivered and sighed. His face softened. 'Sally,' he said. 'Why did you lie to me? You swore there was nothing else you hadn't told me.' He pulled up the chair and sank into it.

Oh. He'd found out about that other loan. 'It had meant to be short term. I was going to pay it back within a couple of months of the wedding.' She was going to claim she'd done some shopping or something and pay it off on one of his credit cards.

She shrugged. It was only a few hundred quid. Not a big deal. She would have won it back in no time. 'There's lots of shit I haven't told you, you idiot. You're so trusting, you never thought anyone would lie to you. How your business associates don't hoodwink you, I have no idea.'

Peter put his head in his hands for a moment before sighing again and looking up. 'You didn't have to lie to me. I would have understood. I don't know what it's like to have grown up with an alcoholic parent, but I would have tried to understand. We could have helped her, like I helped you.'

'What?' Sally sat bolt upright. 'What alcoholic parent? I don't have an alcoholic parent. What are you on about?'

How the hell had he found out about her mother? Glenda must have broken her promise and talked to Peter. She should have known better than to trust a bloody alkie. 'I'll bloody kill her.'

'We could have taken her to Alcoholics Anonymous.' Peter continued talking. 'We could have helped her beat it. It's an addiction. There's things that can be done to help. Just like Gamblers Anonymous helped you.'

'And you know all about addiction do you? You think you can just drag someone to some limp wristed support group and then voila, everything's better. You think addiction is just a bad habit you can drop? Like giving up chocolate? I've got news for you, Peter. It's not like that in the real world. It's all very well for you, with your mum that cooks you food all week and your dad with his golf buddies. You've never had to find your old man hanging from the banister because he couldn't bring in enough money to pay the rent.'

Peter sighed again. 'I can't help wondering,' he said, staring at the body in the bed. 'What else you've lied to me about. She said she came to see you on our wedding day. You never said. She's my mother in law. Didn't you think I should have the right to meet her?'

'No. Even I don't want to bloody meet her. She just won't go away. Like a bad smell.'

'I feel like I don't know you any more.'

'Well, darling, you don't. Not a bit. What's more, I don't think you ever did want to know me. You just wanted your bit of fluff wife. So long as you had the long hair to play with and the body to shag, I'm sure you were all right. I would have kept the house for you and cultivated your contacts and we'd have both been happy. Just wait until I get my body back. I'm going to show Glenda what happens when she interferes.'

Peter was silent for a while longer. Sally jumped off the bed and paced. What had her mother told Peter? He was clearly upset about whatever it was. Every so often, she glanced at him. He was still staring at the body in the bed. Sally resumed pacing. There had to be a way to find out what Glenda had told him.

Peter stood up. 'I'm sorry Sally. I have to go.' He blew a kiss to the woman on the bed and strode out, pulling his jacket tighter as he went.

Sally stared after him. His head was bowed. She went back into her room and sat on the bed. This was not good. When she got her body to wake up, she needed Peter to still be in love with her. She needed to do something. The only way she was going to get anything done, was by enlisting Grace's help. 'Well that's just bloody awesome, isn't it?'

* * *

Grace was on her knees, painting a skirting board when Sally popped up behind her. She was so used to it now, that she didn't even jump. 'Hi,' she said, not taking her eyes off her brush.

Sally paced, her big wedding skirts swishing around her as she walked. Grace sat up and put her brush down. 'What's up?'

'My mother went to see Peter.' More pacing.

Grace went back over what she knew about Sally. She knew her father had killed himself. The horror of that explained a lot about Sally's need to pursue a dream. But her mother? Sally rarely mentioned her mother. Grace had assumed her mother was dead, but clearly, she wasn't. 'I didn't know your mum was living around here,' she said, carefully.

Sally swung round. 'I don't like to talk about her. She's … awful. I'd rather pretend she wasn't around.'

Grace thought about her own mother and felt a pang of sadness for the time she'd had with her. She couldn't imagine having her mother and ignoring her. 'Why?'

'You have to help me. I need to know what she said to Peter.'

Grace shook her head. 'I don't understand. You don't want your husband to know about your mother? I can understand you don't get on with her, but to pretend she doesn't exist? That's just not normal.'

'But you'll help me, right?' said Sally.

'No. Not until you explain.'

Sally gave a theatrical sigh. 'Fine.' She sank to the floor in a pouf of wedding dress.

Grace slid the lid back onto the paint tin and settled to listen. Sally started talking. She told Grace about her mother. And her father. And about a small posy of forget-me-nots.

Chapter Fifteen

The neighbourhood was one Grace had never been to before. The tidy suburban front gardens had given way to places with wonky garden fences and weedy tangles. There were cars with no tyres and rotting sofas where flower beds should have been.

'Are you sure about this?' Grace's whole body was tense. As she drove along the road, avoiding as many pot holes as she could, people turned to look at her. She half expected a brick though the windscreen any minute.

Sally was waiting for her outside a crumbling Victorian house with a garden that looked like the Congo. Grace pulled in, hoping the crunching under the wheels was caused by gravel and not broken glass. She checked she hadn't left anything lying around in the car before she got out to stand next to Sally.

Sally was looking at the house, her shoulders set as though she were psyching herself up to go in. 'Now, do you remember what to say?'

'I'm looking for Glenda and I have a message for her from the other side,' said Grace.

'Don't let her talk you round to her side. She is the most convincing liar I've ever met. She can talk anyone against anyone. She pretty much drove my Dad to suicide. When he finally caved in and killed himself, she was all "oh no, poor me. I can't live without him".' Sally went towards the door, delicately lifting her feet to avoid the dog excrement on the path. 'She only started drinking so that she could hang out in bars to meet another man.'

Grace manoeuvred her way along the path, watching

where she placed her feet. She had been reluctant to get involved with whatever this was that Sally was doing, but after a half an hour of being cajoled, pleaded with and pouted at, she'd agreed to go with Sally, just to get a bit of peace.

Sally waited for Grace to reach the broken doorstep. 'Ready?'

Grace nodded. Sally's relationship with her mother seemed to be a very confused one. Her own life had been so sheltered and loved. Sally's life, she realised, was about as different from her own as it was possible to get. She rang the bell. The noise sounded strained, as though the bell chime was being strangled.

The door opened and a skinny girl in a vest top and shorts stared out at them with wide, vacant eyes. She seemed to look right through Grace.

'Hi. I'm ... er ... looking for Glenda ...' Grace noticed the girl's hugely dilated pupils. Either she'd been somewhere very dark indeed, or she was stoned. Given her expression, Grace was willing to bet it was the latter.

The girl didn't reply, just walked unsteadily back into the house, leaving the door wide open.

Grace looked at Sally, who shrugged. Grace stepped into the house. The smell smacked her in the face. It smelled of damp and stale food and marijuana. But overlaying it was the smell of air freshener, which made it all the more sickly. Swallowing down the urge to gag, Grace ventured into the hall.

'Glenda is upstairs on the left,' said Sally. 'Come on.'

She led the way up. The windows above the stairwell shed a smoky sort of light in the gloom. Grace whispered, 'Are you sure about this?'

'I've been here before,' said Sally. 'Of course I'm sure. This is Glenda's room.' Sally's eyes gleamed. Her face was set in a hard scowl. The combination of the expression, the wedding dress and the fact that she was standing through a cardboard box left on the landing made Sally look downright sinister. Grace shuddered.

'Well, what are you waiting for? Knock,' Sally said.

Grace raised an eyebrow. She was doing Sally a favour being here. 'Pardon?'

Sally rolled her eyes. 'Please.'

Grace nodded and rapped on the wooden door. There was a pause and someone rustled inside. Sally gave a tut and marched through the door before it was opened, leaving Grace on the landing alone.

'Hey—' Grace was interrupted when the door opened and a pair of watery eyes looked out. 'Oh. Hi.'

'Who are you? What do you want?' The voice that went with the eyes seemed watery too.

'Um … Glenda? My name's Grace. I'm a friend of Sally's. I need to talk to you.'

Glenda looked her up and down and let her in.

The first thing that Grace noticed was how empty the room was. There was a bed, a chair and some blankets. Not even a pillow. A coin operated heater in a corner seemed to be the only source of heat. Sally was looking at the mantelpiece where there was a photo of a family and a collection of empty bottles.

'What do you want from me?' Glenda sat down on the bed.

'It's a bit difficult to describe,' said Grace. 'I have … a message from Sally. She wants to talk to you.'

'Oh my god. She died?' What little colour there was in Glenda's face drained away. 'I didn't see a notice in the paper. Peter promised he'd put an obituary in the *Times*. Did it only happen today?'

Grace looked at Sally for help. She didn't like to lie to this woman. Sally made encouraging motions with her hands. 'It's ... difficult to explain. I ... can hear her.' There. She'd not actually said Sally was dead.

Glenda stared at her for a moment before her face cleared. 'Oh. You're a medium.'

To Grace, the noun medium was synonymous with charlatan, but this was probably the best way to help Glenda understand. She sighed. 'Yes. I suppose you could describe me as that.'

Glenda looked her up and down. 'Don't get me wrong, darling, but you don't look like a medium.'

'No. I don't. The point is, Sally has some questions.'

'I mean, there's usually jewellery and stuff. And more ... floaty clothes. I don't think I've ever heard of a medium in jeans.'

Grace shot Sally another plea for help. 'Tell me something that only you know.'

'Is she here?' Glenda followed Grace's gaze. 'Sal? Are you there? Really?' She raised her eyes to the ceiling, as though expecting Sally to be floating up there.

'Don't call me Sal. I bloody hate being called Sal.'

'She says, please don't call her Sal,' said Grace. 'I think she prefers Sally.'

Glenda's eyes filled with tears. 'Yes. She does. Oh Sally, it is you!'

Okay, so Sally's mother was fairly gullible. 'Yes. It's her.' Grace listened as Sally came up with a tirade of expletives.

'She wants to know why you went to see Peter,' Grace said, when Sally stopped. 'I've removed a few swear words there, in case you thought it was too clean.'

'She did like to swear, did Sal ... I mean, Sally,' said Glenda.

'Stop referring to me in the past tense,' said Sally. 'I'm not bloody dead.' She shot a glare at Grace. 'Do NOT repeat that.'

'Anyway, the answer to the question?' Grace prompted Glenda. This could go on for a while and she didn't really want to leave the car outside for too long.

'I was worried. She's my daughter. I hadn't seen her come or go from the house for a year. I watched all night, sometimes. All I saw was Peter. So I eventually worked up the courage to go and ask him what happened. I worry,' said Glenda. 'I love her.'

Sally gave a loud 'Hah'. Grace ignored her. 'Do you want to tell me what happened?' She asked Glenda gently. 'Why are you and Sally not on friendly terms anymore?' She'd heard Sally's side of the story. She was curious to know Glenda's.

Glenda sighed. 'We were happy, once. We really were. But then he lost his job.' She spread her hands. 'He thought he was failing us ... and he started to borrow money and couldn't pay it back. In the end he just couldn't face it.' Her face was a picture of misery. Grace felt sorry for her.

'Don't listen to her sob story,' said Sally. 'She made him feel like crap. She used to come home and not talk to him all evening. He tried and tried and she didn't give him anything to hold on to. No wonder he gave up. She knew he was borrowing money. All she had to do was go and talk to her sodding parents and they would have bailed us out. But no. She was too bloody proud for that. She cared more about her pride than she did about us.'

'I think Sally wants to know why you didn't go to your parents for help.' Grace frantically tried to fill in the gaps. Were Glenda's parents rich? Had she married against their wishes?

Glenda looked down at her hands. 'I did. When Sally was at school and he was out looking for work. I went twice. Both times they wouldn't let me in the door.'

Sally stopped mid curse. 'I didn't know that.'

'I loved him,' said Grace. 'I genuinely did. He and Sally were the centre of my world.'

'That's a load of bollocks,' said Sally.

The door opened and the stoned girl from before walked in. 'Glenda. There's some visitors for you. They're downstairs … oh. How did you get up here?' She swayed a little on her feet.

'Thanks, Chloe.' Glenda made a little shooing motion to get the girl to leave the room.

'Are you going to a wedding?' said the girl, looking at where Sally was standing. 'I want a big dress like that when I get married.'

Sally's eyes widened. 'You can see me?'

'Durr, yeah. You look a bit weird though. The way you're all faint at the edges. How'd you do that?' She took a step closer.

Glenda looked from the girl to Grace and back again. 'Wh—?'

Grace opened her mouth to speak, but Sally silenced her with an upraised hand. 'You can see me,' she said to the girl. She put her hand out and touched the girl's face.

'That tickles.'

'You don't feel cold?' said Grace. Her mind was whirring. This girl was clearly stoned out of her mind. Perhaps she was able to comprehend all those things that the normal brain filtered out in order to be able to function normally. The professional in her tried to rationalise things. Perhaps this could lead to an explanation as to how Sally was visible to her.

'A bit cold.' The girl wriggled. 'Stop it, it tickles. Ohh.' Sally had just put an arm through her stomach. 'That's weeeeeird.'

Sally's eyes narrowed. 'I wonder.' She stepped behind the girl and put her hands on her shoulders.

'Sally, what are you doing?' Grace didn't like Sally's expression. There was determination and something like malice in it.

'An experiment.' Sally stepped forward and disappeared. The girl's eyes shot wider and then she fell over.

'Oh my god.' Grace sprang forward.

'What happened?' said Glenda. 'Don't worry about her, she's always falling over. Has something happened to Sally?'

The girl lifted up her head. 'Sorry about that. Not sure I can work the legs.' She sounded different somehow. It was the same voice but the tone and cadences were different. No slurring, for a start. Her head turned slowly to look at Glenda.

'Sally?' said Glenda. 'Sally, is that you?'

'Of course it's me, you stupid bat. Your idiot friend couldn't string a sentence together, could she?' the girl said in Sally's voice. 'Why don't you tell her the truth about you and Dad?'

'But I did,' said Glenda, speaking to the girl on the floor as though it was completely normal for someone to take over someone else's body. 'When Patrick died, I just couldn't bear it. I felt I'd lost my main reason for living. I married him for love. I left everything for him. I would have done it all again to have him and Sally back.'

'That's not even remotely true!' The girl's head turned unsteadily to look at Grace. 'She left me to cope with everything after Dad snuffed himself. I was fourteen, for Christ's sake. She was supposed to be looking after me.

She could barely look after herself. And then she started drinking. So I had another thing to worry about.'

'I'm not strong like you, Sally. I couldn't cope. I would have come out of it, eventually, but there wasn't time.'

'Well, I did okay without you. I've built myself a life and the last thing I need is you poking your drunken nose in and ruining it. You stay away from my Peter, or I swear to god I'll make you sorry.'

Glenda let out wail and buried her head in her hands. The poor woman was clearly in anguish. Grace took in the pallor of the girl who was currently hosting Sally. What was the process doing to her? Could Sally hurt her host?

'Sally,' said Grace, as authoritatively as she could. 'If you haven't got anything constructive to say, perhaps we should leave that girl alone.'

'You can sod off and all,' said Sally.

'Not unless I take you with me,' said Grace. She couldn't leave these poor women with an angry ghost. If Sally figured out how to use the girl's limbs there was no telling what she might do to Glenda. 'I think you've made your feelings perfectly clear to your mother. Now, please leave that girl's body alone. I'm worried that you'll damage her. She doesn't look good.'

Sally said nothing. The girl's body twitched. The eyes rolled back, leaving just the whites showing.

'Sally, get out. If she dies ...'

A sort of growl left the girl and suddenly, Sally was standing over her. 'Fine. Just make that bitch promise never to come sniffing around my husband again.' She pointed a finger at her mother.

Grace knelt on the floor and checked the girl's pulse. It was slow, but clear. She patted her on the cheek. 'Wake up. Come on.' When the girl failed to respond, she gave her a sharp slap. The girl's eyes flew open. She stared at Grace for a moment before focus returned.

'Woo. That was some strong stuff,' the girl murmured. 'Cooool.'

Grace wondered what she should do next. The girl put a hand on her chest and breathed deeply. After a minute or so, she struggled into a sitting position. 'You got any food on ya?'

All right. If she had the munchies, she was probably going to be okay. Now to deal with the other two. Sally was still shouting and Glenda still sobbing. Grace put a hand on Glenda's shoulder and passed on a toned down version of Sally's message. 'We're going now,' she added. 'I won't come back again, but Sally might.' She stood up, ignoring Sally's glare. 'She can only go to places she's been before, so you may want to move out of this room. And tell your friend the same. It may not be safe for her otherwise.'

By the time Grace got back to her place, Sally was already there, pacing around the kitchen.

'What was that all about?' said Grace. 'I thought you said you wanted to make things better between you and your mother.'

'Oh, come on. You didn't buy that sob story she gave you? She's always doing that. Whenever I need to talk to her about something, she turns it round and makes it all about her.'

Grace frowned and thought back over the conversation. 'No. I don't think she did that. Not until after you lost it.' She dropped into a kitchen chair and gestured for Sally to do the same. 'Want to me tell what's going on? If you want me to help, you're going to have to stop playing games with me.'

'I'm not playing games.'

Grace merely raised an eyebrow.

Sally stopped pacing and stared at her. 'You don't believe me?' For a moment she stared at Grace, then her shoulders dropped. 'Shit.' She sank down into a chair, making the white fabric billow out around her.

Grace leaned forward. 'Convince me then.'

Sally stared down at her hands and twiddled the wedding ring. 'What I said was true. She got more and more withdrawn from Dad. He tried to make it better. That's why he got into debt, trying to get stuff for her to make it better. Then when he died, she crumbled and left me to deal with it. She ruined him. She would have ruined me too, if I'd stayed.'

Grace nodded as encouragingly as she could.

Sally was staring at her hands and seemed to be seeing something else entirely.

'Sally?'

'Peter's my new start. He's all I've got. I don't want her to ruin him too.' When Sally looked up her eyes were desperate. Grace felt a surge of pity.

'I didn't mean to lose it like that,' said Sally. 'All I wanted to do was tell her to stay away from Peter. But she ... she just pushes my buttons like no one else can. I just snapped. I didn't mean to. I'm sorry.'

She looked so wretched that Grace felt sorry for her. 'I believe you,' she said. 'But you've got to promise me that you'll never go back there. When you took over that poor girl, I really thought you were going to hurt somebody.'

'I couldn't have, even if I wanted to,' said Sally. 'Her head was easy enough to get into, she wanted me there. But I couldn't do much with the rest of the body. Not unless I had a chance to be in there a while and experimented a bit.'

Scientific interest stirred. 'What happened there anyway?'

'I'm not sure, I stepped through her and if I lined myself up right, my eyes were where hers were and I could see what she saw. I've not tried to make anyone talk before. Lucky she was totally spaced out.'

'Wait. You've tried this before?'

Sally looked sheepish. 'Only by mistake.'

Grace wasn't sure she believed that, but she thought the sentiments about Peter were genuine. Whatever her issues with her mother, Sally seemed to genuinely love her husband. No matter how much Grace wanted things to be different, Sally and Peter belonged together. She would not be the other who came between them. 'Sally, you need to let me tell Peter about you.'

'No. I don't think it's the right time yet.'

'Why not, Sally? You love him. He doesn't know you're around. Why don't you let me tell him?'

'No. I can't let him see me like this.'

'I don't get it.' Grace refrained from pointing out that he couldn't see her anyway.

'The last time I saw him, I was warm and alive. I want him to remember that when he thinks of me. Not this... nothingness. I'm not a ghost. I'm not anything. I'm just a chilly draught that makes him shiver. I don't know why this happened. I don't understand any of this, Grace. I just want it to all go back to the way it was. I want my married life. It's not fair.' She sank into a chair and didn't even bother correcting herself when she stopped an inch or so above the surface.

'Oh Sally.' Grace went over to her and, despite the chill, put an arm around her, carefully, so that her arm didn't go through Sally's back. It was cold. She closed her hand into a fist and held her arm there.

Sally was staring into the middle distance. 'Do you know what attracted me to Peter in the first place? It was the way he looked at me like I was the most perfect woman in the universe. No matter how grotty I felt, he'd look at me like that and I'd feel ... amazing.' She looked at her hands and touched the wedding band on her finger. 'Now he can't even see me. He looks at me now and all he sees is someone in coma. There's hurt and sadness and desperation in his eyes. That doesn't make me feel anything good. It's like someone's designed a private hell, just for me.'

'I'm sorry. I wish I could help you.'

'You are helping,' said Sally. She wasn't crying, but her expression was full of pain. 'At least you can see me to talk to me.'

'I really do think you should talk to Peter. If you have any unfinished business at all, it makes sense that it should be with him.' Her arm was starting to shake with cold. She removed it.

Sally didn't seem to notice that her arm was gone. She gave a mirthless laugh. 'I have plenty of unfinished business with Peter. I'm not sure I could have him talk to me without seeing me. Or thinking I was that poor woman in the bed.'

'It will be weird, I guess.' There was no doubting that. 'Don't you think you should at least let him know that you can hear him?'

'Why? He'll only change what he says to me and I don't want him to. He talks to the other me so much more than he did when I was alive.'

How could you be in love with someone and not want to find out every last scrap of information about them? 'But you were getting married. You must have talked lots.' If Peter were hers ... No. She couldn't think that. Peter wasn't hers. He was Sally's. He belonged with her.

'We tried, but we always got distracted with one thing or another.'

Grace opened her mouth to question her, but saw the gleam in Sally's eyes and thought better of it. It was pretty obvious what they got side-tracked doing. 'Ye-es. Well, all I can say is that you never know what will happen until you try.'

'Easy for you to say. What happens if …' she paused and clamped her lips shut.

'If?'

'Doesn't matter. I just don't want to do this.'

'Sally, he's your husband. He loves you. You can't keep avoiding him just because you like spying on him. You've got a chance to fix that now, tell him all the things you were too distracted to talk about.' The minute she said it, she saw the problem. The conversation was hurtling towards one giant problem. Sally couldn't talk to Peter directly. Grace would have to be there as a go between. Quite apart from being a great big gooseberry, she'd have to convey messages of love from Grace to Peter. That would be so very difficult. Shit. Now what.

Sally glared at her. 'How, Grace? How exactly can I do that? He can't even hear me.' She sighed. 'He doesn't know I exist.'

The sadness on Sally's face was heart rending. Grace sighed too. She knew she had to offer to help. No matter what it cost her, she always offered to help. It's what she did. 'I'll tell him,' she said. 'You tell me and I'll tell him.'

Sally frowned, then her brow cleared. 'Really? That would work. I think it will, anyway. You're a good friend, Grace.'

Peter got into the office early. His programmer, Steve wasn't a morning person. He wouldn't rock up until gone nine-thirty, so things were nice and quiet.

Peter rubbed his eyes. The whole thing with being cold at random times meant that he woke up in the middle of the night, either too hot or too cold. He stretched his arms over his head and felt the knots in his shoulders ride up. He needed to keep his mind on the job when he was here. This was his business. He didn't want it to slide into neglect. First he needed caffeine. He grabbed his mug and left for the little kitchen.

The 'kitchen' was merely a little galley with tea making facilities, a fridge and a microwave. As he got his coffee filters out of the cupboard, Peter noticed that there were fewer there than he'd expected. Again. He sighed. What was it with people nicking other people's coffee? It wasn't like it was that expensive to buy your own. He really should do something about it, but it would have to wait until another time.

As the kettle boiled he let his thoughts wander back to Grace. The smell of fresh coffee reminded him of her. He smiled. Everything seemed to remind him of her these days. The harder he tried not to think about her, the more she popped up in his mind. He should be thinking about Sally, not Grace. Peter poured boiling water into the percolator and watched the water sink, slowly. Where Sally had swept over him like a wave of light and sound, being with Grace seemed tranquil and natural. It was as though she'd always been there in his life. But he loved Sally. Didn't he?

Sally had lied to him. She had always maintained that both her parents were dead. Her mother had fallen ill and died soon after her father's suicide. That's what she'd said. Only there her mother was. Large as life. He wondered if Glenda was some sort of imposter, an aunt perhaps, who was trying to get him to give her some money. It was possible, but then why hadn't Sally mentioned her?

He wondered what he really knew about Sally. He thought about the nurse's comment about the blue sheets. Since then he'd noticed that many of Sally's things had blue flowers on them. Even the crockery she'd brought with her when she moved in. If so, why had Sally said she loved roses?

Peter sighed and walked slowly back to his office. If only he could talk to Sally, maybe she could explain. If only he could talk to someone who would understand. His mother would always believe the worst in Sally. Despite his reluctance to admit it, he knew that neither his mother nor his sister liked Sally. He had been too swept up in new found love to let it bother him, but over the last year, with Sally needing him and his family trying to support him, he'd come to see it more and more clearly. He couldn't talk to them about Sally. They would never give her the benefit of the doubt.

The only person who cared enough to understand was Grace. But he couldn't talk to her either. He had to stay away from her. What had happened with her was a mistake. And now he couldn't stop thinking about her and feeling a little kick of yearning every time. He couldn't fall for someone else. He was married. Besides, Grace clearly didn't want to talk to him either. The last time he'd called, she'd wanted nothing more than to get off the phone. He supposed he didn't blame her. If she felt half as attracted to him as he was to her, it would be torture to know that they had no future together.

He sighed. Grace would be the only one who would understand the bone numbing tiredness that he carried around with him. What possessed him? She had become a friend and he'd let his body control him. Now he'd lost her.

In his pocket, his phone rang. He grabbed it, straight away, in case it was the hospital phoning to say something had happened to Sally. Every time it rang there was this split second of panic before he saw the caller ID.

It was Grace.

Peter relaxed, briefly, before his heart picked up again. Why was Grace calling? Despite his best intentions, the thought of talking to her lifted his heart. He hoped she wasn't wanting to meet up. He didn't think he could handle being so near her and not being able to reach across and touch her cheek. Grace seemed so sensible. She wouldn't put either of them in such a position of temptation. He sat up straight, ready to handle anything and said, 'Hello Grace.'

'Hi Peter. I ... need to talk to you about something.'

'Sure. What can I do for you?' He cringed. He sounded like he was talking to client, not to a woman he cared about. All the things he wanted to say clamoured around in his head. He had to force himself to focus so that he could hear what she said.

'It's about Sally.'

He hadn't been expecting that. Of all the things he and Grace had to discuss, Sally wasn't the first topic that came to mind. 'What about Sally?'

'It's a bit awkward. Um ...' There was a pause, when she said 'okay' to someone in the background. 'Peter, if you could talk to Sally again ... what would you say to her?'

'Grace, what's going on? What are you talking about? Are you at the hospice?' He was already on his feet, grabbing for his coat. 'Has Sally woken up?' Why hadn't someone from the hospice called?

'No. No. Nothing like that. It's ... weirder,' said Grace. 'I think we've found a way that you can talk to Sally from ... wherever she is.'

Peter stopped moving. 'What are you talking about? Is this some sort of new brain imaging thing?'

'No. More like …' Grace gave an annoyed sounding click of the tongue. 'It's not the sort of thing I can explain over the phone. Can I meet you at the hospice tonight? Say around six-thirty? In Sally's room.'

'Grace—'

'Please? Can you be there?'

Peter sat back down, his coat crumpling on the floor. 'Sure. I'll be there.'

'Great.' She sounded relieved. 'See you later.' And she was gone.

Peter stared at the red 'call ended' sign on the phone. What was all that about? He spent a moment frowning at it until he realised it wasn't going to give him any answers. Sighing, he placed it on the table and returned to his computer. There was work to do.

Chapter Sixteen

Grace chatted to the security guard while she waited for Peter. He brought her up to date on all the latest news. All the big and small bits of news that made up the community that lived and worked in the hospice.

Normally, Grace would have listened, but all she could think about at the moment was the mission she was here to fulfil. Sally was waiting upstairs, although Grace didn't put it past her to pop up at any point. Sally seemed to think that Grace's nerves were because Peter might think she was crazy. Grace knew that being thought insane was only part of it. She had expected to have more time before she saw Peter again. She was only seeing him again this soon because his wife, whom they had both betrayed, was insisting on it. The irony didn't escape her.

She fidgeted with the zip on her coat, worrying it with her finger. It was hard, being on her guard all the time, in case she let slip something that revealed too much to Sally. She didn't want to help Sally with this madness about her mother, but she felt so guilty, it was hard for her to refuse Sally's plea for help. Besides, she was starting to like having Sally around. It was a long time since she'd had company at home and it was rather nice – even if Sally was slightly over the top at times.

The guard was talking about how Captain Windell, who used to wear highly polished army boots with his pyjamas had passed away in his sleep, when Peter arrived, looking windswept and harassed.

'Hello Mr Wesley,' said the guard, displaying his uncanny knack of remembering people.

Peter looked surprised to be greeted by name. 'Er … hello.' He looked at Grace. 'What's going on Grace?'

'I didn't know you knew each other,' said the guard, raising his eyebrows quizzically at Grace.

'Only through the hospice,' said Grace firmly. 'I need to talk to Mr Wesley about Mrs Wesley.'

The guard's expression normalised. 'Ah.' He glanced at Peter with sympathy. 'Is everything okay with her? We haven't had a call down or anything.' He reached for the ledger to check for calls to the emergency services.

'Everything's okay,' said Grace. 'Well, you know what I mean.' She turned to Peter and managed a tight smile. 'Shall we go up to Sally's room?'

Peter waited until they were in the lift before he said again, 'Grace? What's going on?' He looked wild eyed. His hair was mussed up as though he'd been running his fingers through it. There were dark circles under his eyes. When he frowned, his scar puckered.

'It's hard to explain,' she said. She watched the display as the floors ticked past. How did she start this conversation? It was an impossible thing to just casually bring up. The lift stopped and someone got in, saving her from having to explain. They shuffled to the back and no one said anything.

They got out of the lift together and walked down the corridor. Sally was waiting at the doorway to her room, watching TV over the duty nurse's shoulder. 'Oh good,' she said. 'You're here.' She looked at Peter as he stopped to get an update from the nurse. 'God, Peter looks like he hasn't slept. Again. Poor baby, he looks knackered.'

Grace nodded her head, but only slightly so that no one noticed. She wondered how Peter would take the news that his wife was wandering around being a ghost. She smiled at the nurse, who waved in recognition. Had the fact that she and Peter were friends made it into the hospice gossip? If it had, Sally would know. Sally hadn't mentioned anything, so hopefully not.

She followed Peter into the room. He went straight to the bedside to kiss Sally's pale forehead. The ghost Sally stood by the bed, fidgeting. Grace shut the door behind her.

'You ready to do this?' Sally asked Grace. She wasn't exactly sure she was herself. She had liked being about to observe Peter's life without him being aware of her. It was a window on what it would have been like if she had died in the accident. Peter wouldn't have shrugged it off and found someone else. He would have pined. The thought was satisfying. She had chosen well. He was truly in love with her.

'So, what did you want to talk to me about?' said Peter, turning to Grace. 'What's so hard to explain? And why here?'

'Er. Perhaps you should sit down,' said Grace.

'Good idea,' said Sally. She sat down in the middle of the bed. 'It's hard to take in this sort of stuff. Peter's never been that great at absorbing ideas outside his usual area.' She was impressed at how well Grace was dealing with all this. Perhaps she didn't have designs on Peter after all. If she did, why would she agree to this conversation so readily? Maybe she had been worrying about nothing.

'Grace, you're starting to scare me,' said Peter. He didn't move from where he was.

'Best to get on with it,' said Sally. 'There's no point wasting time.'

Grace took a deep breath. 'Okay. You know that night with the lightning storm.'

'Yes ...' He was looking worried and suspicious at the same time. Good boy. Be suspicious of other women.

'Something weird happened that night. I saw Sally's ghost.'

Sally raised her eyebrows. 'Not softening the news or anything there, Grace.'

'She's sitting on the bed, right now.' Grace nodded to where Sally was.

Peter looked at the spot on the bed, then back at Grace. 'Grace ... I know you've been under a lot of stress lately.' He started to step towards her, but seemed to change his mind. 'I think you should really take what happened at the abseil seriously. I think it's affected you more than you think.'

Sally jumped off the bed and stalked towards Grace. 'Wait. What happened at the abseil? What's this?' She thought back to the weeks before. She'd been with Grace most evenings. So this must have been something that happened before she came back as a ghost. Peter had mentioned the abseil. He hadn't come to see her that night. Hmmm ...

Grace looked at Sally 'I had a bit of a panic attack. Peter was there.'

Peter looked alarmed. 'Grace.' He stepped forward carefully, as though approaching a skittish animal. 'Sally can't speak to you. She's in a coma. Now, you're clearly under a lot of strain. I'm sorry if —'

'I'm not going nuts, Peter.' Grace took a step away. 'I know it's hard to believe, but she's here. You said you've been feeling cold. That's Sally. Wherever she goes, it seems to make people cold. There's nothing wrong with the thermostat. It's Sally's ghost.'

'Sally's ghost.' He frowned. He looked around the room and back at the person asleep on the bed. 'Grace, Sally's not dead. You can't be seeing her ghost. Have you been put back on any anti-depressants? Perhaps there's some side effect ...'

Grace ploughed on. 'She wanted to talk to you. I think I'm the only one who can see or hear her, so—'

Peter was staring at Grace with concern. Sally felt a stab of anger. Getting him to feel sorry for Grace had not been part of the plan. This meeting was supposed to be about her. Not Grace. 'I don't think he believes you,' said Sally.

'Of course he doesn't believe me. I didn't believe in you to start with and I can see you.'

Peter looked in the general direction of Sally and back again. 'Grace. I think you should sit down.' He walked over and gave her shoulder a gentle squeeze. There was some sort of familiarity there. Like he'd touched her before. Sally felt the jealousy stirring again. Perhaps she should stay shtum and let Grace make a fool of herself. Peter would be far less attracted to a mad woman. If he was attracted to her at all, that is. So far, all the attraction seemed to be on Grace's side.

Grace turned to face Sally. 'Tell him something only you could know.'

Peter seemed to hesitate a moment, then he removed his hand from Grace's shoulder.

On the other hand, the idea that his wife was around might make Peter less likely to look elsewhere. Even if she was only a ghost. Like in *Truly, Madly, Deeply*. He could end up just talking to her and loving her as a ghost.

'Um ... we were going to go to Thailand on honeymoon. We danced to Doris Day on the radio the day we moved into the house. We had takeaway Italian delivered.'

Grace relayed the information to Peter. He narrowed his eyes. 'How did you know that?'

'She told me. She's standing right next to you.'

Sally reached out and stroked his cheek. Peter shivered.

'She's touching your cheek,' said Grace.

Peter raised his hand to his face, his fingers brushing through Sally's hand. He looked back at his empty hand. He looked so confused Sally almost laughed.

'I know it's hard to believe,' said Grace. 'I don't even believe in ghosts, but it's hard not to believe Sally when she's standing in the middle of the furniture in her wedding dress.'

'Her wedding dress?' He sounded dazed now. There was a catch in his voice.

'She was in her wedding dress when the accident happened.'

Peter moved over to the windowsill and sat on it. 'She was.'

'Oh, darling,' said Sally, perching on the sill next to him. 'It's all true. I wish you could see me.'

Peter rubbed his arm absent-mindedly. 'I want to believe you, but ...' His gaze drifted towards the figure on the bed. For a minute, Sally thought he was talking to her.

'She can hear you,' said Grace, looking at the bed. 'When you talk to her, she can hear you. She's been able to hear you for a few months.'

'Since around the time your mum made that horrible aubergine stuff,' said Sally. She was studying Peter intently.

'Since your mum made the aubergine dish,' Grace repeated.

'You bagged it and threw it out because the smell made you feel ill,' said Sally, smiling. Grace relayed that too.

Peter gave a short laugh. 'She told you that?'

Grace nodded.

'And you can hear her, but I can't?' He was staring right

176

through Sally, at her body on the bed. 'Why can't I hear her?'

Grace explained about the lightning and the weird connection between them. Sally helpfully suggested a couple more things that Grace could convey to him. Peter looked from Grace to the figure on the bed.

When Grace looked like she was about to speak, Sally put up her hand and stopped her. Peter was clearly working something through in his head. They had to wait. They couldn't force him to believe Grace. It was a conclusion he had to come to himself.

It took a few more minutes before Peter looked up. His eyes seemed to have a manic sort of light in them. 'Since the lightning strike?' he said to Grace.

Grace nodded.

'That was two weeks ago.'

Sally frowned. He was going to wonder why she hadn't spoken to him before. This talking through Grace was a good first step, but she needed to talk to him directly, respond to what he said without Grace getting in the way. 'I want to talk to him,' Sally said to Grace. 'Not through you. Really talk to him.'

'But how can you do that? He can't hear you.'

'I could take you over, like I did with that girl.' Only better, she added to herself.

'No. No way.'

'What?' said Peter. Sally was about to snap 'keep up' at him, before she realised that he could only hear Grace's side of the conversation.

'She wants to talk to you,' said Grace. 'Directly.'

Peter sighed. 'I want to talk to her as well.' He glanced again at the figure on the bed. 'So, so much.'

Sally looked pleadingly at Grace. Grace was a soft touch.

These people who felt the constant need to be of help usually were. She would give in.

Grace sighed. She indicated that he should sit in the chair. 'Close your eyes,' she said. 'Close your eyes and I'll relay what she says.' She pulled up a chair and sat opposite him. After a moment, she closed her own eyes and turned her head away, as though focusing.

Peter stared at her for a minute. 'Okay,' he said. There was hope in his voice. He pulled the other plastic chair and sat down, facing Grace. 'Okay.' He closed his eyes.

'Hello, Peter, it's Sally here,' Grace repeated after Sally.

'Hello, Sally.' He smiled. 'This is weird,' he said in a confidential tone. Sally wasn't sure which one of them he was talking to.

'You're telling me,' said Grace. They both smiled behind their closed eyes, and Sally realised he hadn't been speaking to her just then. The shared moment of intimacy between them annoyed her. He was supposed to be concentrating on his wife, not the messenger.

'It's ... nice to see you,' she said, uncertainly. 'I'm sorry I've been making you feel cold. I can't help it.' Grace relayed the message, her voice low.

'I'm ... it's okay,' said Peter. 'I can't believe ...'

'She's not making it up,' said Sally, quickly. 'It really is me. I've been listening to you talking to me for so long and I couldn't say or do anything. I would have given you some sort of sign if I could. You know that, right?'

Peter listened, frowning slightly as Grace repeated it. 'Sally. Does it hurt? Are you in pain?'

The question surprised her. She had expected questions about other things. Not about her body. She glanced over at the shell that used to be hers. It carried on breathing, oblivious to the world. 'No,' she said. 'I'm not in any pain.

Not the physical kind anyway.' She turned back to Peter and reached out to trace the scar on his cheek. He sucked in a breath at her touch. 'How about you?' she said.

Sally ran a finger along the line of his jaw and watched a shiver run down the side of him. She had been able to make him thrill with just a touch and now her hands made his shudder. That hurt.

'I'm okay. Missing you, you know.' Peter frowned. There was a slight hesitation as though he was trying to decide what to say, then, 'Your mum came by. You know, the one you told me was dead.' The note of sarcasm was unmistakeable.

'I'm sorry about that. I wanted to keep her away from you. To forget all the stuff she put me through.' Sally noticed the way Grace's lips tightened before she spoke. Being caught in this domestic conversation was clearly uncomfortable for her. Good. It'll teach her to think twice before trying anything with Peter.

'I would have understood, you know. We could have helped her. I would have supported you both,' Peter said.

Sally laughed. He was so middle class sometimes. Like they had the solution to everything. 'Oh Peter. You have such faith in the twelve step plans. You can't reform addicts unless they want to be reformed.'

'You changed,' said Peter.

Sally said nothing. If he thought that, it was brilliant. She had been worried that the whole thing with the lottery ticket might have given the game away. Good. One less thing to worry about.

'I wanted to change, because I found a man worth changing for.' Sally blew gently in his ear and watched the shiver go all the way down his spine.

'Why didn't you tell me?' he said, rubbing a hand down

his neck as though to brush off her touch. 'And why didn't you tell me when you came back? You could have told Grace to tell me. I would have believed her, eventually.'

Sally glanced over at Grace who seemed to have relaxed a little. How easy would it be to take over her? Possess her and talk directly to Peter. Sally suspected it would not be as easy as when she'd practised. All the people she'd practised on were already in a trance like place, most of them too focused on the slot machines to notice her slipping behind their eyes. That girl at Glenda's house had practically invited her in. Grace was focusing too, at this moment. Maybe if ... but it was risky. If Grace realised what was happening, she'd have her guard up and she'd stop helping. The only other way to talk to Peter directly would be to persuade Grace to let her in.

'Oh Peter!' Sally allowed a catch into her voice. 'I wanted to. But think of what it's like. I can see you, I can hear you, but you can't see or hear me. How can I ask Grace to talk to you on my behalf? I couldn't bear it being so close and not being able to touch you, to feel your warm skin. To kiss you. It hurts more that you can imagine. I couldn't drag you down to this living hell with me.'

Grace's eyes snapped open. She shook her head. 'I can't do it,' she said. 'I can't possibly tell him that and do it justice.'

Sally let her lip wobble a bit and spread her hands out in a gesture of helplessness. 'It's what I need him to know.'

Grace didn't say anything. She looked like she was going to cry. Her eyes seemed to be watering. Christ, what a sap. This was almost too easy.

'Maybe if you let me ...' said Sally. 'You're not like the other girl, she was out of her head. You're sober and you're expecting it. I can't possibly do you any harm.'

'What's going on?' said Peter. His eyes were open. He was watching Grace.

'Sally was asking if I'd let her ... possess me,' said Grace. 'She wants to talk to you. Properly.'

'*Possess* you?' Peter's voice surged with incredulity.

Grace shrugged.

'It's not that hard,' said Sally. 'I'll just step in behind your eyes and we'll share. I can feel everything you feel and see everything you see. But you'll be able to see too.'

Grace hesitated, her eyes going from Peter to Sally and back again.

'Grace?' Peter said. He was probably wanting to know what Sally was saying, but it sounded for a moment like he was prompting her to agree.

Grace sighed. 'Okay,' she said. 'I'm going to let Sally take me over,' she explained to Peter. 'It'll be my voice, but it'll sound like Sally. I've seen her do this before.'

'Is it safe?'

'Yes. Perfectly,' said Sally. 'You saw that girl. She was fine. She wanted to have another go, in fact.'

'Yes,' said Grace. She sat up straighter in her chair and laid her hands on her knees. 'Might help to close your eyes again, Peter,' she said. 'It's a bit too weird otherwise.'

'Ready?' said Sally. Before Grace could answer, she slid over until she was behind Grace's eyes. Grace gasped and fought her. She was much stronger than anyone Sally had tried to slip into before. 'Relax,' Sally hissed. 'Stop fighting me.'

She could feel the tension reduce as Grace forced herself to be calm. She let the sensations wash over her for a moment. Warmth, movement, the pull of gravity. Past Grace's eyelids she could see Peter, his face creased with worry. His eyelids fluttered, as though he was fighting to keep them closed.

'It's me now,' said Sally. The voice was Grace's, but it had her manner and pitch, making it sound as though Grace was doing an impression of her. 'Oh, god, Peter, I've missed you. It's been so strange, listening to you and not being able to see you or respond. Then I could see you and follow you, but I couldn't touch you or let you know I was there. I've missed you so much.'

Peter caught his breath when she started speaking. 'Sally,' he whispered.

Sally gave a little laugh. 'Darling, I don't know what to say. It's been so long and I finally get to talk to you and I don't know what to say.'

'Come back,' said Peter. 'The doctors say you're doing well. We just need you to come back and wake up.'

'If I knew how to, sweetheart, I would. I really would. I don't want to be like this. I would love to pick up my life where I left off.' She gave a little laugh. 'I'm desperate to see a hairdresser, for a start.'

Peter smiled. 'Yes, I'm sorry. I didn't mean to imply you had a choice. It's just that I want you back so badly ...'

'Me too.'

'This isn't quite what I expected from married life,' said Peter, still smiling.

Sally stifled a sigh. She could feel Grace struggling to hold back. She only had a short time before Grace's body rebelled. 'Would it be okay, if I touched you?' she said. 'It's the thing I miss the most. The feeling of you.'

Without waiting for an answer, she coaxed Grace's arm to move. To her surprise it moved quite easily. She reached out and touched his face. He angled his face slightly, so that his cheek rested against her palm. She could feel the warmth of his skin, the beginnings of stubble. 'Oh Peter.' She ran her thumb along his lip, he used to like that. Judging by the intake of breath, he still did. Sally smiled.

She pushed forward, there was a moment of resistance before Grace leaned far enough for Sally to plant a small kiss on Peter's mouth. For the first time in ages, she could kiss him without him shivering and wondering why it was so cold. She pushed again bringing Grace's face closer to Peter. For a moment, there was cooperation and then a surge of emotion. Excitement, surprise, fear and ... familiarity. The thought arrived just as Grace fought back. The bitch had kissed Peter before.

'Shit!' Sally was hurled away from Grace's body.

Grace fell forwards, off her chair. Peter caught her.

'Grace? Are you okay? Grace.' Peter was kneeling on the floor, Grace cradled awkwardly in his arms.

'Never mind Grace,' said Sally, scrabbling to her feet. 'What about me?'

'I'm okay.' Grace steadied herself. Peter helped her to her feet. 'I'm just a bit freaked out, that's all,' she said to him.

'*You're* bloody freaked out?' said Sally.

But neither of them was listening to her. Peter's hand was still on Grace's elbow. Grace was rubbing her forehead and assuring him she was fine. They seemed completely comfortable in each other's presence. There was no sense of awkwardness that Grace showed with other people, no distance that befits strangers.

'What is going on?' Sally demanded.

But Grace pretended not to hear. She left the room, claiming to need a bit of air. After a moment of hesitation, Peter went after her.

Anger bubbled up inside Sally. Grace had clearly made some sort of move on Peter in the past. Otherwise they would never be so cosy. She had to do something about this. But what? She was stuck in limbo. No one could hear her apart from Grace. How could she get to Peter?

Sally kicked the bed and screamed with frustration when her foot went straight through it.

Grace watched the tea gurgle into the small mug and fought down a wave of nausea. The whole experience with Sally had left her feeling as though she were coming down with the flu. 'I'm sorry,' she said to Peter. 'I didn't expect Sally to do that. Silly of me, really. Of course she'd want to kiss you. You're her husband.'

'I'm just grateful you let me talk to her,' he said. 'It sounds like it wasn't easy letting her do that. I really appreciate it.'

Not that his wife did. Sally had been glaring at her when she left. She hadn't expected Peter to follow her out. At least Sally couldn't come into the common room. She hadn't been there before.

'You should go back,' said Grace. 'Talk to her. She can hear you.' She couldn't look at Peter. Being near him was more difficult than she'd imagined. The brief kiss had brought back a rush of feelings that she'd been trying very hard to squash.

'But I can't see her. How will I know she's there?'

'You'll feel the cold.' Grace blew on the tea. 'Besides, now that you know she's there, maybe you'll be able to see her. Or sense her or something.'

'You think?'

Grace lowered the tea and said, thoughtfully, 'I reckon it's something to do with perception. Something happened to me when the lightning struck and my perceptions changed so I can see her. There was another girl who saw her, but she was so stoned, god knows what her perception was like. Anyway, things might have changed with you now. That's my half-baked theory about it.'

Peter considered it. 'I don't think that's too half baked,'

184

he said. 'Are you sure you're going to be okay?' He had half turned to go. He was standing apart from her, as though afraid to come too close.

'Yes. I'll be fine.' Grace looked around the room. The only other occupant appeared to be asleep. 'Peter.'

He turned back.

'I don't think you and I should meet again. Without Sally around, I mean. I don't think she likes that we're ...' She stopped. What were they? They weren't seeing each other. They barely even spoke to each other. What did that make them?

'Friends,' said Peter. 'That's all. Just friends.' She thought he sounded relieved.

She avoided looking at him. Could you be just friends with someone you were in love with? 'Yes,' she said. 'I don't think Sally likes us being friends.'

Peter laughed. 'She always was a bit on the jealous side. She used to guard me pretty carefully if I met any of her old work colleagues. She likes to be clear about what's hers, if you see what I mean.'

Grace knew exactly what he meant.

Back in the room, Peter felt the chill as soon as he approached the bed. Sally lay there, her breathing regular and calm. The machine beeped out her heart beats, slow and rhythmic. All was as it had been before. But now he knew that there was another Sally out there, walking around, listening and maybe talking, if only he could hear her. He sighed and sank into a chair. He leaned his elbows on his knees. 'Sally, are you here?'

A chill ran down his side. So yes, she was there.

'I ...' He stopped. He didn't know what to say. 'It was nice to talk to you.'

A good start. What else? This was a chance for him to talk to Sally in the full knowledge that she could hear him. She wouldn't be able to interrupt or change the subject, so maybe he should use the opportunity to talk to her about stuff that was bothering him. 'Sally, can you move anything? Maybe we can figure out a way to signal yes or no at least. Move something.'

He looked around the room. Nothing changed. Nothing moved. The regular beep of the machine didn't falter. 'Oh. Okay. I'm not sure how to talk to you now.' Another scan of the room and he could see nothing to indicate where in the room she might be. The chill was still there, so she must still be around.

'How about if I pretend you're on the bed. Just like... your body.' He nodded to the prone figure. He couldn't think of anything to say. For nearly a year now he'd been talking to this comatose woman, never knowing whether she could hear him or not. Now that he knew she could hear, he had suddenly run out of words. It was as though the fact that she was listening made her a different person. Perhaps it did. Perhaps the whole out of body experience thing had changed her.

He couldn't see Sally and imagined her to be exactly the same. He gazed at the woman on the bed and realised just how much she had changed. The Sally he'd first been to see had been pale and blonde and covered in cuts and bandages. The cuts had healed, the blonde had grown out, the pinkness of her skin had been replaced with pallor. Where there had once been health and vivacity there was this.

For the first time, he wondered if he himself had changed. He thought of himself as being much the same as he'd always been, but he had been semi-widowed for a year.

His life had gone from high colour to something drab and grey. Had the same thing happened to him? He couldn't remember the last time he'd been in the sunshine. The last normal thing he'd done was having a cup of tea with Grace. And that had ended up being not so normal in the end.

'I don't know what to say to you,' he said. He groaned and put his head in his hands. 'I'm sorry. I'm so, so sorry.' Ice gripped him by the shoulders. It should have been comforting to know that Sally was there. But suddenly, it just wasn't.

Chapter Seventeen

Grace opened the only wardrobe in her parents' room that she hadn't cleared, and stared at the carefully ironed clothes. Despite what had happened with Sally and Peter the week before, she still intended to go to the fundraiser the following weekend. Peter's marriage was his problem. She couldn't let it stop her from doing fun things. Margaret was right. She had spent years doing things that other people needed. It was time she stopped that. Maybe Margaret was right about the holiday too. Perhaps that was something she should think about.

But first she had to decide what to wear for the ball. She pulled out a burgundy dress and held it up against herself. It was far too short and too wide. It had been her mother's. She turned to hang it back up.

'What are you doing?' Sally's voice made Grace jump.

She looked around to see Sally sitting on the bed. 'Hello.' Things had been a bit cooler between herself and Sally since the whole possession experience. They had reached an understanding where Sally knew not to ask Grace to let her possess her, and Grace knew not to mention Peter.

'I'm trying to figure out what I'm going to wear to a party.'

'Ooh. I'll help. I love party clothes.' Sally stretched her legs out and settled back against the headboard. Grace was about to tell her to take her shoes off the bed when she remembered that it didn't matter. She hung the dress back in the cupboard.

Sally looked around. 'It looks good in here,' she said. 'Don't you think?'

'It does,' said Grace. The room had been decluttered

and repainted. Changing the curtains had done wonders to increase the level of light in the room. Sally had suggested moving the furniture around to make better use of the space, but that was a two person job and Sally wasn't much help on that score, so she'd moved things a few inches away from the walls and painted behind them. It felt odd, having the same old furniture in a room that was a completely different colour to before.

She pulled out another dress and eyed it.

'Let's see that one. It's a nice colour,' said Sally.

'It doesn't fit. It was my mum's.' She took another one out and held it up against her. 'So was this one, by the looks of it.'

Sally gave her an appraising glare. 'Clearly, you and your mother were very different shapes. She had boobs by the look of it.'

Grace raised an eyebrow.

Sally shook her head. 'I'm told that anything more than a mouthful is a waste.' She looked pointedly at Grace's chest.

Grace let the comment pass.

'How about that green one?' said Sally.

'Mum's.'

'Why are your nice clothes in the same cupboard as your mum's?'

'It's the nice clothes wardrobe,' said Grace. 'Mum always complained that I didn't look after my dresses properly. So she kept the nice ones in here.'

'That makes no sense,' said Sally.

Grace shrugged. 'No, guess it doesn't.' She pushed her mother's things along. 'Oh, here's mine.' She pulled out a snug fitting black dress. 'I wore this to the final year ball at uni.'

Sally shook her head. 'Too black. Next.'

'This?' She pulled out a bottle green dress with a scoop neck and white trim at the bottom.

'Looks like an elf.'

Grace laughed. 'Okay. Not that one then.' She put it back. Part of her was enjoying this banter. It was something she hadn't had in a long time. Not since uni, which had been far too long ago. 'I don't think I have anything else that isn't black.'

'You're not wearing black,' said Sally. 'It's too dull.'

'I haven't got much else,' said Grace. She pulled the clothes across one by one.

'Stop, stop! How about that one?' said Sally, pointing.

'What this?' Grace pulled out a long bright orange salwar kameez. 'It's orange.'

'It's great.' Sally slid off the bed and examined it.

'My Dad bought that for my mum when they were going out. She said she never wore it. You know, white woman in Asian clothes …' It was eye-wateringly orange and far too bling for Grace's taste.

Sally ignored her. 'I reckon this would fit you.'

'The trousers would be too short.'

'No they won't. Your mum didn't actually shorten this one. Just ironed the hems flat. See.' She ran a finger along the line of a folded hem. 'You'll have to iron the creases out, but it should be fine. Go on, try it on.'

'Sally, it's orange.' Bright, ridiculous orange. No wonder her mother had never worn it.

'So? You'll look great in it. Go on, try it on.'

'Fine.' Grace picked up the hanger and stalked into the bathroom.

The trousers were a little too wide at the waist, but the top fitted well. She tried to imagine her mother in this outfit, the orange bright against her pink arms. Grace lifted up her own arms. Her dark hair and brown eyes she'd inherited from her father, but her skin colour lay half way between her two parents, a light bronze that deepened when she caught the sun. The sleeves looked less orange on her than she'd first thought. She glanced in the mirror. The light reflected off the top and made her eyes look golden brown. The effect wasn't too bad at all. Grace realised she'd been frowning without noticing. She pulled up a smile. Much better. She stepped out of the bathroom and went back into the room.

Sally stared at her. 'You're right. It's too orange,' she said. 'What else have you got?'

'Only black.' Grace moved around a bit to get the feel of the outfit. 'I rather like it, actually. With a wrap, I should be okay.'

'I don't know ...' Sally looked dubious.

'It's not like I'm swamped with choice,' said Grace. 'I think I will wear it.'

Sally pulled a face. 'Suit yourself. It's your party.' She shrugged. 'What are you going to do with your hair? You can't have it down, it would get everywhere.'

'You think?' Grace looked at herself in the mirror on the wardrobe. Her hair lay in a neat plait by her shoulder. She twisted the plait up and held it onto her head.

Sally appeared over her shoulder. She looked different in the mirror. More substantial, somehow. As though she'd moved from plain TV to HD. Grace glanced over her shoulder, where the 'real' Sally appeared less defined than in the mirror. How strange. Perception was a funny thing.

'What sort of a party is it?' said Sally. She seemed absorbed in looking at Grace's clothes and didn't meet her eye.

'Just a fundraising thing. Nothing special. I just thought I should make an effort,' said Grace. She felt bad about being evasive, but she realised she was looking forward to the party and she didn't want Sally there. It might be the last time she got to see Peter alone. She wondered if Sally had been to Fredrino's Casino before. If she hadn't then they were safe. She could just ask, but that would tip Sally off about the venue. She fidgeted with the sleeve of her top.

'Your hair could do with some styling,' said Sally. 'This long hair down to the waist thing is just ... geeky.'

'Geeky?' Grace forgot her thoughts on perception and focused on her hair. She didn't think about her hair much, just pulled it up and left it, usually. Now that she thought about it, it was a bit of a waste. Before her parents fell ill, she'd had it shoulder length. She remembered the difference it made when she wore it loose. 'Hmm.' She pulled out the hair band and started to unravel the plait. A flash of memory reminded her of Peter running his fingers through her hair. She looked down, hoping that Sally didn't notice the flush on her face.

If Sally noticed, she didn't comment. Instead she assessed Grace critically and said, 'Your hair needs a cut. It's started to get dry at the ends.' She put her hands on her hips. 'Maybe you should go for a completely different hairstyle. You'd suit a nice short bob,' she said. 'All that long hair just swamps you.'

Grace wasn't so sure. 'I don't think I've got time to have my hair cut. There's only a couple of days until the party. Most decent places would be booked up.'

'Oh, I know a place that'll fit you in. There's a trainee there. Or there was when I was still in circulation. She doesn't get much work because she's a trainee, but that kid is a genius with a pair of scissors. She was my hidden jewel.'

Grace raised an eyebrow, sceptical. She wasn't sure she wanted a haircut, but Sally's ideas about home décor had been so good, perhaps it was worth following her advice on this too.

'Don't you trust me?' said Sally.

Grace looked contemplatively at Sally. There was no malice in her face. Just amusement and the gently teasing smile she often had when she gave Grace advice. Grace took the number down.

Sally beamed. 'Ask for Cerise,' she said. 'I only hope she hasn't moved on to set up business for herself.'

The next evening, Sally stood waiting outside the hairdresser's. The wind had got up and there was promise of rain in the air. It was as though the world was charging up, waiting to unleash something torrential.

She watched as Grace parked up and fed the meter. She glanced up at the sky as she hurried towards the door. She gave Sally a little smile and swept past.

'I've got an appointment with Cerise,' she said to the girl in reception.

The girl gave her an amused look. 'Yeah. Take a seat. I'll tell her you're here.'

Sally grinned. It had been a stroke of luck getting Cerise for Grace. Cerise, bless her, was a lovely little thing but she was a terrible hairdresser. Her mother, who owned the salon, had tried to train her up, but Cerise lacked any creative flair. She could cut hair passably well, but she could rarely manage to do anything with any panache. Sally usually avoided her like the plague.

Even better, Grace was trying to fit it into her lunch hour, so there wouldn't be time for her to change her mind.

Grace fidgeted while she was waiting to be called in. Sally tried to picture what Grace would look like with a short bob. With that long neck of hers, she'd look like a lollipop. Good.

Eventually, a slim girl with a pleasant face arrived and introduced herself as Cerise. She looked at Grace's long hair that hung over the back of the chair. 'Just a trim?' she suggested, almost hopefully.

'Actually,' said Grace. 'I'd like something different. Could you make it shorter? Around here.' She gestured to her shoulders.

Cerise bit her lip. 'I'm not sure … all that lovely hair …'

'You've got a meeting in fifty minutes,' Sally reminded Grace.

Grace sighed. 'I'm sure,' she said. 'Something shoulder length. Something that will suit my face.'

'Oh. Okay. If you're sure.'

Sally watched with satisfaction as lengths of hair fell to the ground under Cerise's scissors. She was pretty sure that Grace's hair had been at least part of the attraction to Peter. He had loved playing with Sally's hair. Brushing it, teasing it, twining it in his fingers as she lay next to him. He probably took one look at Grace's Rapunzel locks and fell under her spell instantly. He wouldn't find her so attractive now.

'Maybe you should go for something really different,' said Sally. 'Like a chin length bob.'

Grace's eyes flicked to hers in the mirror. 'I like that idea,' she said, aloud.

'Pardon?' Cerise stopped working.

'Would you be able to do it shorter? A nice short bob, maybe?' said Grace. 'I can feel the weight falling off as you cut. I quite like the lightness it brings.'

'Oh. Okay.'

It didn't take too long. The end result was an uninspiring

bob, which was exactly what Sally had hoped for. She saw Grace's horrified expression and retreated to the other end of the salon, so that Grace didn't see her grin. To her surprise, she felt a twinge of guilt. Grace had been kind. Now she'd made her look like a scarecrow. All's fair in love and war, she told herself. She liked Grace, but keeping Peter's thoughts in the right place was more important. Someone walked briskly through her.

'You're not happy are you?' said Cerise to Grace.

Grace made an apologetic face.

'It doesn't really suit you …' Cerise said. 'Could you wait just a minute, I'll have a chat with one of the senior stylists and see what they say.' She ran off to talk to one of the other stylists. Soon there were two of them, assessing Grace's hair.

'What if you make it even shorter?' said Grace. 'Would that help?'

'It might.'

Sally watched in horror as they discussed it. This wasn't part of her plan. She had hoped that Cerise would take so long that Grace would have to rush back to work with her hair all hacked and short. Bugger.

She sidled up to Grace. 'You've got a meeting to go to,' she reminded her. 'It doesn't look too bad.'

Grace looked at her watch. 'I'm going to be late for my meeting,' she said. She looked close to tears. Pathetic.

'I'll sort it out,' said the senior stylist. 'Cerise, can you finish the blow drying on my client please?' She picked up the scissors and efficiently set to work on Grace's hair. 'Don't worry madam, we can sort this out in no time.'

While she was talking, inch after inch of hair was being cut away. Sally started to relax. Maybe the plan wasn't going so badly after all. Grace's hair was now very short. By the time the stylist held up the mirror and showed Grace the back, Grace looked like a boy. Her features, already slightly too large, looked huge now. She looked like a cartoon woman. Hah. Let Peter try and get his kicks off that.

Grace touched the back of her neck; her expression was slightly stunned. Unless that was just the lack of hair making her look bug eyed. Sally stepped behind Grace and whispered in her ear, 'You look fabulous.' In the mirror their eyes met.

She put her hands on Grace's shoulders and felt the tremor of cold go through her. She smiled. Grace's returning smile was tense, as though she were afraid.

Good. She should be afraid.

Grace got into the car, grateful to escape Sally's scrutiny. The way Sally had looked at her in the mirror had cut through her completely. It was as though Sally knew what had happened between her and Peter. Oh, Sally knew that she and Peter were attracted to each other, Grace was pretty certain of that. She had felt the shock when they had kissed Peter, both in the one body. But did she know about the rest? Had she guessed how close they had come to sleeping together?

She twisted in her seat and checked all around. Sally had disappeared. She was probably already somewhere miles away. Grace pulled out her phone and dialled Peter.

'Grace?' He sounded surprised to hear from her.

'Peter, I think Sally knows ... about us.'

'What do you mean?'

Grace rolled her eyes. 'I think she knows.'

There was silence from the other end of the line. 'Grace ...'

'I'm not making this up ...' She suddenly realised how

mad it sounded. What possible reason did Sally have to suspect anything? Was she letting her conscience run away with her?

'Has … she been to Fredrino's before?' She knew what she was asking. Although Peter had mentioned Sally's problem to her they had never really discussed it. It was clearly a sensitive subject.

'No. She won't have.' His reply was quick and firm.

'Are you sure?'

'Yes. It opened a couple of weeks before the wedding. She started going to the GA meetings a few weeks beforehand. It's the one casino I can be sure she hasn't been to.'

'Oh.' Grace felt some of the tension in her release a bit. Even if Sally knew where the party was, she wouldn't be able to go there. 'That's okay then.'

'Grace, are you alright? You sound a bit strung out.'

Grace looked in the rear view mirror and was relieved to see no flash of white. 'I am a bit,' she admitted. 'I think it's just nerves. I haven't been out socially for a long time.'

'Me either,' said Peter. 'Unless you count meeting a bunch of people who volunteer to clean a hospice socialising.'

'You mean it isn't?'

It was a weak attempt at humour, but it made Peter chuckle. 'I guess it is,' he said. 'Is Sally bothering you?'

'No. Not really. I mean, she's been hanging around my house and generally mooching about, but she's no trouble really.'

'I think she's been around here a lot too. I keep turning the heating on because I'm so cold and then a few minutes later, the house is boiling because she's left. It's making me have a permanent sore throat. I hate not knowing whether she's there or not. I wish I could see her.'

Of course he did. She was his wife. Whatever had

happened between him and Grace, Sally was still the one he loved. Grace felt her heart settling inside her like a lump of lead. Peter was never going to be hers. She would always be the one that wasn't quite good enough to replace Sally. She touched the space where her hair used to be and was surprised to find nothing there.

'Grace? Are you still there?'

'Yes. I should get back to work,' she said.

'I'll see you tomorrow night then. Bye.'

'Bye.' After he hung up, she sat for a moment, staring at the phone. She was torn between aching to see him and feeling the terrible loss of not being able to touch him. She sighed again and pushed her phone back into her handbag.

Chapter Eighteen

The upstairs rooms of Fredrino's casino were a sort of mezzanine, where the main open area overlooked the casino floor below. Peter looked around at the very modern décor with the glass and chrome balcony railings and the alcoves containing small Greek statues. The place was glamorous, but had no charm whatsoever.

The party was filling up slowly. He spotted some familiar faces from helping redecorate the common room. From across the way, Harry waved to him. He grabbed a drink. The last time he'd been at one of these things, he'd had Sally on his arm. It felt weird being there by himself.

He had walked through the main casino floor on his way up, past the sad punters and the early birds who were loosening their suit collars and putting up their money already. What attracted them? What made someone like Sally get sucked into this sort of place? She was bright and cheery and … he stopped mid thought. But was she really like that? That was the Sally he thought he knew. The real Sally lied to him. Not just about big things like the death of her mother or a debt, but about the little things too. How much of what she said could he really believe? He didn't even know her favourite flower anymore.

He looked around for Grace. He had been thinking about her a lot. It was strange to think that Sally was still around. Weirder still, she was talking to Grace. Which meant that Sally and Grace were friends. Women talked about all sorts of things. What had Sally told Grace about him?

It worried him that he was more bothered about what Grace thought of him than about Sally. He felt guilty as hell.

He had never considered himself the sort to cheat. Then again, he'd never considered himself an easy target either. Sally had betrayed his trust, but it didn't mean it was right for him to betray hers. He sighed. At least in this casino, he knew Sally wasn't there.

He thought of Sally, sitting on their bed, looking so small and vulnerable, confessing about her addiction. She couldn't have been acting then. She just couldn't. He believed that she had been telling the truth when she told him she wanted to stop gambling. That loan must have been her last. Perhaps she forgot to tell him about it. Or maybe she had used it to buy him a present. Or perhaps she was even meaning to pay it off. It must have been a mistake.

He spotted Harry and started to wave, but Harry's attention was on something behind him. Peter turned around. And the world paled. Grace walked into the room. She was wearing some sort of Asian floaty outfit, which made it look like she was gliding. The deep orange of her clothes made her glow as though she were made of gold. Her hair. Her hair was gone. For a moment Peter felt the plunge of disappointment. Her beautiful, silky hair! Almost instantly, he realised that, where Grace had been attractive before, she was now stunning. The boyish haircut accentuated her graceful neck and high cheekbones. Her eyes looked incredible.

As he stood there, staring at her, she spotted him and smiled. He almost stopped breathing.

'Hi,' she said.

It took a few seconds for him to gather his wits enough to speak. Grace mistook his surprise. 'It is a bit drastic, isn't it?' She ran a hand on her neck. 'I haven't got used to it yet.'

'You look amazing,' he said.

'Thanks.' She flushed a little and looked sheepish. There

was a moment of awkwardness when he wasn't sure how to greet her. He couldn't very well give her a peck on the cheek. In the end they shook hands.

'Oh my god, my darling you look incredible.' Harry swooped down on Grace. 'That hair style really suits you.' He kissed her on the cheek and fussed over her.

Peter stepped back and let Harry escort Grace further into the room and introduce her to people. He had to be careful. He couldn't afford to lose control with Grace again. A one-off incident when he thought Sally was dying was one thing, doing it again when he knew Sally was alive in some way was completely another. It wouldn't do anyone any good for him to touch Grace again. The trouble was, he didn't trust himself to be able to resist.

Sally stared at Peter's post, lying open in a heap on the kitchen table. The corner of one poked out, gilded and looking like a ticket for something. Probably the ticket to the fundraiser he was at right now. The one that Grace was going to. Sally wasn't fooled for a minute about Grace's claim not to know where the place was. She knew alright. She just wasn't telling Sally because she was afraid she'd turn up. She had flitted through all the usual party places she could think of, but they weren't there. It sounded like a big enough event that the hospice committee would have chosen a biggish venue. But where?

If only she could move that letter lying on top of the ticket, obscuring the details. Sally glared at it. If only she could just … She took a swipe at it. Nothing happened.

'Ugh.' She looked around to see if there was anything she could use. Anything … Nothing.

The only way she was going to see any more was if Diane came and started tidying up. Even the prospect of information wasn't enough to make her wish Diane in her kitchen. She plonked down into a chair.

She knew, *knew*, that Grace had kissed Peter before. Judging by the rush of arousal that had flooded Grace's system the minute their lips touched, she'd done more than just kiss him. Sally recalled the intensity of the body's response. Grace's response, she reminded herself. By the time Peter's lips made contact Sally had no longer been in charge.

The thought that Grace had been anywhere around Peter, *her* Peter, made Sally furious. She felt it inside her boiling her up like a fever. The thing that made it so much worse, was that she had felt everything twinge in Grace's body in response to that small kiss. And she'd realised that her own body had never responded to Peter like that.

Anger rolled, higher and higher until she lunged at the pile of paper with a furious scream. The papers flew off the table and landed on the floor. Sally stared, anger forgotten. Had she really just done that?

She rushed through the table and crouched on the floor. There was only one ticket. It was a fundraiser for the hospice. Yes! It was to be held at … the top floor at Fredrino's. Fredrino's. The casino.

Sally grinned. She would be there. If Grace tried anything on with Peter, she would know how to take care of it.

Now, all she had to do was figure out how she'd moved those papers.

Grace looked out over the people swarming around the roulette tables. She watched the collective intake of breath and straining forward as the wheel spun round. The ripple of disappointment that followed the ball landing was broken by one woman shouting 'Yesss!' and punching the air. The man standing next to her rubbed his hands together as the croupier pushed chips in his direction. As Grace watched, they exchanged a glance before pushing most of the chips back out again. The possibility of stopping while they were winning never even occurred to them.

She didn't really understand what drove these people and she wasn't really interested. They were, however, a welcome distraction from the party behind her. It had been a struggle to stop herself from glancing over at Peter during the meal. Wherever he was, it was as though they were connected by an invisible thread. Yet he had been cool towards her. She could understand that. When he kissed her he had thought that his wife was as good as dead. Now that Sally was back, in a way, his feelings were bound to have changed. Grace wasn't sure what she'd expected from this evening, but it wasn't shaping up to be a huge bundle of laughs.

There was a movement next to her. Peter leaned his elbows against the railing. 'Hey.'

'Hi.'

'Enjoying yourself?'

Grace smiled. 'Yes. Thanks. I don't go out that often, it's weird … but in a good way.'

She reached up to push back her hair, only to realise it wasn't there any more. Her fingers brushed her neck and she felt silly.

'Missing your hair?' said Peter. 'It really suits you short, you know.'

'Thanks.' She fiddled with a short tendril. 'It was Sally's idea. She said it would look better short. Although, I don't think she meant quite this short. I got a bit carried away.'

'Does Sally follow you around all the time?' Peter's voice lost momentum towards the end of the sentence.

He was still watching her fingers tease her hair. There was something intense about the way he was watching her.

Grace suddenly felt hot. She dropped her hand back onto the railing. It felt reassuringly cold. 'Not all the time. Just most of the time.'

Peter seemed to come back to the present and glanced over his shoulder. 'It is fairly liberating knowing that she's not here. I feel really tense at home wondering if she's watching me.'

'I thought you could tell.'

'Sometimes I can. It's almost worse when I can't because I'm not sure if she's not there, or if she's just in another room. It's a bit ... stalky.'

'It must be weird not being able to see her. At least I can see and hear who's in the room.' Below her there was another shout of triumph as the gambler's luck held. Grace glanced down at the crowd, which had grown larger as people came to share the excitement.

Grace could see the excitement ripple through the crowd. They leaned closer, straining to join in and be touched by the good fortune of those winning. Looking at those hungry faces, Grace wondered if Peter's faith in Sally was justified. Sally had shown herself to be an accomplished liar. How could Peter be so sure?

As though reading her mind, Peter said, 'Sally swore on our love that she was quitting and she signed up to Gamblers Anonymous straight away. She didn't have to do that. She didn't even have to tell me, but she did. She made a solemn promise to me. No matter what went before that, I believe in her promise.' He sounded distant, as though his mind was elsewhere.

Grace glanced across. Peter's mouth was set in a hard line. He needed to believe in that. She remembered him saying her last words to him had been 'don't you trust me'. He needed to trust her. To have trusted her before the accident.

She nodded. 'Okay. Well, I haven't seen her all evening.'

Peter nodded, his mouth still set firmly.

It was time to change the subject. 'So, do you know many of the people here?'

'Not really, just the people who were there doing the painting. And you and Harry, obviously.' Peter blew out his cheeks and made a visible effort to relax.

'Harry's had a bit to drink, I think,' said Grace. She looked away. Harry had been quizzing her about Peter, trying to work out what to report back to Margaret, no doubt. He had seemed to think they were an item. Grace had her work cut out to persuade him that there was nothing going on. If only there were. She sighed.

'Was he giving you a hard time?' said Peter. 'About being friends with me.'

'We're friends. I guess it's understandable that they think we're … you know … together,' she said, still avoiding looking at him.

Peter drew a sharp breath. 'Grace …' She felt the leaden weight of her heart sink a bit more. She didn't want to hear what he had to say, it couldn't be anything that would make her feel better. But she couldn't bring herself to move away. Just to hear him say her name was something special. How pathetic to want someone that much. It was all just chemistry, she told herself. Glands and chemicals. That's all it was.

When she didn't look at him, Peter touched her hand. 'I wish things could be different. Grace, look at me.'

The glands and chemicals were making her feel wretched. Her heart squeezed in her chest. She blinked back tears. She had been longing to be near him all evening and now the proximity of him was unbearable. She had thought it was difficult being near Peter when Sally was there, but now, without her to keep them apart, it was infinitely worse.

'I'm sorry,' she said. She reached up to wipe away a tear that had escaped. Peter pulled a paper napkin out of his pocket and handed it to her. 'Thanks.' She dabbed the tear away.

'Keep it,' he said when she offered it back. 'I've got another.'

Grace forced a laugh, even though her heart was breaking. 'I won't ask why.'

Peter scrutinised her face. 'Are you okay?'

She tried to make light of it. 'Serves me right. Hanging out with a married man.'

He smiled, but his eyes didn't seem to get the message. 'Yes. Let's face it, he's never going to leave his wife.'

It wasn't funny. Neither of them was laughing. Peter's smile gave up the struggle and disappeared. 'I can't,' he said. 'Even if I wanted to. And I do … want to.' His hand rested next to hers on the rail, the wedding band glinting in the lights from the casino. 'It was bad enough when I thought she was gone. But now… she's my wife. I loved her once. And … I don't know if she's alive or dead. I need to work out where I am.' He looked up. 'I'm so sorry.'

His eyes looked straight into hers and the wretchedness in them wrung Grace's heart. She and Sally were tearing him apart between them. Next to that, her own agony seemed small and overblown.

'If only there was something we could do. Get her back with her body. Maybe bring her back.' If Sally came back, she would never see Peter again, but he could be happy. He wanted to stay with his wife. He clearly felt terrible about what almost happened between them. And, thinking about it, she wouldn't want it any other way.

Peter shrugged one shoulder. 'But we can't.'

She put her hand over his and gave it a squeeze. 'No. We can't.'

Peter turned his hand over so that their fingers interlaced. 'I'm sorry,' he said, again.

'I know.'

They stood together, hands resting together on the banister. This was a goodbye, of sorts. It was all Grace could do not to put her face on his shoulder and cry. She understood, she really did, but it didn't make the hurt any easier to bear. Peter's fingers uncurled from around her hand and she knew that the fragile contact between them had to break.

Suddenly, there was a chill at her back. Sally's voice said, 'What the fuck do you think you're doing?'

Chapter Nineteen

The bitch was holding Peter's hand. Sally's world thrummed with anger. So this is what they got up to when they thought she couldn't see them. If she hadn't managed to dislodge those papers, she wouldn't have been any the wiser.

Grace dropped Peter's hand and spun round, her face red with guilt. Peter was looking around wildly.

'You wait until my back is turned and you seduce my husband? You husband stealing bitch.'

Grace started to speak. 'Sally, it's not what—'

'Not what it looks like? Don't lie to me, I saw you. Holding hands.'

'Is she here?' said Peter. 'Where?' He squinted vaguely at the place where she was standing.

Grace gestured. Peter frowned as though he would be able to see her, just by concentrating. Moron.

'I thought you were my friend!' To Sally's surprise, that actually hurt. Until the words left her mouth, she hadn't realised that Grace was her friend. Someone to chat to and watch TV with. She hadn't had that sort of friend in … well, ever. Somehow, that made it all a hundred times worse. No wonder she'd stayed away from female friends before. 'You back-stabbing bitch.'

Grace put her hands up in front of her. 'Sally, calm down. Let me explain.' Her voice was low and her movements were understated, as though she were trying to avoid drawing attention to them.

Oh no. There was no way she was letting Grace get away with this. No way. Pain and fury boiled up inside Sally. She could almost feel the heat against her skin now. She looked around her and spotted a small statue in an alcove next to her. Acting on instinct, she lunged at it. To her surprise it moved easily. She picked it up and spun on her heel back to Grace. She'd teach her to move onto HER Peter. 'Explain?' she screeched. 'Explain this!'

Peter moved before the statue left her hands. It flew across the short space. Grace's eyes widened. There was a shout. And Peter was there, throwing himself in front of Grace. The statue connected with the side of his head. Momentum carried him onward and his head crashed into the balcony wall. He slid to the ground, eyes closed, blood oozing from his head.

'Peter!' Both Sally and Grace were at his side. Grace knelt beside him and put a hand under his neck.

The anger was suddenly quenched by fear. Sally fell to her knees on the other side of Peter.

'Peter, talk to me,' said Grace. Her voice quavered.

'Peter. My darling. What have I done to you? I didn't mean to,' said Sally.

Peter's eyes opened. He was looking straight through Sally.

'Peter, Peter, darling. Are you okay?' Sally thrust her hands to his face. His eyes suddenly focused and she knew he could see her. For a brief moment they stared at each other. Then a shudder ran through the length of his body and his eyes closed again.

'Get away from him,' Grace hissed. 'Haven't you done enough?'

Sally staggered backwards, through a man who was coming to help. For months she'd been wanting Peter to look at her again. Now she wished he hadn't.

Peter woke up with a splitting headache. He lay there with

his eyes shut. He could hear Grace's voice and other, male voices. No Sally. He was warm. So, definitely no Sally. In his mind, he pieced together what had happened. The last thing he'd seen was Sally, her hair all golden and her wedding veil billowing around her. It was over a year since he'd seen her. He'd looked into her wide open blue eyes and seen anger and malice and deception. There had been only one thing he'd wanted to ask her. 'What are you doing here?'

He knew the casino had opened after Sally started going to GA meetings. He knew because he'd carefully shredded the invitation to the grand opening before Sally saw it. He'd thought it unfair to put such temptation in her path. Grace had told him that Sally could only go to places that she'd been to before. So the only way Sally could have arrived at the casino was if she'd been there before. After she'd promised not to gamble again. Either he was missing something, or she'd lied to him. Again.

He thought back to the evenings when he'd dropped her off at the doors of the meeting hall. She'd always waved him off and set off to go inside. She always insisted on getting home by herself. He hadn't thought anything of it then, but what if she'd never really gone in? What if she'd come here to gamble instead? He knew now that was what had happened. He'd trusted her, but she'd shown him, over and over, that she couldn't be trusted.

What else had she lied to him about? He'd been right to try to throw away that blasted lottery ticket. 'Don't you trust me?' she'd asked. Now he knew the correct answer was no. Somehow that made him feel less guilty. Not totally, but just a little.

He had been so in love with Sally and now he felt ... pity. Sadness. A sense of his life wasted. If all this hadn't happened, would he still be married to Sally? Perhaps, if he hadn't found out. But then, his whole life with her had been a lie. A mirage projected by Sally. He would have found out at some point. They would have argued. They would have gone their separate ways. In a flash of insight he realised that Sally wasn't the sort to have a family. He was just a stepping stone for her dreams. He could have been anyone.

And now? What now? He was still married to Sally. She was still around, stalking him and anyone who came near him. He was trapped.

Peter groaned. There was a swish and Grace was instantly at his side. He could feel the warmth of her next to him and smell her perfume. He opened his eyes. She drew back, ever so slightly. It was as though a thin veil had descended between them.

'Peter. How are you feeling?' She looked worried, but was not, he noticed, touching him. He remembered the last conversation they'd had. He took in the sight of her, so close. The short wisps of hair at the nape of her neck, the wide mouth that was so delightful to kiss, the kindness in her eyes. He was in love with her – this clever, serious woman who was so unlike his wife. He was in love with her, but he'd asked her to keep her distance. He knew that she would keep her word.

'Peter?' A small frown appeared and the smile faded.

They were in an office of some kind. A man appeared behind Grace. 'Concussion?' he said. They both peered at him with concern.

'No,' said Peter. He pushed himself up so that he was propped on his elbows. 'My head. Ow!'

'We're not sure what happened,' said Grace. 'I think you tripped and fell and hit your head.' She was telling him the cover story, which was sensible, but she looked so guilty, it was laughable. She was a terrible liar. The other man didn't look like he believed her either, but he didn't say anything. He looked from one to the other and shrugged, probably deciding it to be a private argument.

'You've ... got a nasty cut on your forehead,' said Grace. 'On the other side to the scar.'

He sat up further and touched the plaster on his head. 'It'll make a nice addition to the collection. I'll look like a proper hard man within a couple of weeks.'

Grace gave him an unconvincing smile. 'How are you feeling?' she said again. 'Any dizziness?'

He shook his head and winced. 'Ouch.'

'I think you should sit still for a while,' said the man. 'You took a nasty blow. I think we should take you into A & E, just to be on the safe side.'

Oh no. The last time he went to A & E he had been taken in a separate ambulance to his bride. He had spent far too long sitting in a wheelchair, waiting and waiting for news. 'No. No need. I'm fine. I just need some water.'

The man looked unconvinced. "There's a glass of water. Can I get you something else?'

'Painkillers.' Peter sat up, slowly.

'Actually, I'd love something to drink,' said Grace. She took a seat a safe distance away from him. 'Coffee, if you have it?'

'Right you are, miss.' The man left, looking slightly relieved.

Peter gingerly took a sip of water. Once the man was out of the room, he looked around. 'She's not here, is she?'

'No. I guess she's never been in this room before.'

But she had been in the casino. He had been right. 'I need to talk to her,' he said.

'She'll probably be at your house. Or just outside.' Grace

was looking at the floor. 'When you're feeling well enough, I'll see you home. You can talk to her then.'

She meant that he should talk to the empty air, hoping that Sally was listening. But he needed to talk to Sally properly. To interact with her. To hear the excuses as she made them. 'No, I mean, I need to talk to her … face to face. Directly.'

Grace stiffened. Too late, he realised his mistake.

'You want her to possess me?' Her voice was cold. It was as though a door had clanged shut. There was no more awkwardness. Just a cold distance. 'No. I have no intention of coming between you and your wife. Not in any sense.'

Shit. The last time Sally had taken over Grace it had been a disaster. For everyone. Grace had just been attacked by Sally and now he was asking her to do something she didn't want to, just so that he could argue with Sally. He felt like a completely insensitive git. 'Grace, I'm sorry. I didn't mean—'

Grace put up a hand. 'When you feel well enough, I'll leave. I won't bother you again.' Her eyes met his and he saw the anger and hurt in them. 'You and Sally need to sort things out between yourselves. I am not part of this.'

The bouncer returned with a mug of coffee and a couple of ibuprofen for Peter. Grace stood up and crossed the room.

Peter took the pills and swallowed them with more water.

'How are you feeling now, Peter?' the bouncer said.

Peter sighed. 'Better, actually.' He nodded as though to prove it.

The bouncer looked relieved. 'No nausea? Dizziness?'

'No. Nothing like that. Just a really stingy cut.' Peter attempted to smile.

Grace had turned her back to him and was examining the pictures on the walls.

'I still think you need to go to A & E,' said the bouncer. His eyes darted from Grace to Peter and back again. 'I know you said you were okay, but I have to call—'

'I'll sign a disclaimer if you like,' Peter interrupted. He needed to get this sorted out. The last thing he needed was a trip to hospital. 'I understand you have procedures, but I really am fine. Just a small cut, that's all.'

'I ... actually, we do have a form for that.' The man brightened. 'Let me find it for you.'

It took only a few minutes to sign the paperwork. The bouncer seemed relieved to have sorted it all out. 'Let me call you a taxi.' He picked up the phone.

Grace turned. 'Could you make that two please?' She gave Peter an appraising look. 'Unless you need someone to come in the taxi with you.' Her voice made it clear she would rather not.

'No. I'll be fine. I'm sure.' His head was shooting with pain, but he didn't feel ill enough to force her to stay. Spending a journey sitting next to her would be agony. Not the sort of pain that drugs would help with.

The look of relief on her face made him want to weep.

Grace went to the bathroom to wash her face and hands. In the mirror she saw Sally. She would have been startled if she wasn't so angry with her.

'How is he?' said Sally. There seemed to be genuine concern.

'He'll live, no thanks to you.' She spoke to the reflection, rather than the ghost. Somehow the reflection seemed truer. 'You could have killed him.'

'I didn't mean to hit him,' Sally bit back. 'My so called friend is trying to steal my husband. I was angry. Who wouldn't be?'

'We were talking. Nothing more.' Somewhere inside, Grace felt a familiar stab of guilt, but at that moment, she was too angry and worried to care.

'Oh yeah? I may be a ghost, but I'm not blind you know. You were holding hands. Getting cosy. I don't know which of you I'm more hacked off with. You for sneaking behind my back. Or Peter for going off with someone before I'm even cold in my grave.'

'Oh for heaven's sake. Don't be so melodramatic.'

'Melodramatic, my arse. You knew exactly what you were doing. I should have known the cutesy friend act was too good to be true. Sneaky bitch.'

'You know what? I don't have time for this.' Grace turned around and faced her. 'He's a good man. You've used him and lied to him. You don't deserve him. He certainly doesn't deserve what just happened.'

'Hah. Saint Peter. If he's so hard done by, why did he marry me in the first place? It's not like I forced him to.'

'How the hell should I know why he married you?' said Grace. Sally had probably manipulated him into it. Goodness knows, she'd told him enough lies.

'You've been lying there in a coma and life moves on. People change, Sally. Deal with it.'

'If he's changed so much, why doesn't he divorce me?' Sally was shouting in her face now.

'He can't divorce you. You're in a coma. And he's not a widow because you won't bloody well die!'

There was a moment of silence as the enormity of what she'd said sank in. There it was, in a nutshell. They both wanted Peter. Neither of them could have him because Sally was neither alive, nor dead.

Sally recovered first. 'Oh you'd like that, wouldn't you? If I died.'

No, she realised. She wouldn't. She didn't want anyone to die. There had been enough death and loss. She didn't need to deal with that sort of thing anymore. 'You know what? I've had enough of this. This is not my problem.' She walked around Sally and stamped off.

'Don't you walk away from me,' Sally screamed from behind her. 'You can't run away from me.'

'Watch me,' Grace muttered.

Sally popped up ahead of her. 'You can't run away from me because I will haunt you.' Her narrowed eyes gleamed. 'I will follow you. Wherever you go. You can't get away from me.'

Grace ignored her.

Sally faltered. 'I'll wait for you at your house. You've got to come home eventually.'

'I can move. Then what are you going to do?' She walked up until she was nose to nose with Sally. The cold bit into her face. Goosebumps rose on her arms. She could feel the outside of her fists tingling with it. 'Don't threaten me Sally. You need me. Far more than you realise. Without me, you're nothing. A ghost that no one can hear or see. All you can do is make people feel uncomfortable. The most famous you'll get is if you end up on Paranormal Activity.'

Sally glared at her, but Grace knew she was right. Sally needed her. Getting away from Sally would be difficult, but it wasn't impossible. In fact, it might just be the catalyst she needed to change her life. Ordinarily, she would have balked at the idea, but now she was tired and heartbroken and very, very angry.

'Now kindly get out of my way.' She walked through Sally. It took all her self control not to gasp out loud as the cold seared through her. Once through, she walked briskly until the blood pumping around her body warmed her up. When she got to the door, she risked a glance behind her and saw Sally glaring at her, with murder in her eyes.

Chapter Twenty

Sally watched Peter get into a taxi. He had cuts all over his face and there were flecks of blood on his shirt. He looked pale. She had done that to him. She noted, with some satisfaction, that Grace didn't go with him. She too stood watching the taxi drive away, her back straight, her shoulders set back too stiffly.

Sally drew back into the shadows, carefully pulling her skirts back so that Grace wouldn't see her. When Peter and Grace had come out of the building, with the big man in tow, there had been a space between them. The intimacy she had seen as they stood together hand in hand was gone. Instead there was an odd formality. Sally felt a flare of satisfaction.

She wondered what would have happened if the statue had hit Grace, as she'd intended. At least now, Sally was the one wronged. Sure, she'd chucked things, but who wouldn't do that if they'd found out their husband was being poached by another woman. While the poor wife was in a coma for Christ's sake. She had no doubt that Grace would have come up with an explanation so that no one thought she was a bonkers, ghost spotting, freaking nutso, but Peter had known Sally was there. He had seen her.

She needed to do something about Peter now. As she remembered the look in Peter's eyes, Sally shuddered. All this time following him around and he had finally seen her when she'd lost control. All the work she'd done, carefully being all sweetness and light to him. Making sure he was so totally swept up in life and love and sex that he didn't have time to stop and think. All that laughing and simpering and sucking. All that couldn't be unravelled by a single moment where she lost her temper. Not now. In that brief moment between waking and unconsciousness, Peter had looked at her. She'd spent all this time yearning for him to look at her again. Yet the look he'd given her was anything but adoring. There had been shock, anger, fear and ... contempt.

Sally knew that, for the moment, he was falling out of love with her. He had been looking at the poor cow in the bed for too long. She needed to talk to him. To talk him round. She couldn't do that without a body.

Another taxi drew up and Grace spoke to the driver. She looked like she was going to cry. Well good. She should cry. Bitch.

Once the taxi had driven safely out of sight, Sally emerged from the shadow of the wall and returned to the casino foyer. She plonked herself down on one of the plush seats. A nervous looking woman who was sitting there shivered and moved to a warmer seat. Sally scowled at her, which of course, the woman didn't see. Bloody annoying.

She needed a body. Grace's wouldn't do. She needed to find that girl that lived in her mother's house. Sally frowned. The girl was fairly attractive. If she could get her stoned enough to let Sally take control, but not so stoned that the limbs were hard to work ... then she'd have to get her to Peter. She wondered what it would be like to seduce Peter in someone else's body. A plan started to form.

Grace didn't cry until she got home. She went straight up to her room and tore off the orange clothes. Tears fell, silent and unchallenged down her face. She got into her comfy old pyjamas and sat on her bed. It was late, but she knew she wouldn't sleep. She drew her knees up and leaned her head against the wall.

219

The house was silent apart from the usual creaks and thumps. No Sally. Thank god. Hopefully, Sally's sense of outrage was such that she'd stay away. Grace didn't want to have to explain. To tell Sally that yes, she was in love with Peter, but that Peter wasn't in love with her. He had let her down gently, telling her that he couldn't leave his wife.

If Grace had been in any doubt about his feelings towards her, the moment when he asked her to let Sally possess her had put her straight. Sally had nearly killed him, but all he thought about was her. He wanted to explain to Sally that he wasn't intending to stray. Grace was nothing to him. Just a vessel for communicating with his wife.

'I'm such an idiot,' Grace said to the empty room. 'What was I thinking?'

There was no answer. The house felt big and empty. A few weeks ago, she'd have felt her mother's stamp in the walls and the furniture, but not any more. The house smelled of new paint and dust. In revamping the house, all she'd managed to do was clear her parents away from it. Nothing had come in to replace them.

Grace wiped a palm across her face. She hoped Sally wasn't going to come back here either. Which meant no more unexpected chills. No one watching her, commenting on her choices. No one demanding to watch TV. No one chatting, incessantly about things that Grace couldn't care less about. Finally there would be peace and tranquillity.

And silence. There was silence. Grace slid off the bed and padded downstairs. A hot chocolate should help get her to sleep. She turned on the kitchen lights, half expecting to see Sally standing there holding a knife. No one. When she heated up the milk, the whirr of the microwave seemed too loud. The ping bounced off the walls.

She made the drink quickly, feeling slightly uneasy.

Having got used to the ghost being around, now the house seemed creepy without her. When she turned the kitchen light out, she had to force herself not to run up the stairs in a panic.

Sally got to the house her mother lived in to find it in darkness. Of course, it was well past midnight now. Sally stepped through the closed door. Now then, where could she find the girl, Chloe? She lived in this house, but where? In the past few weeks, Sally had been back in search of Chloe and twice, she had been lucky enough to find her in the hall. It was easy enough to possess her, but it was still not easy to control her limbs. Tonight, Sally was worked up enough to throw an object, so she would surely be more powerful than before.

Sally had been in the hall, the kitchen and Glenda's room, but nowhere else. So even if she found out which room Chloe was in, she couldn't get into the room.

There was a light on in the kitchen. Sally drifted along to look in the door. The fridge door was open. A skinny body was silhouetted against the light that spilled out of it. Sally couldn't believe her luck. It was her. It had to be. There couldn't be two people who were as skinny as that. She cleared her throat.

Chloe turned around. It was a peculiar movement, like a startled spin, but in slow motion. Her face was slack and her mouth hung open. She was wearing nothing but a pair of knickers and a vest. When she saw Sally, she grinned. 'Oh, it's you. You gave me a fright.' She pulled out what looked like cold takeaway rice and kicked the fridge door shut behind her. 'I'm just getting food. You want some?'

She opened the plastic container and started to shove handfuls of cold rice into her mouth. 'Haven't seen you in ages,' she said, through a mouthful. 'You been okay? Going to another wedding?'

'Actually,' said Sally. 'I've just come from a party.' The girl was stoned. Good. That would make her body easier to control.

'Wow. You have such a cool life. What kind of party? Did they like your dress?' She was swaying. 'Your name's Sarah, right?'

'Sally. And it was a very nice party. A bit intense.'

Chloe nodded. 'Oh yeah. Things can get intense around here too.'

'I bet. Look … er … Chloe. I need your help. I need to get into your head again.'

'Oh can't do that.' She shook her head gravely.

'Why not?'

'Got to eat this rice.'

Sally glared at her. Bloody dopehead. What was she on about? 'Oh for God's sake.' She walked around the girl and stepped into her.

The girl went rigid and dropped the box of rice. There was a moment when there was a spark of a struggle and she tried to keep Sally out. Angry and strong, Sally easily displaced her. With the control gone, Chloe's body started to fold. Sally caught up with it as the knees hit the ground. Ouch. Sally felt the pain second hand through Chloe. Sally managed to persuade the hands forward so that Chloe didn't land on her face.

Now, on her hands and knees, Sally tried to move Chloe's body upright. It was harder work than she'd expected. She was stronger now than she'd been before, but still not quite strong enough to override Chloe. This made her angrier. Angry, she realised, meant strong.

'Grace,' she growled. 'She pretended to be my friend and

222

then she nicked my husband. Bitch.' She was able to lift Chloe's head.

Suddenly, the body started to respond to the threat of Sally. Something flooded into the blood. Despite her anger, Sally felt the stomach drop away. The heart rate rose, pounding and roaring in the head.

'Ugh. Stop it.' Sally tried to turn the heart rate down. But nothing would stop the galloping pulse. She could feel the heart, contracting faster than she could breathe. She tried to influence it. Slow it. But it only beat faster. She lost control of Chloe's head, which crashed to the floor. As Sally grappled with slowing the heart back to normal, the arms gave way and Chloe crumpled. Sally pushed and pulled and kicked, no longer knowing what she was doing. The noise in Chloe was deafening. It suddenly occurred to Sally that something was going very wrong. She had to get out before whatever was happening affected her too. She leapt forward, like a runner leaving the blocks. Her momentum took her through into the corridor.

A gagging noise came from inside the kitchen. Sally peered back in. Chloe made another gargling noise, ending in a sob. And then went still. Liquid trickled onto floor. The stupid cow had wet herself.

'Oh for god's sake,' said Sally. 'Wake up you silly bint. I need you.' She aimed a kick at the prostrate form. There was no response. She hunkered down to look at Chloe. She couldn't move her.

Sally scrambled back. 'Oh my god.' Chloe was dead. Sally stood up and backed away. She had killed someone. 'Oh my god.'

She stood there for minutes, staring at the body on the floor. She looked around for signs of another ghost in the room, but there was nothing. She shuddered, not from cold, but from habit from when she had a body. She could see Chloe's spine pressing against her skin, which just brought home how vulnerable she had been. Chloe was just a drug-addled, sick teenager. And she had killed her. She felt sick. She had to go home.

At her feet, Chloe made a noise. Not dead. Oh thank god. She was in enough trouble without adding murder to her list. Chloe's body jerked and a stream of vomit ran into the hem of Sally's dress. Disgusted, Sally took herself back to her home. She looked down at her dress. 'Still clean,' she said.

Chapter Twenty-One

Peter finished his tumbler of whiskey and felt the liquid burn in his chest. He needed to talk to someone. The person he really wanted to talk to was Grace.

He had really blown it with her. Before, she had understood his reasoning, but now she thought he was still in love with Sally. Thoughts clamoured around in his head. He had told Grace he wouldn't leave his wife. But his wife wasn't the woman he'd thought she was. The memory of Sally's hate-crazed face frightened and shamed him at the same time. How had he been so wrong about her? How could he have ever thought he loved her?

He took the bottle with him into the kitchen and poured himself another glass. Resting his elbows on the table, he stared at his phone. He needed to clear things up with Grace. He couldn't bear for Grace to think that he didn't care. Because he did. She had somehow found a place in his heart that he hadn't known existed. He had been wrong about Sally, but he had been even more wrong when he thought he could survive without Grace.

He dialled Grace's number. The phone rang and rang. There was no answer. It had been at least an hour since he left the casino, she should have got back to her house by now. He hoped everything was all right. He dialled again. After several more rings, Grace answered.

Her voice was cautious. 'Peter. Is something the matter?' She sounded raw. Like she'd been crying.

'Are you okay?'

There was a pause at the other end. 'I appreciate your concern, but it's hardly necessary.'

'Grace, about—'

'Don't,' said Grace. 'I get it. You and Sally. I don't need to hear any more.'

Peter winced. Grace was polite, but so stiff. He shouldn't expect anything more. 'Grace, I didn't mean to upset you.'

'Was there anything else? It's late.'

'Is Sally there with you?'

'No. I assumed she'd be with you. You are her husband, after all.'

'I was worried ...' He stopped. His thoughts coalesced and the idea that Sally might go after Grace solidified. The hate-twisted Sally that he'd glimpsed was capable of anything.

But Grace was way ahead of him. 'She's not here,' she repeated. 'If she wants to hurt me, there isn't a lot that I can do, is there? She's a ghost. No one else can see her. The only way I can keep her away from me is to move to a motel for the night and I refuse to be driven out of my home by her.'

Peter could hear the slight tremor in her voice. Grace was worried now.

'You could. Just until she calms down. I'll pay for it.'

'No.' No explanation. Just that. Oh Grace.

'Grace. I think she's dangerous. She really meant to hurt you when she threw that statue.'

'I know she did. She was angry. She'll have got over it now. She's not going to hurt me, Peter. She needs me. I'm the only one who can see her. And she's ... we were .... Well, she knows me and I know her.'

Peter gave a short laugh. 'I thought I knew her too,' he said. 'Look how that turned out.'

Grace sighed. 'I appreciate that you're worried, but there's no need. She's not here, okay. Now good night.'

'Grace wait—'

The line went dead.

'Grace. I think I love you.'

He called her again. It went straight to answerphone. Peter stared at the phone in frustration. He drained his glass and poured himself yet another. Where was Sally now? Not at Grace's. So maybe she was here. He sat very still, trying to feel the cold that meant that Sally was around. Nothing. Bloody Sally. She was always hanging around where she wasn't wanted and when he needed to talk to her, she didn't show.

'Sally!' he shouted into the empty house. 'Where the hell are you? Come out here and talk to me.' But there was no response.

'You used me.' Now that he had started, he couldn't stop. 'I thought you loved me, but all you wanted was money and this …' he waved his hands around. 'This bloody house. It's too big. It's too fancy and you wanted it just so that you could stick a finger up to the world and say "hey look, this is mine!" You didn't love me. It could have been anyone. You only chose me because I was stupid enough to fall in love with you.'

He stopped and looked around again. Still nothing. She wasn't there. The words boiled inside him. 'I alienated my family for you. I've put my company at risk for you. I'd have given up my life for you. Now I find out that it's all a lie. And Grace. She likes you. She actually thinks you're her friend. And you tried to kill her. I saw you. I saw your face. You wanted to harm her. I know you did.'

The realisation punched him in the chest. If he hadn't intercepted it, the statue could have done serious damage to Grace. Given her height and how close she had been standing to the balcony, it was quite possible it would have taken her over the railing. Then he would be in hospital visiting two women. He would probably have ended up being charged for murder.

Was that what Sally wanted? It certainly wasn't what he wanted. The idea of a life without Grace to talk to was so enormous, it made him dizzy. He had told her he couldn't be with her because of Sally. But could he really keep away?

'I don't love you, Sally,' he said, quietly now. 'I love Grace. But I can't have her. Because of you.' He gritted his teeth. 'And you're not worth it.' He reached for the bottle again and stopped. That wasn't the way out. He'd seen what addiction could do. It could get you in a fight over a stupid lottery ticket, for a start. Sighing, he pushed the bottle away. He groaned, 'Shit,' and laid his head on his arms. Just for a minute. When his head stopped throbbing, he would go to bed.

Sitting in the far corner of the kitchen, Sally watched. She would have cried. But ghosts don't have real tears.

Grace woke up feeling stiff and shattered. She had slept huddled up in the top corner of the bed, safe up against the walls that Sally couldn't walk through.

Even though she didn't think that Sally would really harm her, she'd removed all the heavy things from the shelves and put them in piles on the floor, just in case. There was nothing left to fly off a shelf and hurt her. Now, looking at everything lying as she had left it, she felt silly.

She stretched, her arms and back complaining with the night's tension. Her throat and eyes stung from crying the night before. She felt as though she hadn't slept at all. She needed a shower and a coffee before she could face anything.

As she showered, she thought about Peter's phone call in the night. He had seemed genuinely concerned that Sally would want to hurt her. She had assumed that it was a momentary flare of temper that had caused Sally's outburst. It was probably the strength of emotion that had suddenly given her the ability fling things. She wouldn't be able to do it again now. Probably.

A few minutes later, she ventured downstairs, feeling much better for having washed the previous night off. The house was still. She turned into the kitchen and her breath caught. Sally was sitting on the kitchen table, head bowed.

Grace hesitated, not sure what to say after the argument the night before. She hadn't said anything wrong. The one person who should apologise was Sally. So why should she feel bad? Grace took a step into the kitchen.

Sally raised her head. Her expression was utter misery. 'Morning.' Her voice was barely a whisper.

They stared at each other for a moment. Grace couldn't think of anything to say. She didn't know how she felt towards Sally right now. Nor how Sally felt towards her.

'I've lost him,' Sally said. 'After all this, I've lost him.' She raised her hands and dropped them again in a gesture of helplessness.

Grace felt a stab of alarm. Had Sally done something? Had Peter hit his head harder than anyone thought? 'What are you talking about? In what way have you lost him?'

'He doesn't love me any more.' Sally's voice was a wail.

The first thing Grace felt was relief. Peter was okay. The next feeling was, unexpectedly, sympathy. Peter had rejected her for Sally. Now Sally thought he'd rejected her too. 'Are you sure?' she said.

Sally looked so miserable that there was no doubt. Grace decided that she needed caffeine before she could handle this.

She watched Sally out of the corner of her eye, as she filled the kettle. The ghost sat hunched on the table. She seemed somehow diminished. It was as though her personality had shrunk until she was just a woman in a wedding dress, not the bright, in your face Sally she was used to.

'He saw me,' said Sally, not turning around.

'Just before he passed out? Yes. He mentioned.' Grace sat down and pulled the sleeves down on her jumper as she felt the chill emanating from Sally.

Sally turned. 'No. Before that. When I ...'

'When you threw a heavy object at me?' said Grace.

Sally nodded her head and looked down again. It was a few seconds before she looked Grace in the eye. 'I'm sorry about that,' she said. 'I was angry.'

'You can't go around throwing furniture at people just for talking to your husband. That's just mental.' Grace stared at her. 'You could have killed someone.'

Sally looked like she was going to say something else, but then shrugged. 'You're right. I overreacted. I knew he was falling for you and when I saw you guys together, holding hands, I just ... lost it.' She nodded towards the kettle. 'Your kettle's boiled.'

That was probably the closest thing to an apology that she could expect. Grace made her coffee. The words 'he was falling for you' went round and round in her head. Had he been? If he had, he'd certainly got over it now. She turned around when Sally began to talk again.

'The thing I really loved about Peter was the way he looked at me,' Sally said, playing with her wedding ring again. 'But last night, he looked at me like he hated me. Like he was scared of me. It was ... horrible.'

'You're a ghost. It's pretty normal to be scared of ghosts, especially when they're hurling things around.'

'No, there was more than that. He ... There was some

stuff I didn't tell him. About me and my addiction. And he found out.'

'I gathered.' She sat back down. 'Sally, I'm out of this, okay? You and Peter are going to have to sort things out on your own.'

'But you—'

'Look, if it's any consolation, Peter told me to stay away from him. That's what we were talking about last night.' Grace felt tears prickling again. This was hard. She should be used to losing people by now. And Peter wasn't ill or dying. Why was this so hard? She blew on her coffee, hoping the steam disguised her teary eyes. 'He didn't want to do anything that wasn't right by you.'

'Really?' said Sally. 'He said that? Why?'

'Because he's a decent human being and he loves you. Or he loved you at some point. He said you needed to have a chance to defend yourself.'

'He really said that? Wow.' She looked away. Her posture had changed. Her back was straighter. The hangdog expression had abated. Grace looked away. Good. If Sally and Peter made each other happy, good luck to them. She was better off out of it anyway. Really. She was.

Sally tapped her fingertips on the table, as though she were thinking hard.

Grace blew on her coffee again and took a small sip. So here she was, again. Alone. There was no point moping about it. She had to do what she always did. Get up off the ground and deal with it. She was a fighter. That's what fighters did. Peter didn't want her. If she fought for him, she would never be able to shake Sally. Come to think of it, she was saddled with Sally anyway. No one else apart from drug addicts could see her, so Sally would continue to haunt her. The only way out was to go somewhere she'd never been.

'Sally, have you ever been to Asia?'

'What?' Sally looked over her shoulder. 'Why?'

'Just asking.'

Sally picked something invisible off her sleeve. 'We were going to Thailand for our honeymoon. Peter was going to show me the world.'

Grace nodded, no longer listening. She always faced up to things. Peter had made his position clear and Sally, well, Sally would find someone else to hang out with. Peter would sort himself out too, one way or another. She'd spent years doing stuff for other people. Maybe it was time she stopped.

Sri Lanka. She could go there. Maybe track down her father's family. She wondered if they would want to know her. Probably not, but she'd like to see the country her father remembered so fondly. She could ask for unpaid leave from work and just go. She had some money left from her mother's insurance payout. She could sell the house too. When she got back, she could move to something smaller. She didn't need all this space anyway.

She immediately felt better. A long holiday would be just what she needed. She'd always wanted to see Sri Lanka. She could go and see Thailand and India as well. Who knows, she might like it enough out there to stay. Then everything would work itself out.

Except then Sally would be a ghost, drifting unseen and unheard through the world. She looked again at Sally, who was still thinking. Could she really condemn Sally to that? Sally was a pain in bottom, but did she really deserve that? Grace shook her head. There it was again. That irritating drive to worry about other people.

Peter woke up to hear the key in the front door lock. He

lifted his head and wondered where he was. His arm had gone numb where his head had rested against it. He must have fallen asleep at the kitchen table. He was still dressed in last night's clothes. There was a bottle of whiskey and a glass in front of him. His head felt horrendous and he felt as though he'd lost something. Memory crashed into him. Sally. Grace. Shit. He rubbed his face and felt stubble rasp against his palms.

'Oh my god, Peter!' His mother was standing in the doorway, holding a cool bag in one hand, keys in the other. 'Oh my darling what happened to you?'

He looked down and realised that there was still blood on his shirt. 'Uh ...'

Diane's gaze dropped to the whiskey bottle, which was nearly empty.

'Oh. I left it open overnight.' He grabbed the lid and started to screw it back on. 'I only had a couple of glasses.' He frowned and winced as the cut on his forehead pulled.

Diane dumped her bags on the table. 'What happened?' She picked up the whiskey tumbler with two fingers and moved it.

Peter touched his forehead. 'Oh, you know how it is. The wife beat me up.' He smiled at his own joke. Except of course, it wasn't a joke.

'Stop being facetious Peter. How bad is that?' She was reaching for his forehead. He pulled back.

'I'm okay, Mum. Honestly. I had a bit of a fall at the party last night. I toppled into a statue. It's no big deal.'

'You've got cuts all over your arm and face.' She stretched his arm out and examined it. 'It looks like a big deal. Did you have these cuts cleaned?'

'Yes. They had a very good first aider there. He and Grace sorted everything out.'

'Grace? Your friend from the hospice.'

'Hmm.' His mother's apparent recognition of Grace surprised him. He had mentioned her only in passing. Had Val mentioned something to their mother about Grace? He hoped not.

'How drunk were you?' said Diane, still examining his arm.

Peter gave a small laugh. 'I'm not as hungover as I look,' he said. 'I just need to have a shower and get into some clean clothes, and I'll be as good as new.'

Diane nodded and reluctantly let go. 'I'll make you some breakfast for when you come down. Then you have to tell me all about what happened.'

Peter headed up the stairs. Later, he stood under the stream from the shower and let the previous night wash off him. Who was he trying to kid? He would never be as good as new. He'd seen the madness of his wife. And he'd alienated the one woman he really wanted. An ache settled in his gut. He knew now, without a shadow of a doubt that he loved Grace. He even loved that she didn't argue with him when he told her he couldn't see her. She understood. What an idiot he was not to see that Sally had been playing him for a fool all this time. And how did he not realise that he loved Grace? Now that he did realise, what next? He was married to Sally. Peter tilted his face to the water and groaned.

When he got back downstairs he was greeted by the smell of bacon. 'Mum, you're an angel.' He sat down to the bacon and baked beans his mother set down on the table. 'You read my mind.'

She sat down next to him, a coffee cradled in her hands, and watched as he attacked his plate.

'So,' she said after few minutes. 'Want to talk about it?'

Peter took another mouthful and lowered his fork. He hadn't told anyone other than Val about Sally and Grace. Perhaps he should. 'It's... a bit weird,' he said.

'Okay.' She was watching him with a gentle expression. Suddenly he felt about ten years old.

'Mum. Can you promise you're not going to go crazy?'

'Darling I—' She stopped when she saw his expression. 'I can't imagine what you're going through right now, but I'll do my best to understand.'

So he told her. About Sally's gambling problem, about the argument that crashed the car, about the guilt and the fear, about everything apart from the ghost. It flowed out of him in a torrent of emotion and sadness. His mother listened, quiet and absorbed, just like she'd always done.

'So, in the end, she wasn't at all who I thought she was,' said Peter. 'She lied to me about all these things.' To his surprise, there was pain behind his eyes. He blinked. 'The Sally I thought I knew was ... well, she never really existed. It was just an act for my benefit. I was such an idiot.' His vision was blurring. He clenched his fist around his fork, impatient at himself. 'I feel ...' He lost the battle with emotions and a tear rolled down his cheek.

'Like you're losing her all over again?' Diane finished for him. 'Oh darling.' She stood up and wrapped her arms around him.

'All that time I sat next to her bed and hoped and prayed and wished for her to come back. All that pain and heartache and guilt.' He said into her shoulder. 'I loved her Mum. Really loved her and she's gone. She never even existed in the first place. Which is worse.'

Diane held him. The familiar smell of her perfume and hairspray reminded him of being a child. Of comfort. Of safety. For a few minutes he let himself lean on her and fall apart. Diane patted him on the back and laid her cheek against his head. 'Oh, my darling. If only I could have spared you this, I would. We tried, but you were so in love.'

Peter froze. 'You tried?' He pulled himself away and scraped the tears off his face with the back of his hand. 'What do you mean, you tried?'

His mother looked uncomfortable. 'When you first brought Sally round to see us, I ... didn't feel she was right for you. Neither did Valerie. We talked about it and Val said she'd talk to you.'

'But I just got annoyed with her and told her to butt out of my business.' He remembered the argument all too well.

'Sally was everything you thought you wanted,' said his mother. 'I thought she was calculating and fake. I felt she wanted you for the wrong reasons. She didn't seem that interested in what you wanted and ... I just couldn't imagine her ever having children, could you?'

Come to think of it, no, he couldn't. God, how could he have been so stupid. 'I can't believe I fell for it so completely,' he said.

Diane smiled. 'I can. She was very pretty and I'm sure she could be very persuasive when she wanted to be.'

'I guess.' He picked up his plate and headed over to sink.

'What are you going to do about Grace?' said Diane.

'Grace? Nothing. I don't know. She probably won't want to ever see me again.' The thought felt like lead in his heart.

'That's a shame,' said his mother.

Peter paused. 'Pardon?'

'Oh, come on darling. It's obvious that you like Grace. And she likes you. She sounds like a very nice person. A very ... genuine person.' Diane stood next to her son and put a hand on his arm. 'Apart from all that you've just told me, your wife has been as good as dead for a year. No one would blame you if you started forming other ... friendships.'

This was his mother. Straight down the middle, Scruples-R-Us mother. 'Mother, are you suggesting I be unfaithful to my wife?' Amusement tugged at the corners of his mouth.

She took a breath. 'I ... wouldn't normally ...'

'What if Sally wakes up?'

'What if she doesn't? You need to move on. Accept the possibility that she may never wake up.'

Except of course, she already had, in a manner of speaking. He stilled, trying to sense if she was in the room. Still nothing. 'I wonder where she is.'

Diane misunderstood. 'We all do, darling. We all do.'

Sally watched the nurses changing her catheter bag and changing her. They chatted about their lives and loves and generally handled Sally's body as though it were an object. Although they addressed it occasionally, it was as a matter of training. They didn't expect her to hear.

They tucked her back into the newly changed bed and brushed her hair out so that it lay in a brown fan on the pillow. One of them checked the machines, did the obs while the other messed around changing the water for the flowers. It all took a few minutes and they were gone.

Sally felt the enormous loneliness of being invisible. She watched herself lying there and thought about the difference between someone unconscious and someone dead. The difference was barely noticeable, but it was there. Even the useless body on the bed had something in it. Life. It was a complicated thing. A body and a consciousness, each useless without each other.

Sally felt the sudden need to be with her body. She plonked herself on the bed and lay down. She frowned. Something was different. She carefully shifted herself so that she was in line with her physical body. As arms and legs and middle fell into place, there was a feeling of something changing. A feeling of something being right.

Suddenly, there was a blast of sensation. She could feel neurones firing from all directions. There was heat, there were sounds, there were smells and there was pain. Dear god, there was pain. She screamed.

Her body seemed to suddenly realise she was there. Glands kicked stuff out into her blood. Her heart started to race, just as Chloe's had done.

'No, no, no.' Sally tried to slow things down, but that only made things worse. The machine next to her started beeping. People rushed into the room.

With a little effort, Sally managed to disassociate herself, partially, from herself. She lay there, half in, half out of her body, waiting for the heart to settle down. The room was filling up with doctors, someone had a defibrillator out. It was like something from ER. Except without George Clooney.

Without her to mess things up, her body settled down. The heart monitor went back to pinging gently. The medical staff were still babbling, standing around the bed. Sally ignored them. Now, she had an idea.

Chapter Twenty-Two

Grace fidgeted as she waited for the lift to reach Margaret's floor. The decision to go away, once made, was exhilarating. Grace had spoken to her manager who was considering it. She wouldn't normally be allowed to take six weeks off. Being a senior scientist came with responsibility. She caught herself assessing her team trying to figure out who could take on which aspects of her work.

Then there was Margaret.

Now that it came to telling Margaret, she was starting to feel guilty. Margaret had no one. If Grace disappeared for six weeks, that would be six weeks where no one visited her. As Grace strode along the corridor Harry's father, pushed in his wheelchair by Harry, came out in the opposite direction. The old man was muttering to himself.

'Morning Mr French,' said Grace.

He gave her a nod and grumbled. 'That woman is very rude.'

'Oh stop it, Dad,' said Harry. 'You love it.' He gave Grace a grin. 'I'll see you some other time, my darling, I need to get on. Come on Dad. Let's get you back to your castle.'

Grace waved to the father and son as they hurried off down the corridor.

Margaret was lying propped up on her bed. Grace noticed that she looked well. Her eyes were sparkling and there was a small blush of colour in her cheeks.

'What are you reading?' said Grace, pulling a battered looking paperback towards her to read the cover.

'Oscar and Lucinda,' said Margaret.

'Again?' She knew Margaret had read that at least three times before.

The old lady shrugged with her good shoulder. 'So, what's going on with you, young Grace?'

'Actually ...'

Margaret's good eye narrowed. 'Yes?'

'I'm ... er ... thinking of taking your advice and going away for a bit.'

'Oh, excellent. You're going on holiday. About time too. Where are you going? How long for?' She seemed genuinely pleased.

'About six weeks, if I get the time off work.'

'Oh.' For a moment, Margaret's face clouded. When she looked back up, the sadness was gone. 'Well, you deserve it.'

'And you don't mind?' There would be no one to visit and chat and pretend to sneak in a shot of port for her.

Margaret's gaze met hers. 'Of course I mind, I'll miss you. But that shouldn't stop you going. You need to stop letting other people's needs dictate your life. That includes my own needs. Just get on with it, Grace. I'll still be here when you get back and you'll have more interesting things to tell me.'

'I'll try and find someone else to read to you,' said Grace, feeling wretched now.

Margaret gestured weakly at the tape player. 'I've got the lovely John Turnbull's voice for company. I hate to tell you this, but his is much more soothing than yours. Besides,' she added, with a smile, 'that Mr French is coming to see me again tomorrow.'

'Harry's Dad?' She must have seen them when they were

returning from Margaret's room. Good old Harry, true to his word. 'How did that go?'

'That man is just insufferable,' said Margaret. 'I've never met such a miserable old curmudgeon.' Her eyes took on their sparkle again.

Margaret's demeanour didn't agree with her words. Perhaps she enjoyed having some different company after all. 'Did you enjoy their visit?'

'Absolutely,' said Margaret. 'I like a man who can handle a bit of verbal combat.'

Grace shook her head. If Margaret was being visited by Harry and his father, at least she needn't worry about Margaret being lonely. She pulled out the latest audiobook she'd got out of the library.

'So, if you're thinking of going away, that means things aren't going well with your young man.' Goodness, Margaret didn't miss a thing.

'He's not my young man,' she said, automatically. He definitely wasn't now.

'What happened?' It wasn't so much a question as a demand for an answer. Grace eyed Margaret. For all her frailty, Margaret was a hardy soul and would probably not be surprised by anything. Even a ghost. Perhaps she should tell her.

Margaret was still watching her, waiting for a response. Grace pulled her chair closer. 'Okay,' she said. 'I'll tell you, but you've got to promise not to laugh.'

Margaret didn't laugh. Instead she said, 'How interesting. She's a ghost to all intents and purposes, but she's not dead. Makes you wonder if there is such a thing as a soul.'

Grace was surprised. She hadn't expected that. 'You believe in ghosts?'

Margaret rolled her eyes. 'When you've been sitting

around for as long as I have, you'd be amazed at the things you can believe in!'

Margaret's support had surprised Grace and lightened her, as though the responsibility of visiting Margaret daily had somehow been weighing her down. On the spur of the moment, she'd ordered a Kindle and made a wishlist of novels set in modern day Sri Lanka to load on it. A Kindle. Her father would have been apoplectic. She wondered how he would feel about her going back to see his roots. She suspected he would have been proud. He was always proud of her. He was always proud of where he came from too, despite never going back there once he'd married. He spoke of 'home' in glowing terms, telling her about the island's beauty and fecundity and showing her pictures in the big coffee table books that she hadn't had the heart to throw out.

She dug those same books out now and settled down in the living room, with a mug of tea, to look at the pictures and work out what she wanted to see while she was there. She was engrossed in reading about the cultural triangle when a small noise made her look up. Sally was sitting on the sofa opposite her, watching. How had she not noticed the chill? She was about to comment, when she realised that something was different. Sally's appearance never changed, her hair and make-up were always frozen in time from the day of the accident. But something in her demeanour was wrong. It was little details, the way she was curled up in her seat, the downturned corners of her mouth, the lack of bravado. All these gave off the impression of defeat. For the want of a better description she looked … haunted.

'How long have you been here?' said Grace.

'A while.' Sally didn't move from her position nestled in the armchair. 'You look happy.' She raised her chin in the direction of the book that was on the table. 'Looking at your dad's book?'

If she needed a time to tell Sally, now would be it. Grace drew a deep breath. 'I'm going to go there on holiday. '

Without Grace around, Sally would be utterly alone. She felt as though she was abandoning her.

'That sounds nice.' There was no enthusiasm in Sally's voice.

Grace waited for Sally to voice her opinion. She always had an opinion on everything. None came. Sally seemed preoccupied, as though she wasn't really paying attention.

'Are you okay?'

Sally finally made eye contact and Grace was shocked to see the fear in her friend's eyes. 'Sally, what's wrong?'

'I need a favour.'

'Okay. What is it?'

'I want you to let me talk to Peter. Just one more time.'

Oh no. Not this again. She thought she'd made everything clear. No more possessing. 'I told you—'

Sally held a hand up to stop her. 'I want to say goodbye.'

'What?' The implication was that Sally was going somewhere. Perhaps she'd decided to go and live in the casino permanently. Or found another ghost to hang out with. 'Where are you going?'

Sally rolled her head back dramatically and stared at the ceiling. 'I can't carry on like this anymore. No one can hear me. No one can see me. I'm turning into my mother. And Peter doesn't love me anymore.'

'Sally …' Where to start? Did Peter not love her any more, or was it Sally being over dramatic again? Grace could understand the horror of realising that you'd nearly killed the man you love in a fit of anger. But what did she mean by 'turning into her mother'?

'If I could come back now,' Sally continued as though Grace hadn't spoken. 'If I could come back now, I might be crippled. I'll have crap hair and crap skin and I'll probably pile the weight on as soon as I eat a bit. And there's the risk that parts of me might have been ruined by the accident. Oh, Peter would stick by me. Everyone will. But that would only be because they felt they had to. I would be the object of pity.' Her mouth twisted. 'And I'd be revolted with myself, lying there weeing and crapping into a bag. It's disgusting.'

'You might not have anything wrong with you,' Grace suggested, not sure how to steer the conversation back to something positive. If Sally were to die, properly, Peter would be a widow, free to be with someone else. But then what? Just because he was able to see someone, it didn't mean that he would want to see her.

'You don't know that,' said Sally, still staring at the ceiling. 'Peter doesn't look at me in the same way he did before. So what have I got left? There's nobody who would miss me.'

Okay, now Sally was just feeling sorry for herself. 'You've got your friends ...' she was about to say 'Your mum,' but resisted just in time.

'I haven't got any friends,' said Sally. 'Never really bothered with them. Except you.' She looked away again. 'And look what happened there.'

No. she was not going to have that conversation again. Grace shook her head. 'So, what are you saying?'

'If I died now, I'd just be the girl who was cruelly and tragically snatched away on her wedding day. Her man grieved for her for over a year and finally, she died. It's a beautiful and aching story.' Sally made a sweeping gesture with her hand.

Sally was going for the full tragic heroine now, like a teenager in full strop. Grace decided she wasn't in the mood for that either. 'Sally, that's all very well, but you're stuck as ghost. You can't die just because you've had enough.'

'Yes I can. I know how to do it and I want to go while things are still looking good for me. It's a far far better death that I have now … you know, what that Sydney guy said.'

'It's a far far better thing I do now than I have ever done before?'

'That's it.' Sally sat up, suddenly animated again. 'What do you say? Will you let me talk to Peter, so that I can say goodbye?'

The sudden change of mood put Grace on her guard. What if the whole 'I want to die' thing was just a trick to get her to agree? Sally was clearly stronger now than she had been before. What if she'd figured out a way to stay in Grace's head?

She gazed thoughtfully at Sally, who leaned forward, waiting for an answer.

'No,' said Grace.

'What? Why not? It's just for me to say goodbye to my husband!'

'No. I said no and I meant it.'

Sally rose to her feet. Grace braced herself for a barrage of abuse. Without taking her eyes off Sally, she gripped the edges of the book harder, preparing to use it to deflect whatever Sally was going to throw at her.

But the abuse never came.

'Okay,' said Sally. 'I suppose I can understand that after what happened. I just want to say, thank you, Grace. For letting me hang out with you, and taking me to talk to people and all that stuff. You're not the sort of person I'd normally talk to. It's been interesting getting to know you.'

Grace blinked, not sure what to make of that speech. 'Um … okay.'

'And I really am sorry about the whole thing with the statue. I lost my temper. I shouldn't have.'

This wasn't like Sally. There was no bluster. No insistence that she was right. What was going on? Grace looked at Sally's face again and saw something she'd never seen in her before. Calm. As though she'd found something she'd been looking for. There was sadness too, but mostly, she looked … calm. Somehow that was more creepy than the barely controlled rage vibe that Sally usually gave out. 'Sally, what's going on? You're starting to scare me.'

'I'm a ghost.' Sally gave her a thin smile. 'It's what I do.'

She drew herself up and clasped her hands in front of her. 'Do me a favour, Grace?'

Grace hesitated, still wondering if this was some elaborate trick of Sally's to get what she wanted. 'What is it?'

'Look after Peter.'

And Sally disappeared.

Grace stared at the spot Sally had just vacated. What was that all about? She ran through the conversation in her mind. Without the suspicion that she was being tricked, she realised the melancholy of what Sally had said. It wasn't a trick. It was a farewell.

But how? Had Sally figured out a way to die? Would that even work?

She pulled out her phone and called Peter. 'Where are you?' she demanded when he answered.

'Grace? I'm at work.' He sounded surprised.

'You need to get to the hospital.'

'What? Why? They haven't called—'

246

'Sally's up to something. I'm not sure what, but I think she's going to commit suicide.'

'Commit ...' He stopped. 'That's ridiculous. She's in a coma.'

'I know how stupid it sounds.' She grabbed her handbag and fished about for her car keys, the phone wedged between her jaw and her shoulder. The phone beeped as her cheek made contact with the screen. 'She just came and gave me a long speech about how it was nice knowing me.'

'Are you sure she's—' said Peter.

'Peter! I'm going to the hospital. Before she does something stupid.' She hung up on him and ran to the car. She couldn't let Sally just slip away like that. For all the problems they had with each other, Sally was still her friend. As she slammed the car into gear she realised that she'd miss Sally. Without her around the house would always echo, just like it had done before. Without Sally, Grace would be alone again.

Sally drifted back through the places in her life. The house she and Peter had furnished. The old flat which was now full of someone else's stuff, the bedsits, the shared houses until eventually, she stood outside the small house she'd grown up in. She'd stood there before, looking up at the house and feeling that same mixture of loneliness and loathing that she'd carried with her, ever since her father died. No wonder she'd left when she could. Sometimes it was less lonely being alone.

The house was empty. The residents were presumably out, doing whatever menial jobs they could find. She stepped through the door. A few steps in and she looked up. In front of her was the stairway where she'd found her father, hanging from a short rope, his eyes and tongue protruding. She could almost see it. 'Dad?' she said, just in case his ghost was hanging about still. She waved a hand through the space his body had been in.

There was no answer.

'I'm going, Dad. I just wanted to say – I think I understand what you did. You thought we would be better off without you. I get that. But you were wrong. We weren't. Things got worse. Just so that you know. It didn't help. It just made everything worse.'

She paused, listening for an answer. When there was no response, she turned to leave. As she stepped back out into the overcast afternoon, she realised that, for the first time in a long time, she felt okay. No anger burning, no tears being throttled. She smiled to herself and she swept down the path and through the gate, not bothering to make contact with the ground. There was a park she wanted to go to, just around the corner, where the forget-me-nots grew.

She didn't look back at the house. There was nothing left there for her to see.

Peter ran out of the office. Something in Grace's voice disturbed him. It was ridiculous that Sally was planning on committing suicide. For a start, she was a ghost already and her body was in a coma. For seconds, she was so into her drama. There was no way she'd make a quiet exit like that. Even a huge car crash on her wedding day wasn't enough for her. There was no way she'd go out without a bang.

As he got into the car, he realised that there would be drama. Sally had him and Grace rushing over to the hospital for no apparent reason already. What did she have planned?

As he drove up to a traffic light, he wondered how he would feel if Sally really were to die. He had been grieving her loss for so long that it had sunk into his very bones. He had loved her, lost her, loved her more, then realised that the woman he'd loved had been a fabrication. He no longer knew what was truth and what was mirage. If she died now, would he really be losing anything that he hadn't already lost over the past year?

Sally waited. Grace would come. She knew she would. She wasn't sure if Peter would though, which was telling in itself. A few weeks ago there was no doubt that he would drop everything and rush over at the slightest twitch from her. But now, she wasn't sure.

She looked over at the pale creature in the bed, with her crappy hair that was mostly brown now and sallow skin. It wasn't a bad body. It had been in much better condition while she was looking after it. She stretched her arms out in front of her and admired the sleek tan and perfect manicure. The photo at the side of her bed was testimony to what a beautiful bride she had been. On that day she had been at the peak of life, with a fabulous future ahead of her. She had such promise. Not like the poor cow in the bed.

The creature in the bed had no future. If she ever woke up, she would be a broken thing – weak from being in bed for over a year, maybe damaged in other ways. She would have to suffer the embarrassment of having to wee into a tube and being rolled around by nurses. She would have to go to a home that was too smart for her to look after and to live with a husband who didn't love her any more. No, that wasn't a life. That was a life sentence.

'I'm not going to let you win,' Sally said. She pointed to the silent body. 'You are going to die.' She pointed to herself. 'I am going to be the one they remember. Me. The beautiful bride who was so tragically whisked away on the happiest day of her life.'

Outside, the sun came out from behind a cloud and pale light flooded the room. Sally moved, shadowless, to the window and checked out the sky. There was a patch of blue. She hoped that lasted until she died. In a few more minutes, the sun would start to set and the room would be flooded in gold. It would look stunning.

'A perfect send off,' she whispered to herself. That made her think of a good last sentence. She would turn her head, if she could manage it, and whisper 'It's a beautiful day to die.' She repeated it to herself and savoured the pathos of it. Yes. Those would be fitting last words.

Chapter Twenty-Three

When Peter got to the hospice, Grace was already there, waiting at the door, fidgeting. Seeing her immediately made him feel guilty. Was every visit to this place destined to be linked with guilt and pain?

'I thought I'd wait five minutes to see if you turned up.' She turned and walked with him into the entrance.

'What's going on Grace?'

She explained as they strode up to the lift. Peter had to admit it all sounded rather odd, but very Sally. 'She wants to die while she's still the tragic heroine, rather than as a dried out invalid? That makes sense in a weird way.'

'Won't you miss her?' Grace demanded. As the doors to the lift slid shut, she jabbed floor three.

'I would,' said Peter. 'But I'm not convinced this isn't a ploy to get us to her room so that she can have another pop at you. Or me.'

Grace looked down. 'The thought occurred to me too. But there was something about the way she was ...'

'Well, I guess we'll see in a minute.'

Silence followed and they avoided eye contact. Grace looked drawn and worried. The skin under her eyes was bluish and there were creases as though she hadn't slept. Her ultra short hair was sticking out messily, as though she'd run her fingers through it too quickly. He remembered the expression on her face when she'd backed away from him. He'd done this to her.

'Grace—'

'Don't.' She moved away from him, squashing up hard against the wall of the lift. 'Just ... don't. Okay.'

What could he say? The knowledge that he didn't love Sally any more didn't change anything. He was still married to Sally and she needed him. He stepped back, so that there was a good distance between him and Grace. Would he miss Sally if she went? He had been saying goodbye to her for over a year now, would her death really make a difference, apart from making life less stressful?

When the doors opened, Grace was out first. Peter followed her as she dashed along the corridor. A nurse came out of Sally's room.

'Hello Peter. Grace.' She nodded to them both. No one seemed to question that Grace was coming to visit Sally anymore. 'I've just done her obs. She's stable. Although, there was some activity early this morning. Would you like to see the charts, Peter?'

Peter followed the nurse back into the room to look at the charts. Grace stood by the bed, her head to one side. He was acutely aware of her, shifting her weight impatiently as she waited until it was safe to speak to Sally without the nurse hearing.

The nurse explained that Sally's heart rate had gone up, then down, then stabilised. 'When the team came in, she had her hand raised. There was still no sign of recognition or response from her, but she put the hand back down by herself.' She ran though what the doctors had said, but Peter wasn't really focusing. A few months ago, something like this would have left him clinging on to every word, searching for a glimmer of hope that Sally was coming back. But now, the chill in the room was enough to tell him that Sally was nearby. He looked at the woman lying on the bed and wondered what Grace saw there.

Sally sat on the bed, careful not to line herself up completely with her body. Peter was trying to look interested as the nurse ran through obs charts. Grace was staring at Sally, as though trying to read her mind. It was kind of funny.

With the filter of anger removed, Sally could see how Peter and Grace would be perfect for each other. They were both organised and boring. Grace would probably be genuinely interested in Peter's charts and arrows and things. Peter would love the sciencey whatever it was that Grace did. She hoped they didn't move into her house though. She had lovingly decorated that house to be the perfect place. She'd known what was going where before she'd even met Peter. Grace could have Peter and the money and the lifestyle, but not the house.

The nurse left, assuring Peter that they'd keep him up to date if anything else happened. Grace moved to the foot of the bed. 'Sally, what are you doing?' she said softly.

'I don't know what you mean,' said Sally.

'Sounds to me like you're getting better.' said Grace. 'Is that what you were trying to tell me before?'

'Nope,' said Sally. 'This little carcass is useless.' She patted the silent, breathing body next to her on the bed. 'Her legs don't work. In fact, nothing works from …' she hovered her finger over her body and jabbed it in, somewhere just below the diaphragm. '… there downwards. Even the arms are a bit of an effort to be honest.'

Grace's mouth made an 'o' as she took in the information. She looked over her shoulder at Peter.

'What? What did she say?' Peter came to stand next to her. Sally was pleased to see that he left a decent space between them, as though he were afraid of touching her. If Grace wanted Peter now, she'd have to work for it. Too bloody right. No one should get a man that easily. If she, Sally, had to put so much work into grabbing Peter, it was only fair that plain, gangly Grace should have to work a little harder.

'Sally, what are you up to?' said Grace.

'Isn't it obvious? I'm going to die.'

'She says she's ... dying.' Grace half turned her head so that she could speak to Peter, but her eyes remained on Sally. 'But Sally, why? Why now?'

Sally carefully sat down and stretched her legs so that they aligned perfectly with her body's legs. She couldn't feel anything in them, but somehow, as soon as the two bodies linked, she felt a sense of rightness. She leaned forward, so that her chest remained free from her body. 'I'm tired,' she said. 'I don't want to stay and live in limbo. I've had enough. I'm getting out.'

Grace looked at a loss for what to say. Her lips moved and she shook her head slowly. Much to Sally's amazement, there were tears gathering in her eyes.

'Don't.' Grace's voice wavered.

Why was Grace getting upset? She could get her mitts on Peter once the funeral was over.

'Grace?' Peter, poor darling had no idea what was going on.

'Tell him,' said Sally. 'Tell him to remember me as I was, not how I am now. Tell him I loved him. I still ... love him. I know I'm not the easiest person to love back, but I hope that, at some level he loves me too.'

Grace repeated it in a broken whisper.

Peter looked at the bed, his face impassive. He didn't believe her. 'What is she doing?'

'I think she's found a way to die,' said Grace.

Peter edged a little closer to the bed. His eyes darted to the wall. Sally realised he was getting within arm's reach of the emergency call button. If she needed any more confirmation that Peter no longer loved or trusted her, this was it. He thought she was going to cause more trouble.

The cheer she'd felt vanished. This was how it ended. With her husband eyeing her with suspicion. Suddenly, she wanted to cry. She turned back to Grace and saw that she was gripping the metal end of the bed so hard that the sinews on her hands were pushing out under her skin. With sudden clarity, Sally realised that the person who would miss her the most was Grace. Grace whom she'd tricked, used and ultimately tried to hurt. Grace whom she'd spent the evenings chatting with. Grace, who genuinely cared. And she'd taken that as a weakness to be exploited.

'I'm sorry,' she blurted out. 'You've been a good friend to me, Grace, and I've been horrible towards you.'

Grace shook her head and blinked back tears. 'I'll miss you,' she said.

The need to cry got worse. It built up behind her ductless eyes. When she could feel again, it would probably hurt. Well, there was no point hanging around, she told herself. She had to get on with it or she'd miss the light. She reminded herself of the last words she'd planned.

'Well, bye then,' she said. She lowered herself down, her arms first, then her torso. Partway down she paused. 'You don't get to have my house,' she said to Grace.

Grace gave a half sob, half laugh. 'No.'

'Look after him.' Sally nodded towards Peter, whose gaze was flitting between Grace and the woman on the bed.

'I will.'

Peter said something, but Sally didn't make out what it was. She reconnected with her body and the rush of signals overwhelmed her. Her world exploded with sensation and taste and sound and pain. When at last it bubbled down to a manageable level, she realised the alarm was going off and there were more people in the room. Peter must have pushed the button. She found her heart and concentrated, trying to slow it down, but it galloped away as her body's automatic systems spurred it on. She tried to force it faster instead. Suddenly, there was pain, rising fast. Sally desperately located her lips and vocal chords. Time for the last words.

As pain and ice rolled up on her, her mouth opened for her last words to the world. 'Ohhh Fuuuuuuuck!'

And then it was over. There was tranquillity.

Peter stared at Sally, lying on the bed. Her scream drowned out the noise of the heart monitor and the alarm. Her body seemed to convulse once, twice, and then lay still. The heart monitor subsided to a long flat note. Nurses shouted to each other. Someone turned up with a defibrillator and shouted 'clear'. Sally's body jerked up in the air as they tried to resuscitate her. He could no longer see her; the medical people were in the way.

Someone touched his arm. He turned to see Grace, tears running down her face. Without thinking, he took her hand. They stood together backed against the wall as people tried to bring Sally back. In the end, they gave up.

'She's gone,' said the doctor, quietly. 'Time of death. 3.54.' She turned and faced Peter. 'I'm so sorry.'

Peter nodded, suddenly numb.

'Would you … like a few minutes?'

He nodded again. He felt Grace's hand leave his. He didn't stop her. There was a general shuffling and the room emptied, leaving him with the body of his wife. He stepped towards the bed and looked at her. Her oxygen mask had been removed and someone had put her arms on her middle so that she looked like she was in repose. There were faint blue marks on her face from where the mask had rested and thin veins showed on her pale cheeks. He touched her face and found that it was still warm. She could almost be asleep.

'Sally,' he said. He wasn't sure which one he should grieve for. The woman he remembered from what seemed like years ago, or the one he'd glimpsed of late. Either way, someone had died. Someone he had loved. Once.

'Goodbye, Sally.' He leaned forward to kiss her. He was surprised to find that her cheek was salty with tears.

Chapter Twenty-Four

It was a quiet funeral. Peter stood with his family gathered around him. There were a few family friends, people who barely knew Sally, but were close enough to show sympathy for Peter's widowing. He had told Sally's work and one man had turned up. A little way apart, trying to keep in the background was Glenda, in her blue coat. Grace stood next to her, also keeping apart from his family group.

As the coffin was lowered, Peter looked up at the two women. Glenda was sobbing. Grace had put an arm around her, but looked uncomfortable doing so. Apart from him, they were the only people who really knew Sally. But, in the end, who really knew Sally? He wondered if even Sally knew herself.

Looking around at the carefully sombre faces around him, he realised he didn't feel anything. He had been grieving the loss of his Sally for so long, that now she had actually died, it didn't feel any different. He had dreaded feeling relief, but that hadn't materialised either. He wondered if he was in shock and there was some emotion waiting to mug him when the whole funeral business was over. Probably. He dutifully scattered some earth over the coffin.

After a few moments he was surrounded by people, touching him gently on the shoulder and saying how sorry they were. He accepted their condolences without saying much. His mother stood beside him, deflecting questions. Dear Mum. She had let him get on with funeral arrangements, for which he was grateful, but she'd reminded him of what needed doing. And, as always, she'd brought food.

His sister came up to give Peter a hug. 'Hey,' she said, gently. 'Are you okay?'

'I'm sorry I've been a crap brother.'

'Don't worry about it.' Val smiled.

He smiled back, suddenly feeling warmth seeping back into his life. 'Thanks.'

'In the meantime, if there's anything I can do... if you fancy a break, there's nothing like playing with kids to take your mind off things.' His sister clearly didn't miss Sally in any way. Being Val, she didn't bother to hide the fact. 'I'll see you back at the house. I'm just going to phone the babysitter and check the kids aren't giving her a hard time.' She placed a light kiss on his cheek and marched off.

Turning, Peter spotted Glenda. He made his way over to her.

When she saw him she burst into tears afresh. He could smell the alcohol on her before he reached her. He held out his hand and she grabbed it. 'Oh Peter. My Sally. My beautiful little girl.'

It occurred to Peter that Glenda hadn't seen Sally since the wedding. It was probably kindest that way. The funeral directors had done their best to restore Sally to her former glow, which had helped disguise how much she'd faded in the year since the accident. He hoped it was a comfort for Glenda to think of Sally as a glowing and beautiful woman.

'Thank you for letting me know, Peter. It was very kind of you.'

He had put an ad in the Times, just as he'd promised her. It had simply read 'the death is announced of Sally Wesley nee Cummings', followed by the funeral details.

'The world won't be the same without her!' Glenda wailed.

People were looking at him. His mother came to stand

next to him. 'Mum, this is Glenda. She was … er … someone Sally knew very well. Glenda this is my mother Diane.'

Glenda blew her nose on a hanky and held her other hand out to shake. Diane looked slightly horrified, but shook hands gingerly.

'We're … er … going back to my house for the wake,' said Peter. Glenda didn't look like she needed any more to drink.

'Actually, Glenda and I can't come.' Grace appeared, seemingly from nowhere. 'Give me a minute to speak to Peter, Glenda, and I'll be right with you.' She stepped neatly in between them and leaned forward to give Peter a stiff and formal hug. 'I'll take her home,' she whispered in his ear.

'Is Sally here?' he whispered back.

'No.' Okay. So that meant Sally wasn't around haunting the place. For the first time something like relief fluttered.

Grace drew back. 'She did love you, you know. In her own way,' she said softly. She pressed something into his hand. 'Glenda and I should get going now. My deepest condolences, again.'

Before he could respond, she was marching Glenda off efficiently. He watched her receding back and wished he could talk to her. Right now, the only person who understood was Grace.

'What was all that about?' said his mother. 'Was that Grace?'

'Yes, that was Grace.' He looked at the thin parcel in his hand. It was packet of forget-me-not seeds.

'What's that?' His mother was frowning.

'That,' said Peter, as he slipped the packet into his pocket. 'Is … was Sally's favourite flower.'

* * *

'Now you make sure you call if you need anything,' Diane said for the fourth time as Peter ushered her out of the door.

'Mum. Relax. I'm okay. I just need to get on with the new normal.' He kissed her on the cheek.

'What are you going to do first?' She paused on the doorstep, still frowning with worry.

That was easy. He'd had time to think about it. 'I'm putting the house up for sale.'

'What?' At this, even his father, who was standing by the car, jiggling his keys, looked up.

'It's full of memories of Sally. We bought this place together. I can't carry on living here.' He didn't mention that every time he felt the slightest bit cold, he wondered if Sally was back. He couldn't relax. And it was true. The house was more Sally's than his. The only mark he'd left on it was crumpled bedlinen in the spare room and a single set of crockery on the draining board.

'Oh darling. It's a major upheaval, moving house. You don't need more stress in your life.'

Peter gave her a bleak smile. 'Right now, upheaval is probably just what I need. I have to work out what I'm going to do without Sally. Start afresh.'

'He's got a point,' his father conceded.

'But ...'

'Give the boy some space, Diane. Now come on. We're going to be late.'

Diane rolled her eyes. 'Be careful darling.' She touched Peter's chest lightly before she turned away.

Peter watched them drive out and felt relief. He was tired of playing the dutiful bereaved husband. He knew he should be sad or relieved, but all he felt was disappointment. All that he'd been through, surely there was some sort of emotional comeback. He shut the door and wandered back into the house. Without his mother fluttering around, it felt tranquil and empty. He walked from room to room, exploring.

The last time he'd had a tour of the house like this, Sally had been there. There were rooms he hadn't been into since before the wedding. There was the dining room, where everything was neatly put away in the dresser that Sally had chosen. A whole dinner service that was never used. The living room which he'd only used when he needed a drink. The house even had a conservatory. He walked into the empty glass room. Sally had wanted to put a sofa in there, but they hadn't got around to it. So now it was an empty rectangle. Peter sat down on the dusty floor and looked up at the sky. Clouds scurried across the clear roof, suggesting there would be rain soon. He lay down and watched them.

He felt guilty for his lack of grief. He should be torn like he had been after the accident. The memory of that pain was there, but at a distance, like a photo of an event he knew he'd been to, but couldn't really remember. All he could think of was that he was glad to be out of it.

If he felt anything, it was anger. Sally had lied to him. She had cheated and manipulated him. She had never loved him. Everything their time together had been built upon was a lie. Even, he thought wryly, her being in a coma. She had been listening to him all along. Listening and plotting.

He watched the white beams of the conservatory glow orange in the evening sun. Should he be grieving for his Sally? The Sally he had once loved had disappeared long ago.

Was she really gone? Really? He thought of Grace's words at the cemetery. If Grace could no longer see Sally, perhaps she really had gone. He hoped so.

The thought of Grace made him smile. She had no

idea how gorgeous she was, that woman. And she was so *nice*. She was about as unlike Sally as you could get. He thought of all the things that had attracted him to Sally – her brightness, the whirlwind rush of being around her, her delicate, almost unreal, beauty.

Grace, on the other hand, was exactly who she said she was. She wasn't mad and vivacious, but she was interesting and warm. When he was with her he felt … grounded. Which wasn't what he'd thought love was all about.

Above him clouds darkened. A few drops of rain splatted against the roof. He winced the first couple of times, then relaxed as the droplets ran off without touching him. He watched the traces of water, like tear tracks, for a moment. Grace had cried when Sally died. He had watched her and wondered why. At some point she had explained that Sally was a friend. Yet Sally had tried to hurt Grace. Some friend.

He ought to miss Sally, but the person he really missed was Grace. He should go and see her. He would. Definitely. Just a few more minutes lying here. And then he'd go.

Peter woke up in the dark. His back was stiff and there was an insistent pattering noise. It took him a minute to remember that he was in the conservatory. He must have fallen asleep. He sat up and stretched. Falling asleep on the floor was really not a great idea. He felt dusty and gritty. He would need to have a shower before he went to see Grace.

Less than an hour later, he pulled up outside Grace's house. The place was in darkness. Puzzled, he got out of the car and ran up to the door to ring the doorbell. Nothing. Maybe she was out. He pulled out his phone and called Grace. It went straight to answerphone.

Where was she? Was she okay? Was he somehow too late? Too late for what?

He went back to the car and was part way home before he remembered. She'd mentioned she was going away for a few weeks. She'd mentioned a holiday. His frown cleared. Of course. He would just have to wait until she came back. That wouldn't be so hard. Would it?

Peter strode up to the reception desk of the hospice. The security guard wasn't there, so he waited. It was odd being here as a visitor, rather than 'family'. The place felt different somehow. Peter noticed things he'd not spotted before. The plaque on the wall. The plants by the main doors. Had those always been there? How come he'd never noticed them when he'd been coming there every day?

The sound of the lift distracted him. A carer rushed outside. A few minutes passed and the carer returned holding the hand of an elderly lady, with the security guard tagging along behind. The guard spotted Peter and came over to the desk.

'Evening, sir. Can I help?' He gave Peter a smile that said he recognised his face, but couldn't place him. How strange. In just a few short weeks, people at the hospice were already forgetting about him. He no longer belonged there.

'I'm here to see Margaret ... er ... I don't know her last name. She's on the fourth floor. Grace Gunaratne used to visit her regularly. Grace is away, so I thought I'd pop by instead.' He gestured at his bag containing an audiobook.

The guard stared at him for a few seconds. 'Mr Wesley, isn't it?' he said. A broad grin. 'Nice to see you back visiting. You're looking for room 417.'

'Thanks.'

Once upstairs, the nurse buzzed him in without comment. As he approached room 417, he felt a rising sense of nervousness. Margaret was the closest thing

Grace had to a living relative. It was like going to meet a girl's parents for the first time. He smiled to himself. He hadn't needed to do that for Sally because she'd pretended she had none.

When he knocked on the door, the old lady in the bed's eyes flew open. She was old. Older than he'd imagined. She looked small and limp, but the eyes that examined him as he entered were sharp.

'Hello, young man. Are you a new doctor?'

The nervousness got worse. Peter cleared his throat, 'I'm Peter Wesley ...' he began.

Margaret's level of alertness seemed to go up. Despite not moving, she seemed to come to attention. 'Peter. With the ghost wife? That Peter?'

'Yes. I ... er ...' Now that he was here, he realised how ridiculous his mission was. 'I was hoping you could tell me about Grace and her holiday. She *is* away on holiday, isn't she? She's not at home.'

'Sit down.' It was a command. Not to be disobeyed.

Peter sat down.

'Why do you want to know where she is? What are you planning to do with that information?'

He marshalled his thoughts. Margaret watched him, sharp eyes boring into him. She must have been terrifying in her heyday. He decided to start with the bare truth. 'I think I'm in love with her.'

'You think? That's not good enough young man. Do you not know?'

Bloody hell, she was tough. He'd thought his sister was blunt, but Val wasn't a patch on this lady. 'Okay, I *know*.' He leaned forward. 'I can't get her out of my head. It's been a weird and confusing time and I know it's too soon, but I miss her. I can feel her absence like it's something solid.' He touched his chest. 'It's like, when she's there, everything is right in the world. And nothing is right without her.'

There was a short pause before Margaret said, 'That's better.' She smiled, with only half her face, but a smile nonetheless. 'I've heard a lot about you Peter Wesley.'

'And I've heard a lot about you.' He smiled back, his nerves ebbing a little bit. Remembering, he said, 'Grace said you liked audiobooks.' He held out the book he'd got for her. 'The woman in the shop said it was very good.'

If possible, Margaret's smile widened. 'That's very good.' She laid the book on her lap. 'So, Peter, why don't you tell me a bit about yourself? Grace means a lot to me and it sounds like she means a lot to you too. I think we should get to know each other a bit better, don't you?'

Chapter Twenty-Five

Grace loaded the clothes from her holiday into the washing machine and looked out of the window. It was grey again. After six weeks in the heat and colour of Sri Lanka, England seemed dreadfully monochrome. On the other hand, it was nice to be back. It was funny how much she'd missed the little things, like the comfort of using her own shower and tea that tasted just right.

Grabbing her latest mug of just right tea, she headed upstairs and stepped into her parents' room. One of the resolutions she'd made whilst on holiday was that she'd stop sleeping in her old room and move into the main bedroom. This was her home, not a mausoleum to her parents. They would have wanted her to have her own life.

She sat on the bed and looked around the room with an assessing eye. Despite all her faults, Sally had been very good with helping her redecorate the house. Her suggestions had definitely improved the look of the place. Grace had got rid of a lot of the old mementoes from the walls. Some of the old photographs were now lovingly framed. On one wall, her father was still skinny and her mother still wore flares. The rest of the walls were bare. They had moved over to make way for her.

There were still things to be done to stamp her own personality on the walls, but it was a start. It no longer felt like she was treading on her mother's belongings.

Sally had suggested that the bed be moved to the other side of the room and the old chest of drawers be replaced by something sleeker to make the most of the light. Unable to think of someone to ask to help move the heavy furniture,

Grace had left it. Now, with her newfound clarity, she realised that there were any number of people at work who would be happy to do her a favour. She had worked late and taken care of their experiments often enough, she was owed a few favours. There was also Peter.

She had thought of him often while she was away, analysing her feelings for him, wondering if he had genuinely liked her at all. There had been days where she only thought of him now and again and days where she missed him so much that it was a physical ache. She hadn't told him when she would be back. She wondered if she should. It was nearly two months since he'd been widowed. Was it still too soon?

So much for her theory that a bit of distance would help her get over him. She sighed and flopped backwards onto the bed.

She wondered whether she should make a start with the new life by simply sleeping in that room that night. Start as she meant to go on. Except all she craved was her own bed. Even if it was narrow and in a small room.

As she rolled off the bed and onto her feet, the doorbell rang. Who could that be? She'd already spoken to Margaret. No one else knew she was back. Frowning, she clattered down the stairs to open the door.

Peter could make out Grace's silhouette as she neared the door. Thank goodness, she was in. He'd been looking forward to seeing her again so much. As the door opened, he felt a moment of panic. The weeks of separation had only made him more certain of his feelings towards her, but what if they'd had the opposite effect on her? What if she'd met someone else on holiday?

He gripped the bunch of tulips in front of him. It was

ridiculous to feel this nervous. He was just going to welcome her back and if she wanted to be left alone, he would go away again. No expectations. Just a friendly visit.

The moment she opened the door, his heart rose a notch.

'Peter.' She seemed surprised to see him, but not annoyed. That was good. Her gaze dropped to the flowers and her expression turned to puzzlement.

'Welcome back.' He held them out and hoped his voice sounded normal.

'Thanks.' She took the bouquet and moved aside to let him in. 'How did you know I was back?'

'Margaret told me.'

'You went to see Margaret?'

'I did.' He smiled. 'She's quite scary.'

Grace laughed. 'She is.' The awkwardness broke. Indicating that he should follow her, she took the flowers in to the kitchen. Laying them carefully in the sink, she started hunting for a vase.

'How was your holiday?' said Peter, watching her as she opened and shut cupboards. She looked amazing. The sun had tanned her skin to a Mediterranean brown. The aura of sadness that he'd got used to seeing was gone; everything about her seemed lighter, happier. 'You look like it suited you.'

'It was good, thanks. Aha.' She pulled out a glass vase and filled it with water. 'How are you keeping?' She looked him in the eye for the first time since he'd got there. 'It's hard, after the funeral.'

'I'm good.' Except he wasn't really. He was shattered all the time. When he finally dropped into bed, all he could think about was Grace and that kept him awake. 'Tired, but good.'

Grace nodded. 'Have you fallen ill yet? That's the first

thing that happened to me when Mum died. I suddenly realised I had all this time to do whatever I wanted with and then bam, I got the flu and about three colds in a row.'

Peter grinned. 'Been there, done that.'

'Apparently, it's the body's response to the release from stress.'

'It's coming to something when falling ill is a luxury you can't afford, isn't it.'

She put the full vase in the middle of the table, next to a pile of post. 'There. That looks lovely. Thank you. You didn't need to bring me flowers.' She fussed with the foliage, tweaking it.

'I wanted to. I never got to thank you for … everything.'

Grace waved it away, still looking at the flowers. 'What are friends for?'

Friends. He didn't want to be just friends. During the long absence, he'd worried whether his feelings for her were just a side effect of his stress and isolation, but the minute he'd seen her again, he'd felt like a weak at the knees teenager again. No. Not just friends.

'I missed you,' he said.

She still wasn't looking at him. 'I missed you too,' she said, softly.

'Grace,' said Peter. 'I was wondering …'

She looked up, but said nothing.

'Would you, like to go out to dinner … one night.'

'You mean, like a date?'

'Yes. Like a date.'

For a moment there was silence. Peter felt his whole body tense in anticipation. If she said no, what would he do?

Grace put her hands on the table and nodded. 'I'd like that.' Finally, she looked up at him and smiled. 'I'd like that very much.'

It was as though he'd grown wings. The world shifted focus and suddenly everything was brighter. He knew he was grinning like a maniac. 'That's great. Thank you. When would be a good day for you?'

Her smile lit up her face, and went straight to his heart. 'I'm not busy,' she said. 'Whenever.'

Peter stood up and took her hands in his. 'Tomorrow? Or do you need a couple of days to—'

'Tomorrow is fine.'

They stared at each other. There was so much he'd wanted to tell her – about how much he'd missed her, how he'd fallen in love with her, how sorry he was for being such a dick – but none of it seemed to matter anymore. She was here, smiling at him, her hands clasping his. There was nothing more that needed to be said.

Grace turned his hands over in hers and looked down at them. Her thumb touched the line of pale skin where his wedding ring had once been.

'I took it off,' he said. 'I'm not married anymore.'

She looked into his eyes and he saw his happiness reflected in hers. He pulled her to him, gently and kissed her. It was a small kiss, one that said 'we have all the time in the world. We'll get it right this time.' When she squeezed his hand and kissed him back, he knew she'd understood. Perfectly.

Chapter Twenty-Six

Grace set the table while she waited for Peter. They had been seeing each other for several months now, discreetly at first, and then openly. They went out, but not regularly. Having a partner that she could take along meant that Grace went to more events organised by her work colleagues and suddenly found she'd been accepted into a new social circle. Peter's family had welcomed her with charm and something like relief. She had got used to being introduced as Peter's partner now and still got a thrill out of it.

They had made it a rule that Friday night was spent together. Neither of them felt comfortable in Peter's house, so they took turns to cook in Grace's kitchen. This Friday, it was her turn.

It was windy and grim outside. Grace checked the oven, where two Parma ham wrapped chicken breasts were roasting. She stood up when she heard Peter's key in the lock.

'Hello,' she called.

He appeared, rubbing the rain out of his hair. He kissed her. 'That smells delicious. What is it?'

She told him. 'With asparagus,' she added. There was some unspoken competition between them, each trying to better the other in their Friday meals. It meant that they ate very well now. For the first time in her life, Grace had started to go running, because she was gaining weight.

'That will go perfectly with this.' He pulled a bottle of champagne out of the carrier bag he was carrying.

'What are we celebrating? Did you land another big contract?' She found a bottle stopper and plugged the neck of the red wine she'd set out.

'Better than that.'

She frowned. 'Better?'

He nodded. 'Guess.'

'You sold the house?'

Peter rolled his eyes. 'You can really take the wind out of a guessing game, can't you? You're too damned good at them. Yes.'

'You sold the house? Oh, that's brilliant!' She threw her arms around him and kissed him. 'That's great news.'

He nodded, keeping his arms around her. They both knew that selling the house was the last step to letting go of Sally. Despite the fact that Sally had only physically lived in it for a few months, it was still very much Sally's house. Peter still slept in the spare room when he was at home. The house, despite its obvious attractions, had been hard to sell. There was probably something about the ambience.

Peter told her the details as he fetched glasses and poured the champagne. Grace had always refrained from asking him what he was going to do once the house was gone. Now she couldn't really avoid it. 'So, what's the plan for afterwards?'

Peter took a gulp of champagne. 'I was rather hoping we could, maybe, get a place together?'

Grace said nothing, thinking about it. She looked at her kitchen. She had made this house her own now, she realised, and she didn't want to leave it. But she wanted to be with Peter. Would he consider moving into this house instead of starting out somewhere fresh?

There was a movement beside her. When she turned, she found Peter kneeling on one knee beside her. 'Oh.'

He looked up at her and gave her a nervous smile. He cleared his throat. Taking a deep breath, he took her free hand. 'Grace. I love you. I want to be with you, grow old with you. Will you marry me?'

She stared at him. Too surprised to answer. She had always assumed that the terrible experience after his last wedding had put Peter off marriage. In fact, she wasn't entirely sure she wanted to take on the label of 'Peter's wife'. It sounded too much like stepping into Sally's shoes.

'I thought you didn't want to get married again?' she said.

Peter's face dropped and she immediately felt bad for her lack of subtlety. He was still for a moment, then he said, 'It's important to you to have these things right. If it's important to you, it's important to me. So ... what do you say?'

She felt her heart lift. She wanted to be with him too. More than anything, it delighted her that he put her needs before his. No one had done that for her in years. But this wasn't about her. It was about both of them. She shook her head. 'No.'

He flinched, hurt. Then he lowered himself so that he was sitting on the floor. 'Why not? What did I get wrong?'

She smiled and sank down to the floor with him. 'Nothing. You didn't do anything wrong. You're just perfect.' She took his face in her hands. 'I want to grow old with you too,' she said. 'But I don't want to be your wife. I'd like to be happily not married to you for as long as I live. Could you do that?'

He grinned. 'I'm happy with that. That IS a yes, of sorts then, isn't it?'

She nodded. He kissed her, a gentle lingering kiss that held a whole future in it. 'Thank you,' he whispered. 'I can't think of anyone I'd rather be not married to.'

He put a small leather pouch in her hand. 'Open it,' he said. 'It's not a ring.'

She opened the pouch and tipped its contents into her palm. A heavy tangle of gold glowed against her skin. She untangled it with one hand. It was a necklace of delicate gold flowers, each with a sapphire at the heart of it. 'It's beautiful.' She turned it and watched the light glinting off it. 'Just … beautiful.'

He picked it out of her hand and put it around her neck. 'They're Ceylon sapphires,' he said. 'They're rare and beautiful, just like you.' He stroked her cheek. 'Grace, you are the most beau—'

She interrupted him by kissing him. They sat together on the kitchen floor, entwined leisurely, until the oven timer went off.

'I love you Peter,' Grace said before she went to check on the food.

They dished out the food and clinked champagne glasses across the table. It was the sort of domesticity Grace had never had before. There was a feeling that everything was just as it should be. She looked at the pictures on the walls. This was her home. It could adapt to her new life with Peter. Maybe even children. Maybe.

'Why don't you move in here,' she said, waving her glass to indicate the place. 'This house is big enough. It's a family home.'

Peter lowered his glass. 'A family home,' he said, carefully. 'Needs a family in it.'

Grace met his gaze. She smiled. 'How about you move in, and we'll see what we can do about that.'

Thank you

Hi

Thank you for reading *Please Release Me*. I hope you enjoyed hanging out with Peter, Grace and Sally as much as I did. This was a difficult book to write because it touched on so many sad themes, but I hope I handled them with care. Writing about Grace and Peter really helped me work out my own feelings about grief and depression, but I worried that those themes wouldn't be welcomed by readers — and boy, was I wrong! I'm eternally grateful to the readers who took the time to get in touch or leave reviews. We writers love feedback (we also like cake, but the less said about that the better).

The next time you're passing on Amazon, Goodreads or any other review website, if you could take a few minutes to write a sentence about what you thought of *Please Release Me*, that would be wonderful. If you enjoyed the book, please tell your friends too.

If you fancy chatting to me directly, you'll find all my details in my author profile. I'd love to hear from you! I'm busy writing another book at the moment. Hopefully, I'll meet you again there.

Take care.

Love
Rhoda

About the Author

Rhoda Baxter likes to write about people who make her laugh. In real life she studied molecular biology at Oxford, which is why her pen name might sound suspiciously similar to the name of a bacterium.

After trying out life in various places, including the Pacific island of Yap (it's a real place!), Nigeria, Sri Lanka and Didcot (also a real place), she now lives in East Yorkshire with one husband, two children and no pets or carnivorous plants. She has a day job working in intellectual property and writes contemporary romantic comedies in whatever spare time she can grab.

She can be found wittering on about science, comedy and cake on her website (www.rhodabaxter.com) or on Twitter (@rhodabaxter) or Facebook (https://www.facebook.com/RhodaBaxterAuthor).

More Choc Lit

From Rhoda Baxter

Girl on the Run

Outrunning her past was never going to be easy ...

A job in a patent law firm is a far cry from the glamorous existence of a popstar's girlfriend. But it's just what Jane Porter needs to distance herself from her cheating ex, Ashby, and the press furore that surrounds the wreckage of her love life.

In a new city with a new look, Jane sets about rebuilding her confidence, and after Ashby's betrayal, she resolves that this will be something she does alone.

That is until she meets patent lawyer, Marshall Winfield. Sweet, clever and dealing with the aftermath of his own romantic disaster, Marsh could be the perfect cure for Jane's broken heart.

But with the paparazzi still hot on Jane's heels and an office troublemaker hell-bent on making things difficult, do Jane and Marsh stand any chance of finding happiness together?

Girl on the Run is available as an eBook.

Visit www.choc-lit.com for more details, or simply scan barcode using your mobile phone QR reader.

Doctor January

If you keep looking back, you might miss what's standing right in front of you …

Six months after a painful break-up from Gordon, Beth's finally getting her life back on track. She has faith in her own scientific theories and is willing to work hard to prove them. She's even beginning to see Hibbs, her dedicated lab partner, as more than just a lousy lothario in a lab-coat and goggles.

So when Gordon arrives back from America without warning and expects to be welcomed back into Beth's arms, she's totally thrown. She also quickly begins to see that Gordon isn't the man she thought he was … Hibbs has always held a candle for Beth, but he can only wait so long for her to realise there's more to life than being patronised and bullied by the one who's meant to love and protect her.

Will Beth foresee the explosive nature beneath Gordon's placid surface before he destroys everything she's worked for, both inside and outside the lab?

Doctor January is available as an eBook, paperback, audio CD and download.

Introducing Choc Lit

We're an independent publisher creating
a delicious selection of fiction.
Where heroes are like chocolate – irresistible!
Quality stories with a romance at the heart.

See our selection here:
www.choc-lit.com

We'd love to hear how you enjoyed *Please Release Me*.
Please leave a review where you purchased the novel
or visit: **www.choc-lit.com** and give your feedback.

Choc Lit novels are selected by genuine readers like yourself.
We only publish stories our Choc Lit Tasting Panel want to
see in print. Our reviews and awards speak for themselves.

Could you be a Star Selector and join our Tasting Panel?
Would you like to play a role in choosing which novels we
decide to publish? Do you enjoy reading romance novels?
Then you could be perfect for our Choc Lit Tasting Panel.

Visit here for more details …
www.choc-lit.com/join-the-choc-lit-tasting-panel

Keep in touch:
Sign up for our monthly newsletter Choc Lit Spread for
all the latest news and offers: www.spread.choc-lit.com.
Follow us on Twitter: @ChocLituk and Facebook: Choc Lit.

Or simply scan barcode using your mobile phone QR reader:

Choc Lit
Spread

Twitter

Facebook